FRACTURES

RISE OF THE ANOINTED

BOOK 2

FRACTURES

RISE OF THE ANOINTED

JASON C. JOYNER

little lamb
BOOKS

Fractures: Book #2 in the *Rise of the Anointed* series
Text copyright © 2020 Jason C. Joyner
ISBN: (Paperback) 978-1-9534560-9-0
ISBN (eBook) 978-1-7332828-9-5
Library of Congress Control Number: 2020943405

little lamb
BOOKS

Published by Little Lamb Books
www.littlelambbooks.com

P.O. Box 211724, Bedford, TX 76021

Scriptures taken from the Holy Bible, New International Version, NIV.
Copyright ©1973, 1978, 1984, 2011 by Biblica, Inc. Used by permission of
Zondervan. All rights reserved worldwide. *www.zondervan.com*

The NIV and New International Version are trademarks registered in the
United States Patent and Trademark Office by Biblica, Inc.
The characters and events in this book are fictional, and any resemblance to
actual persons, living or dead, or events is coincidental

Written by Jason C. Joyner, *jasoncjoyner.com*
Edited by Lindsay Schlegel, *lindsayschlegel.com*
Cover design by Melissa Williams Design, *mwbookdesign.com*
Interior design by Melissa Williams Design

First Edition
Printed in USA

TO BECCY,

My light and the one who spurs me to greater speeds.
Forget superpowers–you're the greatest gift
Jesus has ever given me.

Reader Reviews for *Launch*

"I give *Launch* 5 out of 5 stars and cannot wait to get my hands on book 2!"

—Rayleigh Gray Setser, Amazon

"Love this book! I would highly recommend for middle grade, teens, young adults and adults!"

—Alisa Hope Wagner, Amazon

"Great read for young and old. I can't wait for the next book in the series."

—Steve Eldredge, Amazon

"Mysterious, supernatural, and full of heart ... that's what I felt after reading the first chapter and needed to know more."

—Kara Grant, Amazon

"A quick exciting read! The book starts off with a shot, quickly moving from characterization to the action smoothly."

—Lucas Davies, Amazon

"Joyner has a hit on his hands. High praise for a great story line with a plot that you don't want to stop reading."

—Miles Johnson, Amazon

"Great coming of age story built around superhero powers, mystery, and the battle between good and evil."

—Scott Harsock, Amazon

"From start to finish, I had a tough time putting the book down."

—Jake Tyson, blogger at Creating for the Creator

"Our older boys really enjoyed this book, and can't wait for the continuation!"

—Jean Petersen, author of *Kind Soup*

Jason C. Joyner

Character Key

Demarcus Bartlett: Demarcus is a 16-year-old African American with the gift of super speed and reflexes. He is the son of a single mother working hard to provide a better life. A natural leader, sometimes Demarcus can be overconfident.

Lily Beausoliel: A 16-year-old only child, due to the death of her mother and brother, Lily can manipulate light. Her depression is improving after she joined the Anointed. Her light can turn to heat if her temper flares.

Harry Wales: Fun-loving Harry is sixteen and has the gift of teleportation. Initially he was nervous and jumpy, but practice has given him control and confidence. His mum is from England, so he has some interesting habits.

Sarah Jane Langely: Also called SJ, Sarah Jane is a quiet red-head who has great compassion and the ability to heal. At seventeen, she's shy and finding her voice slowly. As the oldest, she is the conscience of the group.

Simon Mazor: The youngest billionaire and founder of the Alturas Collective, until it collapsed at the failure of the Launch Conference. He can supernaturally influence people, but an injury to his eyes diminished the ability. Now he's trying to find his way back into favor with the Archai, an ancient group that wants to control world events.

John Presbus: The elderly mentor to the Anointed youth, he watches out for them and counsels them in using their gifts. His mysterious past is overlooked due to his immense wisdom and spiritual guidance.

Kashvi: A girl of Indian descent who opposes the Anointed. Her special ability is to manipulate water, which makes her a dangerous opponent to anyone she goes against.

Aasif: An Afghan American teen boy, his fiery demeanor is backed by a sonic attack that can create great force or stop his foes with pain and vertigo.

Pastor Julio Sanchez: The pastor of Living Water Christian Center, his church provides cover for the Anointed youth. He knows their secret and trusts John to guide these youth out of his building.

Roberto Pearce: A researcher of antiquities, especially those with paranormal possibilities, he is recruited by the Archai to go on a special expedition. He is unprepared for the consequences of what he'll find in the ancient chambers of Babylon.

Jason C. Joyner

Ji-young Kim: An investigative journalist for the alternate news source the Bay Area Underground, she stumbles across the Anointed early on and tracks their activities throughout the story.

Dr. Franklin "Ratchet" Lowry: A friend of Pastor Sanchez, Ratchet is a scientist and research at Applied Sciences. His expertise in practical applications in physics and electronics makes him a new ally for the Anointed.

Rosa Gonzalez: An 18-year-old woman who was at the Launch Conference, she has super strength. Her traumatic life leaves her vulnerable to being influenced by Simon Mazor, who keeps her under his control as his unwilling assistant.

Part 1

Chapter 1

Demarcus Bartlett stepped into the street, focused on the latest text on his phone. He had to find the perfect meme to respond to Lily.

"Look out!" Harry's voice caught Demarcus's attention. A car bore down on Demarcus, seconds away from impact. He noticed the driver drinking from a cup, distracted from the road in front of him.

No problem.

The car drove past and Demarcus ended up next to Harry, whose face was redder than usual under the streetlight's beam.

Demarcus finished his text and put away his phone. Distracted walking was really a thing.

Harry pulled Demarcus toward the alley and they ducked into the dark. "What do you think you're doing? Is it my turn to save you now?"

He couldn't hold back a laugh. The first day they met, Demarcus had rescued Harry from an oncoming car.

"Who were you texting anyway?" Harry asked. "Is it a certain girl?"

Thankfully the dark alley would hide his embarrassment. Demarcus's texting Lily shouldn't come as a surprise to Harry, but he felt guilty for not paying attention.

"It's not like you weren't checking in with Sarah Jane earlier," Demarcus said. Harry shot him a look. "Never mind. You're right, we need to keep focused on our patrol. If we're going to find out who is behind the attacks in J-town, we need to be sharp."

Harry exhaled, flipping his bangs into the air. He looked good with his hair grown out shaggy. His crush was changing him into a stylish guy.

"Okay, Demarcus, I'll let you off the hook this time. But if you keep acting braindead, I'll teleport you into a jail cell or something to keep you out of trouble. By the way, where are we?"

Demarcus leaned out of the alley and looked around for a street sign. Laguna Street. The attacks from gang members had been occurring mostly between Broadway Street and Geary Boulevard. All of Japantown was upset with the disturbance, and residents were starting to hide in their apartments at night.

Demarcus and Harry usually didn't wander this far north into San Francisco. Demarcus's mama would be freaking out if she knew he wasn't in the South Bay area. He said he would only be ten minutes away if she needed him.

With his speed, the range was a little farther than Mama realized.

"Let's head for Lafayette Park and see if anything turns up."

They exited the alley and turned north. Demarcus could survey things a lot faster if he did it himself, but he did have to be careful in an urban area. The whole cabbage stand incident at the farmer's market reminded him of that. Harry had his own way of doing things, hopping all around with his teleportation. Tonight, they needed to practice some restraint.

John preached discretion seemingly every chance he got. Their mentor was a godsend, but it got old sometimes when he kept on about the same things. Yes, they had to be careful with their powers and use them responsibly. Yes, they needed to stay humble and trust the Lord instead of their own abilities.

But, it was hard when they could do so much more.

"I wish there were a tall building here to get a good vantage point," Harry said, scanning the roofs of the neighborhood. The local apartments and buildings were only a few stories at most.

"Man, you've changed a ton since the Launch Conference. Remember how hard it was to get you to teleport to the roof of the Alturas HQ?"

"That didn't have to do with heights. It was more about not knowing how to control where I ended up. And I've been practicing on my own time as well. My mum keeps wondering where I'm off to all the time." Harry's mother was British, so he dropped occasional Queen's English terms, which always threw Demarcus off, since Harry didn't have an accent.

They crossed another street and walked past a street café. The employees were pulling the tables in for the night. Scents of stir-fry wafted through the air. Demarcus would have to settle for another protein bar before they left the city. His super speed did tax his metabolism. Between that and his constant need for new shoes, his money disappeared faster than he could run.

Angry shouts sounded from around the corner of the next building. Harry looked at him and grinned. Finally, a little action.

"I'll run ahead and see what's happening. If it's the Jade Dragon gang, then I'll take out their guns. You get any victims or bystanders out of there. Got it?"

Harry held up a hand. "Hold up. First of all, we should stick together. Remember what John says. Second, why do you always get to take out the bad guys?"

Before Demarcus could argue Harry's points, a gunshot rang out in the night air. A scream followed. No time. He had to help.

"Sorry!"

Demarcus pumped his arms and legs, and in a moment, he was around the corner. His shoulder-length dreads whipped around his face as he turned the corner. A woman stood with her hands up to her face.

He skidded to a stop to assess the situation. Right then another crack rang out in the air. A sharp pain tore through his upper thigh and he collapsed onto the sidewalk. Fire burned in his leg and he grabbed for it. Hot, sticky blood pumped out of the wound.

Voices argued back and forth. "You hit a guy!"

"He just appeared out of nowhere."

"Let's get out of here!"

Demarcus glanced up to see three figures in black take off toward the park. The woman sobbed and dropped to her knees.

He screamed for Harry. Demarcus had suffered other wounds with his speed before—nasty road rash and the like. But he'd never had blood pour out like this. Had they hit an artery?

Harry knelt next to him. "Dude, what happened?"

Demarcus clenched his teeth. "I ran right into a bullet. The hoodlums took off. I think they hit something bad. Get me some help."

The redhead nodded. "I'll be right back."

"No, take me with you." Demarcus tried to grab him.

It was too late. Harry disappeared, leaving Demarcus bleeding out on the sidewalk.

Chapter 2

"**I** can't believe you did that."

Lily Beausoliel looked at her nails, nine of them a subtle sky blue. And one of them colored bright blue, apparently the color of some kind of time machine from a TV show. Their friend Harry got Sarah Jane hooked over the summer, and she kept trying to get Lily to watch it. The blue nail was just the latest attempt to push the sci-fi world on her.

Since Harry had gotten the idea of dipping fish sticks in vanilla pudding from the show, Doctor something or other, it didn't sound like her thing.

"Well, you were busy texting, so I took that as approval. You snooze, you lose." SJ put the polish away in her kit, a smile on her face.

Lily blew on her fingers. She didn't have a comeback for the texting. It did distract her. But their break time should probably be over. A glass of water sat on her physics textbook. She drained the glass and picked up the large book.

SJ sighed. "It's really that time?"

"Yes. We have to keep up on our studies. You know it makes us better."

SJ brushed a strawberry-blonde strand of hair away from her face and pulled her anatomy book into her lap. "We're in high school. We should have a better social life. It's Friday night and we're doing our extracurricular studies."

"When would we do it otherwise? You'd be drawing horses or something, and I'd be playing around editing photos," Lily replied.

School had only started a couple of weeks ago. There were English papers to write, algebra problems to solve, and French verbs to conjugate. If they wanted to study physics and medicine, it had to be on their own time.

Lily wrote her name in neon colors in the air. "Did you know my last name is spelled wrong? When my grandfather came over from France, they messed up the 'i' and 'e' on the paperwork. Guess it's too late to fix it now." With a swipe of her hand, the writing dissipated. "Anyway, we don't really have a social life. I'm just trying to keep my head above water at Everett. How are things at your school?"

"I haven't made many friends since moving last year. I did find out about a peer helpers group working with the nearby elementary school. If I joined that, I could maybe work with Danny's class. He'd love that."

That was SJ, always thinking of others. "That would be a good outlet for you. Go for it."

Her cheeks reddened. "I'd have to talk to the advisor."

No wonder she hadn't done it yet. Her quiet friend. Although after Lily's mom died, her desire to be outgoing was buried as well. Only since the Launch Conference last June had it started to surface again.

A knock sounded on the door.

"Lily, do you and Sarah Jane want some milk and cookies?"

Lily's stepmother tried to keep an eye on things, always offering treats. "Thanks Kelly, but we're good."

SJ made a pouty face. Her sweet tooth was legendary.

Lily sighed and flopped off the bed to open the door. "I'm sorry. We'd love a snack."

Kelly beamed at the acceptance of her offer. Over the summer the two had begun breaking the ice in their relationship. Still, there was a ways to go before they had the buddy-buddy relationship Kelly seemed to desire.

"I've got the oven heated up. They'll be ready to go in about fifteen minutes." Kelly walked down the hall and back down the stairs.

Lily shut the door and returned to the bed. A prism hung in front of her mirror. The multi-faceted glass dangled on a thin wire. She pointed her finger at it, concentrating.

A beam of light flashed from her finger and intersected the prism. Tiny rainbows scattered across the room. One landed on SJ's forehead.

"I see you're really into studying tonight." SJ ducked away from the rainbow.

"What's wrong with having a little fun with your studies?"

SJ shrugged, not quite meeting Lily's eyes. "You all have things that you can have fun with. What am I going to do?"

Without warning Harry appeared in the room. Right in front of Lily's beam.

"I'm sorry about . . . Ah! My eyes!" Harry clutched his face and dropped to the floor.

Lily stopped her light show and rushed over to Harry. SJ came to his other side. Their friend moved his hands and blinked his eyes several times.

"What are you doing here? Porting into a girl's room?" Lily spat the words in hushed tones. If her parents found him here it'd be chaos—especially without him coming through the front door.

"I know, I know. Wait, where are you? All I see are flashing spots." Harry flailed his hands around to find them.

Lily caught his face in her hands. "Why. Are. You. Here?"

"Demarcus is hurt. It looks bad. I came to find Sarah Jane. She's here, right?"

The girls gaped at each other. Demarcus was hurt? Lily's stomach lurched at the thought. "What are we doing? Take us to him."

SJ looked down at their clothes. "Lily, we're in our pajamas . . ."

Chapter 3

Harry caught their arms and closed his eyes. The three of them blinked out of the room and appeared in a commercial area with office buildings scattered among trees and grassy areas. Nearby, they could hear cars passing on a highway.

Lily glanced around. "I don't think this is where Demarcus is."

"I had to port halfway." Harry rubbed his eyes. "He's too far, and it's hard to concentrate with my vision blurred."

That's what he gets for teleporting in unannounced. "Hurry! We need to get to him."

The trio disappeared again and then found themselves sitting on the cool concrete of a sidewalk. Lily's thin cotton pajamas offered little resistance to the elements.

Harry scrambled over to a body on the ground. Demarcus! His head was slumped back, and a woman held some kind of cloth against his leg.

God, please touch him. "What happened?" Lily asked.

Demarcus groaned, his breath ragged.

The woman's eyes were wide discs. "I was being held up by a

couple of gang members. One of them fired a shot to frighten me when I told them to back off, but this guy appeared out of nowhere, right into the path of the bullet. At least it scared the jerks away." She turned to Harry. "Did you get help? He doesn't look good."

Harry bit his lips. "Yeah, I kinda got some help." He pointed at Sarah Jane.

SJ took a spot next to Demarcus's injury. "Um, let me take a turn holding pressure on his wound, okay?"

The woman scooted over, but she frowned, looking SJ up and down. "Who are you to help? You're wearing pajamas with kittens on them."

Lily interjected. "We're nursing students and roommates. We finished with a shift and had already changed when this guy came asking for help."

The woman's frown didn't shift, but Lily's intervention gave time for SJ to pray. If she had time to concentrate, everything should be fine. Of course, the lying to cover their powers wasn't cool at all. John would not be pleased—with any of the circumstances. Their next mentor meeting would be really uncomfortable.

Lily examined Demarcus. His color had drained, and his body lay too still. *C'mon Demarcus, SJ's here. God will heal you. He's gifted us for a reason, and He's got a plan for you.*

The plan couldn't be for Demarcus Bartlett to die from a stray bullet when he was just trying to help people.

SJ continued her prayers. The woman wrung her blood-stained hands together. "I don't know what this is doing. Has anyone called 911?"

That wouldn't be good. Lily glanced at Harry, his wide eyes

and gaping mouth matching her own reaction. They had to stall a minute longer. Lily put a hand on the woman's shoulder.

"Don't worry. We've done this before. We just need to give it a minute. What's your name?"

The woman's eyes glistened. "Ji-young. I don't like this. I don't want to see this young man die on my account."

Lily noticed the growing circle of blood under Demarcus's leg. SJ's knees were coated with it now. Her forehead beaded with sweat. Why wasn't this working?

Demarcus exhaled, then his body stilled.

What? Lily grasped his shoulder and gave it a shake. "Demarcus? Wake up!"

Ji-young flashed her a quizzical look. "I thought you were nursing students. You know him? Shouldn't you be doing CPR or something?"

SJ looked up at Harry. "I don't understand. Why isn't this working?" Tears began streaming down her cheeks.

This couldn't be happening. Lily choked back her own sobs. She slid fingers on his neck to see if she could find a pulse.

A gasp escaped from his mouth and he sat up straight.

"Whoa. That was a trippy dream—or did I get knocked out? I dreamt that I got shot."

Ji-young fainted.

Harry caught the woman's limp form before she thudded on the sidewalk. SJ cupped her mouth in shock, her hands forming a ring of blood around her lips. Lily wanted to hug and slap Demarcus all at the same time.

"Are you kidding me? We thought you had died." She couldn't take that again.

Demarcus shook his head and glanced down at his leg. "Oh man. That's a lot of blood, isn't it?"

"I think it hit your femoral artery." SJ looked at the blood on her hands. "You know, even though it's healed, I don't think it takes the bullet out. You're probably going to carry that with you forever."

Demarcus grinned. "Cool."

That was it. Lily slugged his shoulder, but his arm was so buff it only hurt her. "That is not cool, so knock it off. Now what are we going to do with Ji-young? What if someone else comes by?"

Harry shook the woman's shoulder gently. Her eyes started to flutter.

"Looks like she's about to wake up. She'll be safe at least. But we should probably take time to explain to her what happened . . ."

A thought jolted Lily. "Kelly!"

They all looked at her.

"She was making cookies for SJ and me. I think she said they'd be ready in fifteen minutes. How long has it been?"

SJ shrugged. "I didn't look at a clock when she said it. It's probably close, though."

Lily reached over to pull Harry in between them. "We've got to go, now."

They all linked arms. The last thing Lily saw on the street was Ji-young's chin dropping in disbelief.

Back in her room, Lily's rear hung over the edge of her bed, and she tumbled to the floor while the rest of them stayed upright on the mattress. What time was it? Her alarm clock read 9:45 p.m. A rapping sound at the door, followed by Kelly's voice. "Girls? The cookies are ready."

Thank goodness Kelly believed in a sense of privacy. Lily whispered in a frantic voice. "You guys, get out!"

Demarcus hopped off of her bed, revealing a pattern of blood on the comforter. This was getting worse. "Can I wash up first?"

Harry's anxious look at the door showed he understood the seriousness of the situation. "Later, man. C'mon." He caught Demarcus's arm and the two of them vanished.

Now what to do about the blood on SJ and her bedspread?

"Lily?" Kelly's voice squeaked when she questioned something.

SJ shook her head like she had no idea what to do. Lily cast around the room for something. They couldn't hide the bedspread. What about the blood on Sarah Jane's face?

The nail polish.

Lily grabbed the darkest red she could find, twisted off the lid, and thumped the bed with her legs as hard as she could, faking a loud grunt in the process. She whispered, "Sorry." Then she splashed some on her friend and the rest on the bedspread.

Kelly opened the door to SJ standing next to the bed with a dark red dribbling off her face and Lily sprawled out over the comforter.

Chapter 4

Demarcus trudged to the youth room at the back of Living Waters Christian Center of Santa Clara. He passed his new friend Matthew on the way and asked him to send updates on the Dallas Cowboys game. It was nice in the heart of 49ers country to find someone with good taste in teams. Matt had to throw out his latest vocal imitation before leaving. The kid had a good ear for mimicking people.

Normally Demarcus would be excited for this meeting. The cover story was a special group needing mentoring through the church with a retiree who volunteered with them. In reality, John Presbus met with a group he called the "Anointed," a group of gifted teens.

Pretty much a secret club of superheroes.

Today was different. After Friday night's near tragedy, Harry and Demarcus had stopped by a store to get new clothes to replace the ones ruined by the gunshot wound. As Harry explained what happened, Demarcus's embarrassment level blew through the roof. What a fool to charge in and get shot like that.

Luckily the plan was for Harry to spend the night at Demarcus's house, so Mama didn't suspect much. She had eyed his new outfit, even though he'd tried to match the ruined clothes as best he could. His practical mother fussed at times about how much money he spent on shoes, but since he had been working, she'd let him be for the most part.

Too bad he lost his job for a local food delivery place. He initially had great marks for his speedy delivery. Things went south when most of his orders ended up mush from too much speed.

Tonight, it was time to fess up to John. Their mentor was a mysterious guy from Greece, by the sound of his accent. His wisdom explained so much, but Demarcus knew John held back a few secrets of his own.

At least he was patient enough to work with their motley crew.

Demarcus peeked into the kitchen to see if there were any leftovers from the church café. A volunteer named Helen was finishing the dishes and only gave him a look as he nabbed an overripe banana. She knew about his appetite, and liked to give him a hard time.

The youth room's bright orange vinyl couches would look tacky anywhere else, but they matched the eclectic décor of the room. A string of lights hung over the door. Flags from different countries plastered three walls, while a colorful mural of handprints and doodles covered the last one. Isaiah 52:10 adorned the front of the room:

> *"The LORD will lay bare his holy arm*
> *in the sight of all the nations,*
> *that all the ends of the earth will see*
> *the salvation of our God."*

Demarcus was the first one here, as usual. The church was close enough to their different suburbs that it made a central location for them all to meet. He didn't mean to rush it, but he had to fight impatience lately since he could do everything with such speed. Papers from the youth class littered the floor and furniture. A quick dash around the room and he had them all picked up.

A small cramp pinched his right thigh. Sarah Jane had said the healing wouldn't get rid of the bullet. He wondered if it would always be a reminder of his failure on Friday night.

He plopped on the couch and got his phone out. No messages. Where was everyone?

A moment later, Lily and Sarah Jane walked in, chatting away. The two girls had become close friends since their ordeal at the Launch Conference. Lily waved at Demarcus and his stomach fluttered. Her blonde hair fell past her shoulders and stood out against her blue sundress. The girls sat on the loveseat as they finished their conversation.

He and Lily were just friends, he had to remind himself.

John arrived soon after. A few sprigs of white hair stuck out from his head and a thick beard rounded out his face. It was a different look since his clean-shaven days working at Alturas. He carried a notepad and a couple of books with him.

So they were waiting for Harry. Again.

"He's the one who can get here the easiest. The rest of us get rides, use buses, or just run. What's his deal?" Lily asked.

Demarcus reached out to him on a messaging app. "Where RU?"

Thirty seconds later Harry popped into the room. "Sorry I'm late. Did I miss anything?"

John's gentle manner didn't get ruffled, but he motioned for them to sit right away. No time for pleasantries today.

The five of them joined together in prayer. John had taught them to pray all at once out loud, something common in Asia and the Middle East. They prayed for the church, their families, and their neighborhoods. They prayed for illumination for their path together. That one always made Demarcus grin, considering Lily's gift. Finally, John asked for wisdom for them all.

Yeah, they probably needed it.

"What happened on Friday, ladies and gentlemen?" John's voice—a firm baritone with no crack in it; a slight clip to each word—belied his age.

The teens shared looks, daring someone else to go first. Demarcus cleared his throat. It was his blunder and desire to be out patrolling that caused the incident. He raised his hand.

"It was my fault. I wanted to see if we could stop the attacks in J-town, and then when we heard a confrontation, I bolted in without thinking. I'm sorry."

Harry explained how he went to get the girls to help. There wasn't much said about Ji-young, and Demarcus hoped it wouldn't come up. The room sat quiet after they finished filling in the details. Lily's imaginative covering up of the blood impressed him. He felt bad that she had to pay for dry cleaning on her comforter. He should offer to pay for it afterwards. Too bad she didn't post a picture of SJ on Flare . . .

Oh, that's right. Flare didn't exist anymore. Demarcus hated the thought of the Alturas social media channel that died along with Simon Mazor, but it still came to mind at times. Old habits die hard.

John sighed and threaded his fingers together.

"Children, we have a few problems here."

Aw, snap. He called us children. Here we go.

"Demarcus and Harry touched on the obvious—what were they doing out looking for trouble? It seems they found some, yes? There are a few things beyond this, however."

Demarcus started tapping his foot.

"First of all, Harry, why did you teleport away with Demarcus in such critical condition? What if the vagabonds returned? What if he didn't survive?"

Demarcus recalled trying to grab Harry in the confusion. When he ported off, Demarcus was able to put some pressure on the wound for a minute until Ji-young quit panicking, but he was overwhelmed with light-headedness after that. Good thing she was there.

Harry stumbled over a response. "I guess I freaked out. My thought was to get Sarah Jane, but I didn't think of taking him to her."

"Well, what would have happened if you took him straight to her house and she wasn't there? How would you have explained that to her parents? What about Lily's house? Apparently, Lily had to damage personal belongings to cover things up as it were."

Oh, this was worse than he had realized.

John paced in front of the room. "This is why I don't think you're ready to be performing such exploits. At the Launch Conference it was a matter of life and death. Certainly, if there's an emergency right in front of us, you should do what you can to help.

"But remember, you don't go through training like these emergency people do. I wish we'd had police and firefighters like this in my day. When I watch them respond, they focus on safety first. They practice these things.

"The Lord is your shield and strength, an ever-present help in trouble. But we don't need to be looking for trouble. There is a battle coming. You need to be prepared. Yes, you need to work on your abilities, but you need discipline. Wisdom. You need to learn to hear God's voice and how to discern good from evil by studying the Bible. The enemy will not come against you like an army, marching right in front of you. Our adversary has been tricking mankind since Creation. How do you expect to confront his forces when you run blindly into trouble?"

The room deflated. John's tone of voice had changed from calm teacher to bold preacher.

The realization of what he'd done stung—how could he turn back from doing what was right?—but Demarcus knew that being challenged was good. Like his track coach at his old school who'd always pushed him to do his best. Maybe this was what a father was like. If only his real father had stuck around to help him out. The jerk had left his mother struggling for her life when he was born.

Still, their teacher was right. What were a group of teenagers doing fighting crime after school? It wasn't like the comic books, that's for sure.

Sarah Jane spoke up, her voice a nervous, soft-spoken tone. "John, when I prayed for Demarcus, he wasn't healed right away. I've also tried to heal others and it hasn't always worked. Why is that?"

John sat down in the middle of the room. Another one of his Mediterranean habits, it seemed. "Dear one, we don't know why the Lord heals one and allows another to suffer. It is frustrating for all of His servants. We want to see everyone touched."

Demarcus noted the pained look in John's eyes.

"We have to trust that God has a greater plan. How do you think the disciples felt when Jesus died on the cross? Their hopes and dreams, crushed and buried in a tomb. But His power is seen most acutely when something dies and is brought back to life."

Sarah Jane's eyes welled up. "What if I can't heal someone when it's critical? I want to spend my days in the hospital, helping everyone in there, but I'm so afraid that I'll fail and be called a fraud."

"Ah, my tender-hearted Sarah Jane. You know better than the rest of us the power of resurrection. Do you see the word you used so much in that statement? It was all about 'I'. Remember this, all of you. It's not about you. It's about Jesus. When you remember He's gifted you for a reason, then you will walk without fear."

Demarcus's foot tapped so fast he started wearing out the rug. He would never forget Sarah Jane's broken body after she was thrown off the top of Simon Mazor's headquarters on the Alturas Collective's campus. She had stopped breathing. No pulse. Yet John had prayed for her and she now sat with their group.

It was a reminder to Demarcus to never doubt God.

Before they could continue with their discussion, Pastor Julio Sanchez knocked on the door. John waved him in.

"What is it, my brother?" John asked.

Pastor Sanchez was one of the few adults who knew the secret of the Anointed. Somehow John had met him and connected with the passionate minister, who taught his flock with a caring, yet bold hand. His church offered covering for their gatherings over the last few months. Demarcus loved his easy-going laugh and sharp mind.

"Brother John, kids. I think you're going to want to see this."

Chapter 5

Simon Mazor opened the door to his office. The door bounced off something in the way. He had to feel around to find a plastic garbage can, but when he moved it aside, it bumped against his small work desk. If he wedged it diagonally, everything fit. He sighed and carefully made his way to his chair.

His hands found the home keys on his keyboard, and muscle memory took over in booting up his system. After a couple of notification sounds, he could boot up the Bluetooth connection to his glasses.

The glasses that he'd wired into the optic center in his brain.

When Simon operated his computer network, he almost felt normal. He wore a microchip behind each ear that synced with his special hardware. This bypassed the signal his ruined eyes tried to send through the optic nerve, instead beaming direct signals into the visual cortex of his brain.

His brain interpreted images as if there was a computer monitor interface inside his head, which had the precision he couldn't replicate when viewing the real world.

Every time he logged in, a flash of light occurred, which brought back a moment that haunted him. How he wished he could scrub the association from his memory.

Simon shook his head to kick-start his focus. Self-pity wouldn't bring him the answers he needed. He typed some commands and pulled a pen-sized device from his pocket. A click of a button on the side of his new router, and it synced into his system as well.

He experimented with the buttons on the mobile unit. The different controls allowed him to use the glasses as a camera via a Bluetooth connection. He didn't have the clarity of a computer screen, but it was progressing. He could make out shapes and general movements. Faces were unreadable, which would continue to hamper his true gift.

Independence returned step-by-step.

The fateful day almost three months ago repeated on a mental loop, stealing his focus. On the rooftop of his Alturas headquarters, he had stood confronted by three teens from his conference. He'd almost made contact with the girl who could control light. Then she had blasted the Source with a laser, and the resulting explosion had thrown him from the roof.

His retinas were seared.

A battle raged each day to marshal his remaining finances to get back to a functional state. His empire—the rising technology company Alturas Collective and the social network, Flare—crumbled with the fiasco at the conference. He had access to only a fraction of the resources he had then. The world thought he was dead. The Archai, the group that had recruited and trained him for years, ignored him. It was their plot he had set in motion to influence people around the world, but now he was apparently a liability. Somehow he had to claw out of this pit and find a way to a . . . rebirth.

Knock it off, man. He couldn't keep cycling past events in his head. If he could perfect the connection between the real-time camera on the glasses and the neural links, his vision would be restored. That would be a huge improvement.

His fingers reached for his jeans pocket for a gummy bear. Nothing. Where was his intern? He tapped the button on his pen.

"Rosa, where are you?"

A voice sounded from the doorway. "*Hola.* I'm right here, Simon."

He turned, startled, toward her voice. He clicked another button on the pen and the computer display turned off. He was left with his blurry world, because the glasses did not have the processing power of his computer. There she was, standing in the doorway, since there wasn't much room in the office anyway.

"Did you get to the store?" he asked.

The sound of a bag landing on the desk. He had to grope around to find it. This young woman's rebellious nature tested his patience. However, her brokenness made it so he could still control her.

"Have you been watching the Internet?" Rosa wondered.

Simon fumbled with the bag and pulled out the package of gummy bears. His fingers found one. Was it orange or red? The resolution on his glasses had to be adjusted some more. He put whatever color it was into his mouth and chewed in frustration.

After he swallowed, he said, "No, I'm a little busy to be watching the latest on YouTube."

"Too bad. I think you really want to see this one. Do you want to see it on my phone?"

"Sync it via Bluetooth to my mobile router. I'll be able to see it better with my new interface."

"What's the name?" Rosa asked.

"Flickering Flare."

Rosa fiddled with her phone until a video popped up in the lower left corner of his field of vision. A swipe with the pen and he had a full view.

The video featured a Korean girl with hair askew doing a self-interview on her phone. The shaky visual made it hard to focus. "This is Ji-young Kim recording live from San Francisco in Japantown. I was investigating the increase in attacks here lately. Moments ago I was held at gunpoint by three members of the Jade Dragon gang.

"They fired a warning shot to scare me, but it hit a young black man who ran into the path of the bullet. He fell to the ground while the gang members fled. Here you can see the pool of blood on the sidewalk."

The camera swung away from the woman to show a dark stain on the cement.

The woman appeared again. "As I tried to help him, a male teenager appeared out of thin air with two teen girls in their pajamas. They literally showed up out of nowhere. The girls claimed to be nursing students, but they looked too young. One of them put her hands on the wounded leg and appeared to be praying.

"The injured man stopped breathing. One of the girls cried out a name: Demarcus. The girl who prayed stated that whatever she was doing usually worked. Then Demarcus sat up as if nothing had happened and started conversing with the group."

The view now moved to the street signs showing the location of the attack. "In the confusion of this Demarcus possibly dying, then sitting up and suddenly being okay, I took a moment to gather myself. And just like that, all four of them were gone. They didn't run down the street. I'm talking vanished.

"This is the intersection where all of this happened. If you saw any of it, please contact me at my Twitter address on the screen. It was four teens: Demarcus, a black guy with dreadlocks to his shoulders, a white male with shaggy red hair, a girl with long blonde hair, and another girl with more of a reddish-blonde, the one who had blood on her.

"First we had the strange happenings at the Alturas campus in June. There have been reports of strange sightings since then. And now this. Bay Area residents, I am committed to discovering the truth for you. Help me out."

The camera twisted until the woman was on camera again. "This is Ji-young Kim for the Bay Area Underground News: the real news that the other news won't touch. Good night."

Simon minimized the screen and stared into Rosa's blurry face, his mind racing.

"Do you know what this means?" he asked.

"I need to try harder to kill that girl next time?" Rosa replied in a snarky tone.

"No. If Sarah Jane is alive, then she can heal my eyes."

Chapter 6

Pastor Sanchez closed the tab on his computer. Demarcus couldn't believe their bad luck. He had saved a journalist intent on uncovering the strange and unusual. Great. Now his name was out there as well as descriptions of their whole group.

Maybe they should wear masks. That could be cool.

Pastor Sanchez and John looked at each other for a moment, as if daring the other to speak up first. Then Sarah Jane broke the silence.

"What does this mean? Should we avoid going out in public together? I don't want some weirdos looking for us. It's one of the reasons I still don't use social media."

John waved the comment off. "No, that wouldn't do. Let's go back to the youth room and get the answers we need."

They all shuffled back. John wasted no time in going to prayer.

After they finished, Demarcus sighed in relief. The mood in the room had become more tranquil. Harry and Sarah Jane were even teasing each other about who caused the biggest stir to the journalist. Demarcus couldn't help a smile at Harry, whose interest in the thoughtful girl had grown through the summer.

John cleared his throat. "Did anyone get direction from the Lord?"

Harry raised his hand awkwardly. "I could set up some Google Alerts to see if people are searching for this Ji-young Kim or Demarcus. We could at least track some things." That was good. Harry was probably the best on a computer out of all of them.

John rubbed his hand over his fine hair on top. "My goodness, the things you young people come up with. That sounds wonderful."

"We could also have some code names," Harry went on. "I was thinking Radiance for Lily, or maybe Spectra. Demarcus could be Blaze, Zip, Zing . . ."

Lily wagged her finger at him. "No zinging way, Harry. Next?"

Pastor Sanchez turned to John. "Should we tell the kids?"

"If you think he's ready."

The pastor pulled out his phone. "I'll give him a call. He said he was almost done." Pastor Sanchez stepped out of the room, leaving them wondering what the secret was.

Lily traced a flower of light in the air with her finger. The design glowed white and then evolved into more colors, ending with a green stem and pink bud. That was a new trick for her.

"That was way cool. When did you start being able to mix colors?" Demarcus pulled out his phone to take a picture of it as he talked.

"I've been practicing a lot in my room. It's weird keeping my blinds down so no one sees anything—I feel like a shut-in. But the optics section in my physics book has helped also. I didn't realize how much there was to light, and it's fun to figure things out."

Her smile lit up her face in its own way. Demarcus grinned back. "All I can do is run fast. You guys have the cool stuff."

John walked by and patted him on the shoulder. "You have much more to offer than speed, son. Do not let your identity get too caught up in one part of your life."

Pastor Sanchez returned, wearing a sly smile and a mischievous look in his eyes. "Ratchet is ready. He says to bring them tomorrow night. They're going to love this."

Chapter 7

Iraq

Roberto Pearce ducked into the secondary cavern and cold air enveloped him. After the desert sun's rays had pushed his team close to a breaking point, the shelter of the cave brought relief.

Yet a presence hovered in this hallowed ground that struck fear into his heart.

His team entered the cramped quarters behind him. The four bodyguards pulled off the balaclavas that protected their faces from the swirling dust and slid their goggles onto their foreheads. They fanned out to cover the opening, in case they had been followed.

Roberto brushed layers of dust off his shirt and coughed. He had studied mystical artifacts for years, which had cost him tenure at Stanford. After teaching and continuing his research at a small college, he never thought he'd receive a grant to do an expedition as earth-shattering as this. When his benefactor reached out to ask him to lead their team, it had changed his fortune for good. There wasn't a lot of support for his kind of research at any level, so he couldn't pass up this opportunity, despite the dangers it entailed.

Roberto's nerves had become rattled at the first gun battle. Thankfully his mercenary escorts were professional and helped him navigate the chaotic landscape. By the third exchange of gunfire, he had gotten used to the efficient skills of his entourage.

He downed some water and looked around at the cavern. Nothing on the walls pointed to anything significant here. Just another cavern in the midst of barren rock and sand. But the nearby ruins suggested this was the spot he was looking for.

The Archai, the organization that sponsored his trip, said they were a historical society interested in obscure finds. They had already recovered something that should help him finish this journey.

He slid a canister off his shoulder and carefully removed the cap. He retrieved the plastic-wrapped parchment and took it out of the final protective layer. The frayed document crackled as he unrolled it.

Amazing that something so fragile held the key to such power.

Each step echoed as he walked around the wide cavern. The outer chamber they'd passed through could have held a tank. He was surprised there wasn't a cache of weapons in here, but it had probably been looted a long time ago.

Holding the parchment out, Roberto scanned the room, moving carefully. Any rock or curve in the wall could be his target. After he traversed two-thirds of the cavern, a faint design began to glow on the parchment. He was close. Roberto slowed and moved the parchment back and forth to find the source of the signal.

There, behind a protrusion of limestone stalagmites: the symbol of a flaming torch with a line swirling around it luminesced in the dark recesses of the cave.

Was this it? Had he truly found the chamber?

All my research points to this. Roberto called to the guards, "This is where you hold our perimeter. I must proceed alone."

He rolled up the parchment and returned it to the canister. He slid off his glove to feel along the rock wall, tugging each separate stone as he went until one gave way.

After a few minutes of prying other rocks out, a small tunnel opened up. He would barely be able to squeeze through the passage. Nothing extra could come with him. He dropped his pack along the wall, but pushed the canister into the tunnel, climbing in after it.

The tunnel descended at a slight angle. Each foot of progress was a fight. He slid the canister forward and wriggled his body along the dirt floor. Sharp rock fragments jabbed his body as he went. Good thing he wasn't a big guy. None of the mercenaries would be able to reach him if there was trouble.

The beams of the flashlights built into his wrist guards reached only a foot ahead of him. They were supposed to be good for fifty. The sound of rocks scraping together stopped him. If anything shifted at all, he would be trapped. But what was the alternative? He had no choice but to go on.

Roberto pushed the canister ahead again and this time it finally disappeared. The chamber! His fingers clambered for purchase so he could pull himself through. His shoulders wedged in a constriction of the tunnel. He had to squeeze sideways to reach the edges of the opening and drop out of the tunnel and into the chamber, twisting as he fell to avoid landing on his head.

An unceremonious crash on the rough-hewn floor followed. The air held a poisonous chill. His breath came in short, ragged gasps. The adrenaline rush of making it into a place only known in whispers and rumors jolted his body and battled the cold threatening to overpower him.

Fragments of bone littered the floor, while a worn ceremonial altar stood in the middle. His lights barely penetrated the darkness. He carefully searched the walls and found no markings to give him further direction. With no other option, it was time to try the ceremony. The stale air made it hard for Roberto to breathe. He hurried to pull the parchment out of the canister. The air began to swirl around him. His lights dimmed further, and his vision blurred at the edges.

For the first time he wondered if the power the Archai wanted summoned was worth dying for.

The parchment fell to the floor. The rancid air began to choke him. Coughing, he found the parchment and unrolled it. The torch symbol, what the Archai had called the Sign of the Flare, remained. Other symbols on the paper blazed with their secret message now that the document was returned to its origin: the main sacrifice chamber for the ancient temple of Marduk.

Roberto forced out the chant from the parchment with a hoarse voice. He gasped as his knees collapsed and he crumbled to the floor onto his back.

The parchment glowed red until the paper ignited in his hands. The light from the flames illuminated the small chamber. Wisps of smoke coiled from the burning parchment and coalesced into a hulking, humanoid form. The form opened up gaping jaws and appeared to inhale the smoldering remnants of the scroll.

Roberto wanted to scream, but the air wouldn't release from his lungs. What was this creature evolving before him?

Shards of bone poked into Roberto's back as he struggled and wheezed for a few last breaths. The Archai had used him as a tool and condemned to die in a dirt hole in the middle of Iraq, in the remnants of ancient Babylon.

"Help," he whispered. Nothing more would come out.

Burning embers of eyes on the smoke creature stared at him, observing him closely. The red lights seemed to look inside of him. A rumble came from deep within the beast, and words formed in Roberto's mind.

You will be my vessel.

No!

Roberto rolled over and started to claw his way across the floor, away from the creature. His lungs burned as if he had inhaled acid.

The mass of the creature dissipated and smoke snaked around Roberto's body. He tried to call out, but his lungs had no more air. The grey plume found his mouth and nostrils, filling his body. His muscles convulsed and thrashed amongst the remains of the temple's victims.

Roberto tried to fight this . . . thing. He pushed back, even as control was stolen from him. His hands constricted into claws, his back arched, his legs kicked. Making a stand didn't work. He tried to focus his mind, find a center, anything to keep the creature from overwhelming him.

Finally, his body rested. He could sense that the smoke had infiltrated every cell in his body. His life was not his own now.

What had he become?

Roberto could hear whispers in his head, a scratching within his mind. They bid him to stand. His legs obeyed.

Roberto thought about continuing to fight it, but he knew from the way he'd been infected that he couldn't face this force head on. Instead, he retreated into a corner of his mind.

A desire welled up from the voices invading his mind and drowned out his terror. He would wage war against the forces of Light. The whole earth would writhe under his feet. He was a living manifestation of an ancient evil.

A name from ages ago bubbled to the fore of his consciousness.

Hoshek, we have an enemy that would thwart our plans. They have powerful individuals that have stopped us before. An image of the Alturas Collective headquarters crumbling from the destruction of the Source.

The Hoshek acknowledged this. *We must strike them down. Then the rest of the world will quake before us.*

Roberto's body moved with the Hoshek's control. Flexing arms and legs, testing out this new form. Roberto's mind was probed. The guards—they would be dealt with first.

Then the Hoshek provided an image of an old man in a custodian uniform from the collective resources of the Archai.

I understand, Hoshek. He is the key to destroying them.

The nametag on the uniform read, "John."

Part 2

Chapter 8

The church van pulled up to the shiny glass building. Pastor Sanchez parked in the visitors' spot and hopped out to lead the way. Lily couldn't believe he was this excited. She was growing to love the joyful minister because he was really helping her get the hang of the Christian thing. Since her life had been turned around over the summer, she knew she was growing in her faith. It even seemed like her gift was stronger to the degree she focused on God. Was it connected? Or was she naturally growing in it?

Of course, when she let God's light shine in her heart, there were also things that came to mind that made her cringe. She didn't always like what was revealed.

Their group passed the engineers and researchers pouring out for the day. A tall, smiling man in a Chicago Bulls polo held the door open for them with a pleasant, "Allow me. I'm Steve. Ratchet asked me to get you all checked in. He's finishing things upstairs."

Ratchet? What kind of name was that?

The bright lobby appealed to Lily. The cool metallic décor was simple but stylish. It felt very Silicon Valley, at least from what movies and TV showed. Steve led them to a wide silver guard station. A uniformed, heavy-set man sat up straight and clicked a few times on a touchscreen.

"Okay, you're the group that is meeting with Dr. Lowry for an after-hours tour?" The guard's high-pitched voice didn't match his large frame, and Lily stifled a giggle. Pastor Sanchez nodded at the guard.

The guard placed a pad of paper on the counter. "I need someone to list the names of the visitors and sign them in. And I need to collect your electronic devices. We can't have any unexpected electrical interference, and there's no devices with imaging capability allowed."

All the teens groaned.

John shook his head. "I do not understand this fascination with these devices."

Lily heard Pastor Sanchez whisper to the guard, "Does this apply to the adults too?"

"Yes, sir."

The pastor huffed and produced his phone as well. Steve gave a hearty laugh at this. "Employees have a clearance, so they can bring theirs in. Even then, there are areas we can't take them."

Steve finished listing all their names and signing off on the forms. Only a couple of chairs near the door offered a place to sit. How long was this Ratchet going to be?

The elevator pinged and the doors slid open. A stocky man with slicked back brown hair rolled out in a wheelchair, his broad smile gleaming. "Sanchez, is this the group? Amazing! I can't wait to hear—"

Pastor Sanchez interrupted. "Yes, this is the group of advanced science students that wants to see your work. Are you ready for us?"

Ratchet rubbed his hands together. "You bet I'm ready." He wore wheelchair gloves without the fingers. His sleek chair looked lightweight, but Lily was surprised he didn't have a fancy technical one.

"Let's go, gang. I've got some neat things in store for you."

Neat? Even John didn't talk that corny.

They all crowded into the elevator, except for Steve. They waved to him as the doors closed. The ride was so smooth it didn't even feel like they moved. But in a minute, they landed at a different floor and spilled out of the crowded lift. The hallway extended down the length of the building on the left and turned a corner on the right. Ratchet led them around the corner.

"You have no idea what this means. I have been working on some cool things ever since Sanchez mentioned you. Don't worry, despite my near-miss due to excitement downstairs, I haven't breathed a word about the Anointed. This is so rockin' what God is doing here."

Lily and Demarcus both chuckled. This dude was funny. Laugh lines creased his face. There was an energy about him, like he found a lot of joy in what he did.

They rounded another corner and passed some windows that allowed them to look into various labs. Lily imagined they would be meticulous, with things lined up and organized. Instead, there were consoles and hardware stacked in corners, with lots of servers piled into cabinets and tangles of wires sticking out everywhere.

The workers dressed in puffy white suits with hairnets and face shields. It looked more like they were battling an epidemic than doing engineering work.

Lily figured someone might as well ask. "Why are they dressed like that?"

Ratchet did a cool one-eighty to spin around and face them. "Let me explain. Our company does a lot of research with semi-conductors to be used in other electronics. They can't be exposed to contaminants, so we put on those marshmallow suits to work with them." He winked. "Don't worry, you won't have to put those on. My work is a little different."

His chair glided almost soundlessly along the hall. Such an interesting guy—racing around in a wheelchair, a scientist, and very excitable.

They passed another set of semi-conductor rooms before they turned left and reached a door with a keypad and a scanner mounted on the side. Ratchet tapped in a code almost as fast as Demarcus could. The scanner dropped to Ratchet's eye level and he stared into it for a moment.

Harry leaned in. "Cool, a retinal scanner."

"More than that, my young friend. Have you seen the keyboards operated by eye movements for people with ALS? This is a retinal scanner, but I have to enter a special code by looking at the right spots."

Whoa. This was high security.

The doors whooshed open so fast it blew her hair back. Ratchet's eyes grew wide.

"Are you ready for this?"

Chapter 9

The teens filed into the room first. Ratchet wheeled in and did another fast pivot in front of a computer terminal. This lab was a lot different than the other rooms they just passed. The long counters had different equipment lined up for experiments, but they were orderly and shiny in the banks of lights. Over in one corner a pad with a grid glowed with a faint green light.

Pastor Sanchez spread his arms out wide. "Okay, guys and girls, I'm sorry we kept this a secret. When John approached me about being your home church, I was so stoked. Then when he told me about all you could do, I knew the perfect guy to bring into the fold. This is Dr. Franklin 'Ratchet' Lowry. He's a long-time friend and an expert in practical applications for numerous fields: kinetics, optics, and electronics, to name a few. The guy's the resident genius working here at Applied Sciences, and most importantly, you can trust him. He's a Kingdom man."

Lily glanced at her friends. The code word "Kingdom" was John's way of saying that a person understood that God was always at work and advancing His kingdom presently, even when things looked bleak. In fact, Pastor Sanchez was the only other person John labeled as Kingdom.

The excitement in Ratchet's voice was evident when he spoke. "Now I've got some ideas for things that can help you, but they're only theoretical right now. I need to see a little demonstration from each of you to better understand things and how I can help."

A stone dropped in Lily's gut. She noticed her friends seem to deflate, as well.

"Oh, what did I say?"

John snapped his fingers, a new expression he had started using. "I forgot. The kids had to do a similar activity with Simon Mazor at the Launch Conference. It . . . was upsetting. Simon did things in a way that was traumatic."

The mention of Simon made Lily cringe. A flutter of nausea hit her. He was at the controls of the Source, a gadget that almost killed her after his assistants Kelsey and Otto had strapped her in. The last Lily saw of Simon was his body, smoking from the explosion of the Source, falling from the roof of his headquarters. The explosion that Lily had caused when she destroyed the device. She blinked her eyes several times to get rid of the image of Simon's death.

Murder, really. By her hand.

And then there was Rosa . . .

John had explained forgiveness to her several times, and the fact she was defending herself and her friends. It didn't stop the visceral reaction when the idea shoved its way into her head.

Ratchet slumped his shoulders. "Oh, I'm sorry. I had no idea. We can do this another time if it's better for you, but I won't be able to get far without it."

SJ kicked at the floor and Demarcus, usually so eager, held back too. Harry stepped forward.

"It wasn't bad for me. I couldn't control my ability at the time, so I didn't have to demonstrate for him. What do you want me to do?"

The scientist clapped his hands. "Ah, the young teleporter. So amazing, if I may say. I know some theoretical physicists who would love to understand how you do this. But we won't go there right now. Please step on the pad in the corner."

Harry flipped his hair out of his eyes as he made his way over. "Now what?"

Ratchet glanced around. "How is your accuracy?"

"If I've seen a place and have a sense of the layout, I can be right on. If I haven't seen it, then it's more hit or miss."

The scientist pointed to the other corner. "Can you teleport over there?"

Harry appeared before he could even look back. "No problem."

Lily had never seen a grown man squeal before, but she could swear that's what Ratchet did. The dude even gave a wicked fist-pump.

"That was so awesome. Just one problem—can you wait until I calibrate the sensors?"

Harry flushed red. "Oh, sorry."

The clock read 9:30 p.m. Lily couldn't believe how fast the time had gone. Ratchet had done a bunch of tests on both Harry and Demarcus, and without windows to show the dwindling twilight, it didn't register how much time they'd spent doing it.

Ratchet had used a treadmill for part of Demarcus's testing, and he'd asked him to take off his shirt to stick some leads to his chest. Demarcus acted a little shy to take his shirt off, but Lily didn't see why. She knew he'd been working out, but the definition he'd developed was . . . impressive.

The treadmill smoked by the time he had finished running. Ratchet scrambled to override the fire alarm system and sprinklers to prevent his lab from being drenched, all the time with a perma-grin plastered on his face.

Demarcus toweled off his torso and slipped his shirt back on. Lily made sure to avoid watching him directly, to keep her cheeks from burning bright red.

"So how was my speed?" Demarcus asked, excited as a little kid on Christmas morning.

"I wish I could tell you," Ratchet said. "The treadmill is built for industry testing of low-resistance wheels, not for a runner. I'd say north of 200 mph, but that's the best I can do right now. We might have to use a radar gun for the best numbers."

Demarcus nodded. "Oh, yeah."

But was he as fast as light? Seeing the boys test out their powers warmed Lily up to the idea of exploring hers. When Ratchet asked who wanted to go next, Lily turned to SJ. "Are you ready?"

Sarah Jane stood with arms crossed and frowned. "No, you go," she said with a curt tone. Lily wondered what was eating at SJ tonight. That reaction wasn't like her.

"Please step forward, Lily. You're the light manipulator, correct?"

"That's right. Um, do you have some eye protection for everyone?"

"Of course. Let me get the Nano-Fusion goggles out of

this cupboard. They've got special polarized lenses with a nanoparticle coating to absorb or deflect most wavelengths of the electromagnetic spectrum." He wheeled over to a drawer that had eight goggles carefully set in a custom foam insert. They looked as stylish as sunglasses, with a white frame and prismatic lenses. Everyone slipped them on, except Lily.

"Okay, my dear. What can you do?"

This was the fun part.

Lily spread her hands out with palms up. The intensity of the light in the room magnified by a hundred-fold. White light washed over everyone and chased every shadow from the room. The whole group leaned back, their mouths hanging open.

Her friends should know—that was nothing.

She closed her fists and sucked the light out of the room. They were plunged into complete darkness. The electricity still flowed in the light fixtures. But now Lily controlled the output.

Next, she traced patterns in the air, neon lights floating free around the room. With each snap of her fingers she could vary the color and intensity of the different designs. Then a wave sent them all spinning in a strobe pattern.

Harry gulped. "I might be getting sick."

The lights returned to normal. "Mr. Ratchet, is there anything in here I can use to demonstrate my laser capabilities?"

He pointed to a round metallic disc about six inches in thickness. "Call me Ratchet. I'm tinkering with a laser etching process on the side. Will that do?"

She nodded and clapped her hands together, pointing both index fingers toward the disc. A thin beam leapt from her fingers to the disc, causing smoke to rise from it.

"Can you make it stronger?" Ratchet asked.

Her brows furrowed and the muscles in her arms tensed. The laser brightened. In another moment it burned through the back, hitting a mirrored surface of some kind.

And chaos ensued.

The beam reflected off the mirror and hit a computer. The plastic casing melted in seconds and Lily's trick started boring a hole in the wall. She yelped and dropped her hands, shaking them out. The tingling that always accompanied her power returned.

"Um, I can pay for the damage?"

Ratchet rolled over to examine the disc. He peered through the hole, then traced the line from the mirror to the destroyed equipment. "Aw, man. Not this computer."

Oh no. She probably destroyed some critical research or something. "What's wrong?"

He shrugged. "It's my gaming computer. Sometimes I need a mental break to keep the ideas flowing. Nothing like saving the galaxy for inspiration. But don't even worry about it! You guys are so freaking awesome. I won't be bored for months with working on ideas for you."

That turned out all right. She hoped.

They started to return the goggles to the drawer, but Ratchet waved them off. "I have a feeling you guys will want to always keep those handy. You'll never know when they'll be needed."

Demarcus stuck the new eyewear in his pocket. "Doc, you have no idea."

Ratchet wheeled over to her. "Lily, you'll have to be careful with reflecting or refracting light off of surfaces. Obviously, the power you wield is amazing, like my disc proves. But if someone can bend your light, then it could be very dangerous."

She nodded. It made sense from her studies, but she hadn't run into that problem before.

The adults turned to SJ. "Okay, dear," Ratchet said. "What can you do?"

Lily noticed that SJ's face had drained its color to a stark white. "Don't make me do it!" SJ cried.

Before Lily could ask what was wrong, SJ bolted for the door.

Chapter 10

For all their security coming in, the lab doors were much laxer on exiting. They slid open, allowing SJ a quick escape. Lily chased after her. "Wait a second. What's wrong?"

SJ curled up into a ball in the corner of the hallway. "What am I going to do? Ask if someone has a hang nail? You guys can do all this cool stuff. What can I do that compares?"

Lily knelt down and put an arm around her friend. "Hey, don't talk like that. We can't do anything like your gift. Who would have saved Demarcus the other night? Even if Harry had ported Demarcus to a hospital, I'm not sure he would have made it. It was you that saved him."

SJ nervously pushed strands of hair away from her tear-streaked face. "I don't know if I did anything. You saw that."

"No, girl, why are you being so negative? You saved his life. You've healed us all from things. Why don't you show Ratchet what your gift is?"

Her head shook wildly. "No! Don't make me do that."

"Why not?"

SJ's breath came in gulps for a moment before she was composed enough to speak. "How would I show mine off unless someone was injured first? Huh? Simon had to slit his wrist to get me to use my power the first time. I can't handle that."

Of course. The freak was bleeding all over the floor in his conference room when he forced SJ to put her hands on the wound. She hadn't even known she could do it until then. Lily had to remember that the conference was traumatic for all of them.

She stroked SJ's hair. "Hey, it's okay. You don't have to show anyone anything. Let me go explain it to them, and it will be all right."

"No explanation needed."

Lily whirled around, startled by the voice. Ratchet sat behind them, the first time he didn't have a smile on his face. Boy, his wheelchair was quiet.

"I didn't really consider how it would affect you to show me your ability. Biology isn't my strongest suit, so I'm not sure how much I could help you directly. Anyway, are you okay?"

SJ ran her forearm across her nose and stood. "Yeah. I'm sorry for being such a big baby. I'm glad to have my gift, but it is confusing at times. You're right, besides. What more can be done for me?"

Ratchet wheeled over and took her hand. "Remember, God gives good gifts to his children. He blessed you for a reason, and your compassion is much more remarkable than any gift of healing. That's what guides you the most."

He broke out in a wicked grin. His eyes darted back and forth, like he was seeing figures in the air in front of him. "What if . . . I do have an idea for you?"

A hint of a smile formed. "You do? Like what?"

Their new . . . consultant had a wild look in his eye, reminding Lily of a mad scientist. "I need to do a few tests first. Let me see what I come up with."

The rest of the group came down the hall and huddled around them.

John stepped forward and offered a fresh handkerchief. "Just remember, dear. The gift of life is the most important one of all."

Ratchet escorted the group back downstairs to the guard to sign them out. "You guys come back in a week. I work best with a deadline, so I should have some prototypes ready to go then."

Pastor Sanchez groaned under his breath, which Lily heard, standing right next to him. "Oh no, not more prototypes."

They filtered out the glass doors and started across the parking lot. The artificial lights drowned out the stars in the sky, but when Lily focused into the night, she could faintly make some out. She felt almost a kinship with the fantastic lights twinkling in the heavens.

She wished she could get out of the city to a place where she could enjoy the night sky without all the man-made brightness.

"Before we go," Demarcus said, "we need a picture of this."

They all clumped around Demarcus as he held his phone out and called, "Cheese!"

Lily concentrated to apply a lighting effect behind them. When Demarcus slipped his arm across her shoulders, she almost made the picture wash out. They posed and Demarcus showed the result.

"Great! I've got Applied Sciences in the background. Way cool."

"Do you think it's smart to have evidence of our powers in pictures? What if, I don't know, it gets hacked or accidentally posted?" SJ asked.

"I'll be careful with it. I can hide it in a folder with a misleading name or something." Demarcus texted the picture to the group. Lily enjoyed the way everyone smiled. Her heart skipped at the way she and Demarcus looked next to each other.

That would be something, right? Two superheroes, on a date? She laughed off the thought as they climbed in the van.

Chapter 11

The high school really needed a coffee shop.

Lily leaned against her locker, rubbing her eyes. When they had gotten home from their field trip last night, she still had homework to do. The thought of getting up for school this morning was torture. At least the rest of the Anointed were suffering the same way at their schools today.

Her stepmother had to hustle them out in time to pick up Lily's friend Clara. Her best friend at school was always too chipper in the morning, and today was no different. All smiles, she greeted people who walked by and kept up the friendly chatter.

What was her secret?

Clara fished the last of her books out of her locker. "Did you get your media presentation done? I found some cool videos on fire safety and prevention."

Lily closed the locker since Clara had her hands full. "Not yet. I'm in the second group, so I don't have to have it done until next week."

"I hope you've at least picked a topic, instead of waiting until the last minute again."

"Not really. I was busy last night."

The two of them wandered down to first hour, their media class. Lily really wanted to like the class. The teacher, Mr. Hardt, was cool, and the subject intrigued her.

The problem was the presence of Missy Austin.

Hopefully there was no drama today. Lily really didn't want to deal with it.

Clara and Lily slipped into class with a minute before the bell, so Lily checked her phone. The Anointed had all commented on the last pic from Applied Sciences. A smile crept onto her face before she realized it.

Clara leaned over and peeked at her phone. "So you were with your conference friends last night?"

Shoot. Lily wished Clara hadn't seen that. Since school started, it had been impossible to find time for her friend.

"Yeah, we had a special tour of a lab for our youth group. They're, uh, trying to encourage people to go into science fields."

Clara's lips turned down, except on the left side of her face where her scars from a house fire pulled them permanently up. It usually matched her sunny personality, but there was some insecurity now as well. "Lily, are you afraid your new friends won't like me?"

"No way. It's just that with school starting and getting readjusted, it's been hard to get everything scheduled. I'll have you over sometime and introduce you. Soon. Really." Clara and SJ would probably get along great, but Lily worried about too many people knowing their secret.

The bell rang, and she pocketed her phone before Mr. Hardt could say anything about interfering with school time.

"Okay, class, today we'll start sharing our media reports and analyzing them. Do I have a volunteer to go first?"

Lily scooted down in her chair a touch. Even though she wasn't up for a week, the reflex to dodge attention kicked in.

A hand shot up in the front row. Missy? The brat usually tried to avoid real work if she could. As the self-appointed queen of the Hot Tops clique, she had the responsibility of being mean and condescending to everyone else. Lily's cheeks warmed as she thought about Missy befriending her when Lily first moved to the area and met her at school. Before Missy's true nature came out.

Missy stepped up to the computer and slipped a flash drive in. "I found a great website that does underground news in San Francisco. Our grandparents used to only see the evening news or the morning paper. Now, thanks to the Internet, we can learn about things that don't make the mainstream media. There are some crazy things happening out there that we're missing out on.

"This one caught my interest this weekend." Missy glared right at Lily as she spoke. What was her deal? Was she jealous about the Launch Conference? Missy was chosen to go but didn't have special abilities. That meant she didn't get picked for Simon Mazor's special group. Lucky her.

When the video started, Lily's stomach flipped.

It was the Korean girl, Ji-young Kim, that Demarcus had rescued.

The video played and all Lily could do was massage her temples from the headache that had started to throb. She and the rest of the Anointed would have to consider some kind of disguise, a way to escape notice.

Missy pulled her flash drive back out and pocketed it. "I think this woman is on to something. As many of you know, I was at the Launch Conference at Alturas in June. The news covered the explosion that killed Simon Mazor and caused the conference to end, but some strange things happened before that as well. I want to do all I can to expose whatever is going on with these strange sightings."

The rest of the class flew by in a blur. All Lily could think of was having Missy on her trail. Ugh. When Lily told Missy's brother she wasn't interested in him, it turned Missy from friend to enemy overnight. Time wasn't healing that wound.

A thought darted through Lily's head—what if she gave Missy a little scare? Do something with her powers to freak the girl out. A wicked grin crept onto her face as she pictured the possibilities.

Mr. Hardt's voice brought her back to reality. That was not why she had these powers. *Think good thoughts, girl.* John would be so disappointed. He had stressed the responsibility that went with their gifts. She couldn't let anger get the best of her.

The bell rang. Finally, she could head to her next class and get her mind off her rival. She grabbed Clara's elbow and dragged them out before they ran into Missy. They started down the hall to where they split for their different classes.

Clara spoke in a low voice as they walked down the hall. "It's so strange. The description in Missy's video almost matched the friends in your picture. That's crazy, right?"

Oh snap. What was Lily going to do now?

"You know my dad would kill me if I were in San Francisco alone."

Clara laughed. "That's true. Can you imagine what would happen if he found out? My folks would move me to Amish country. Which wouldn't be awesome, because don't they have a lot of wood stoves because the 'no electricity' thing? Yeah, no more fire for me."

Lily laughed at the joke. Clara had a great sense of humor about her burns. But part of the chuckle was relief at dodging the connection there. This secret identity thing was hard.

Chapter 12

The darkness in the office was only cut by the light from Simon's monitor. It was purely habit that he had the monitor on. With his computer viewscreen patched into his optical connection, he was now immersed in the digital world without needing a separate screen.

His fingers ached from spending most of the weekend working on this code. His thumbs and a couple fingers had also started tingling. Developing carpal tunnel syndrome would be worth it if it meant he perfected this new virus. He could get back in good graces with the Archai as well as have a chance at regaining his eyesight.

And his gift.

Simon had spent the first day since seeing that video of Sarah Jane using her powers hacking into Ji-young Kim's accounts. If she had any more proof about the kids that had helped her, she was the type that would plaster it all over the place. After scouring her astonishing number of pictures, reading her texts and messages, and checking all other hidden digital corners, he knew more about her than he wanted to.

What it didn't tell him was the identities of the teens in her story. No visual evidence.

The one definitive piece of evidence she had given, the name Demarcus, had essentially sealed the deal. The special group he had culled from the Launch Conference had five teens in it. Rosa now worked for him and remained under his gift's influence. Demarcus was the speedster. If he was healed, then Sarah Jane was the key Simon needed.

How did she survive when Rosa threw her off the roof? Had she healed herself?

No matter. He intended to find this girl and get her to use her gift on him.

The virus should worm its way into all of the major cellular networks in an hour. Then it would scan for certain types of images. Specifically, images that had a lot of light and exposure to them.

Bile rose in his throat as he recalled how he had discovered Lily at the conference. The girl had barely manifested prior to the conference, but there she blossomed into a magnificent force of nature.

A force that had almost killed him. If Rosa didn't have such strength, she wouldn't have been able to save him.

The dance at the conference was the key. The light show Lily had put on with tracings of light swirling through the air had fooled the attendees. They thought Alturas had put them on. But if the girl showed off like that before, she would do it again.

And there was nothing teens liked better nowadays than to record something like that in a picture.

Chapter 13

Demarcus hopped out of the church van and stretched his legs. Man, it was a pain to have to travel so slowly. He could have made the winding trip through the hills to Santa Cruz in about nine minutes instead of the hour-long trip in the vehicle.

Shoot, if they used the Harry-mobile, it wouldn't even take that long. But the questions wouldn't be worth it.

The salty sea air filled his nostrils. He hadn't made it to the beach in a couple of months. Growing up in San Diego, he was at the beach every weekend. He missed it. It was hard to move away when his mama got the opportunity to get a good-paying job in Silicon Valley. Once they finished catching up from the move, they'd be in a much better place by moving north.

He knew that God was in control, and his new friends proved it.

The rest of the youth group spread out in the parking lot, with a lot of excited chatter going on in different groups.

Pastor Sanchez and the youth pastor, Josh Smith, called everyone together. Demarcus sauntered over to the huddle to hear what the two leaders had to say. These guys were cool to hang out with, although Demarcus still felt bad for giving Josh a black eye when they were doing an object lesson using foam doffers to swordfight.

"Okay, gang," Pastor Sanchez said. "We're here to support Santa Cruz Bible Church in their fall outreach to the homeless. We'll pair up with buddies in our group, then split up with their folks to cover the assigned areas. We have a couple of hours before lunch, so you should be able to finish before then. Meet back at noon and we'll have lunch together, and then you'll have the afternoon to enjoy the beach or boardwalk before dinner."

The other kids paired up quickly. Harry jogged over to Sarah Jane's side. "I've got my partner!" Her face turned pink as he beamed at her. What a goof.

Demarcus and Lily were left looking at each other. She smiled. "I guess we're stuck with each other."

His heartrate kicked up a few beats.

"Oh, and no boy and girl couples. This isn't date night, gang." Josh laughed as Harry dropped his head and shuffled over to Demarcus.

"Maybe next time." Lily turned and joined her friend to get their assignment with a local. Demarcus looked after her, thinking of the good times they had shared since the Launch Conference, exploring their gifts together. Lately, he looked forward more to spending time with his friends than to testing his speed—especially if it meant being with Lily.

"C'mon, Demarcus. Let's go find someone to help," Harry said.

Demarcus had to blink a few times to reset his thoughts. Harry wasn't taking the pairing well. Demarcus slugged his buddy in the shoulder.

"Sorry you got stuck with me. Now let's go do what we're here for—like you said—to help."

The afternoon sun reflected off the water and helped Demarcus dry off faster. He lay on a towel on the beach, taking a break from surfing. The goggles from Ratchet looked like regular sunglasses, so he figured it was no big deal to wear them. The lenses worked as advertised. The view couldn't be clearer and the sun didn't bother his eyes.

He inhaled a deep breath of the ocean air. How refreshing. A service project where he also got to enjoy the beach? It was a perfect way to spend a Saturday. He pushed his fingers through the sand, relishing the chance to be back on the shore. After a long week of school and the stress of the reporter looking for him, it was nice to not worry about anything. And delivering care packages for those in need here in Santa Cruz warmed him more than the sun's rays.

Demarcus rolled over and sat up, scanning the beach. On the left, other members of the youth group played beach volleyball with Josh. Pastor Sanchez had returned to the church van. Then Demarcus swiveled to see where Harry was. His friend had tried out bodyboarding instead of surfing. He caught a glance of Harry's red hair right before a wave engulfed him. Looks like he didn't have the hang of it.

Demarcus was about to jeer Harry when an icy blast of water splashed over him. His back arched and he whirled around to see who had tagged him.

Lily and Sarah Jane scampered through the sand to his left,

dropping a bucket on their way. Lily glanced behind and called out, "Bet you can't catch us."

The girls had a lead. He couldn't use his speed here, but he'd nail them for dousing him with freezing water. The beach wasn't as busy as a summer afternoon, and the crowd was moving to the opposite side for the afternoon concert. That worked to his advantage, as the way the girls chose was almost deserted.

Demarcus jumped to his feet and jogged after them. He felt like he was moving in slow motion, but soon he was close to the girls. They passed under the wharf and weaved in and out of the posts, the low tide giving them room to maneuver. Smart tactics to try and slow him down.

It wouldn't work.

They left the rest of the crowds behind. Lily ran a bit ahead of Sarah Jane as the two girls giggled at their prank. They headed for the hotels that framed the beach from the rocky outlook above, a small cliff with no outlet for tourists. Too bad there was no getaway. Demarcus checked around. This section was empty and it didn't seem like anyone was looking. Time for a sprint.

He concentrated and the force in his legs changed. Power surged in his muscles and he was ready to take off.

Whomp.

Sand flew from the impact of his chest against the ground, and he spit clumps of the grainy stuff out of his mouth. What happened? He pushed himself up to see a large divot where he had tried to start sprinting.

Note to self: sand might be a problem when running.

He stood, brushing his chest off. The girls now stood at the edge of the beach, pointing and laughing.

"Don't know your own power, do you?" Lily teased.

"Ha ha. Don't you know you're trapped? I hope your clothes dry fast, cause you're going for a swim."

Demarcus took a couple of steps and stopped. His mouth dropped open as a huge wave rushed in toward the girls.

Chapter 14

Lily tilted her head and tried to figure out Demarcus's body language. One moment he was teasing about getting them, then he froze like a statue. Wait, now he was waving wildly. His lips moved, but the roar of the surf drowned out his voice.

"SJ, what's his deal?"

SJ grabbed her arm and turned her toward the ocean. "Lily!"

Oh.

A wall of water barreled toward them.

"SJ, run toward the rocks!" They twisted around and ran up the shore towards the hotel above the beach. The rumble of the wave raced up behind them.

"New plan. Duck!" Lily tackled her friend and spun to face the water about to engulf them. If she could heat things up enough . . .

Holding her hands out, she unleashed the best solar flare she could. She imagined it as a shield around them.

Water hit her bubble and vaporized into steam. Salt stung her eyes and coated her face. SJ screamed in her ear.

The water pressed down on them so that Lily couldn't see

anything but the greenish sea enveloping them. But her solar heat seemed to be working.

Then the ground shifted.

Before Lily could react, the sand beneath them gave way and they both tumbled back. The water eroded the shore around them. Her concentration broke and the water crashed in.

"Hold your breath!" Lily cried.

The roaring stopped, replaced by the swirling of water as Lily's body tumbled. Her knee twisted when it hit something hard, causing fire to erupt in it.

God, help us!

Her back slammed up against another object, but this one was tall enough to stop her. Water flowed around her body, pinning it and pressing in. Her lungs screamed for oxygen.

Finally, the torrent halted and she could get her head out of the water. She gasped to suck in some much-needed air. The salty liquid dripping down her head stung her eyes.

Where was SJ?

Lily looked around, her vision blurred by the elements. She had rammed into a wooden post farther up the shore next to the rocks. SJ lay next to her on her belly, her face turned away.

"SJ!"

"You're going to join her," an angry female voice shouted from in front of her.

Lily blinked. A young woman with brown skin and flowing black hair strode out of the water retreating to the ocean, her fists balled. She wore loose-fitting clothes, reminiscent of a Bollywood actress.

The girl raised her arms and two streams of water surged up, looking like snakes coiled and ready to attack.

Lily tried to stand, but her swollen and bloody knee betrayed her. "Who are you?"

She smirked. "I'm Kashvi, and I have been chosen to destroy you."

Chapter 15

Before Lily could do anything, Kashvi thrust her hands forward and the water followed her command. But the water didn't wash Lily away. Instead it wrapped around her like living ropes, gurgling and flowing, holding her to the post. The water squeezed her chest and restricted her breathing.

She tried to do something—anything—with light, but the pressure blocked her concentration.

A blur cut in front of Lily, and Kashvi flew through the air, tumbling to a stop in a small tide pool. The watery restraints washed down Lily's body as well. What was that?

Demarcus stopped next to SJ and picked her up. "Lily, can you run? I've got to get SJ to safety."

Lily shook her head. She could barely put weight on her right leg. "Just get her some help. Now that this Kashvi has lost the element of surprise, I can fight back."

"Are you sure?"

"SJ needs help. Get out of here!"

Demarcus sped off down the beach. Lily didn't know what

was wrong with SJ, but there was a lifeguard station a mile away. Demarcus would have her there in seconds. What would they do without a healer to help them? Lily's knee throbbed with pain. The best she could do was hobble a few steps.

Kashvi pushed herself out of the water, seaweed strewn across her sari.

"Okay, Kashvi, you had your turn. Now it's mine."

Lily unleashed a photon blast. She focused to make it a solid beam.

Kashvi waved her hand, summoning a burst of water like a chariot to carry her out of the way. Lily took her turn to throw a wider beam and caught Kashvi across the abdomen. The girl groaned and crumpled to the sand.

Lily hopped forward another couple of steps. "Why are you attacking us?" She shot a laser blast that singed the ends of Kashvi's hair. "Talk!"

"I think you should've gone for the kill shot right there. You lost your chance."

Lily noticed a black halo around Kashvi's head. Sometimes Lily's power gave her discernment to single out evil.

No, duh. Of course, this girl was bad. If she wasn't going to talk, maybe Lily would have to—

But her world shook. Her thoughts turned to jelly as a piercing sound ripped through her head. The pain was terrible, but it also triggered vertigo and Lily was ready to vomit.

She covered her ears to try and block it, to no avail. She stumbled down in the sand, curling into a ball. Thoughts fell apart and her senses failed her. Was she upside down or right side up?

Her face lay against the cool beach but it felt like she hung in the air.

Lily forced her eyes open in time to see a boy standing by Kashvi, his mouth wide open. The screeching stopped for a moment when he took a breath. Lily stretched her body out to see if she could move again. The dizziness subsided, but she felt like she had a hangover. At least, what she guessed what one would feel like.

The boy's youthful face was punctuated with growing stubble. He knelt by Kashvi to check on her, then turned to Lily. "You hurt her. Now you will know suffering."

This stuff seriously happened?

The boy inhaled, and Lily raised her hand. She couldn't aim with her head still swimming, so she flashed a brilliant pulse of light, as strong as she could manage.

Her two adversaries cursed, so it must have done the trick. Sure enough, they clawed at their eyes. Lily fought to stand up. Where was Demarcus? Two against one—she could use some help.

Another blast of sound hit her, this time catapulting her across the beach. That one didn't cause her nausea, but the force was incredible. She reached for her neck as she tried to lean up and see what was happening.

Now Kashvi and the new kid stalked toward her. Water sloshed up again and a low rumble shook the ground.

Kashvi grinned. "Good job, Aasif. One down."

Chapter 16

L ily tried the flash again but tendrils of water had snaked behind her and pinned her arms. She bucked and kicked her legs, but the water forced her shoulders to the wet sand. Aasif set his feet and started to scream.

A familiar figure appeared behind her assailants. Harry grabbed them both and vanished again.

That was good timing. Lily groaned as the water holding her dissipated. She sat up, her ears ringing and body sore all over. Her t-shirt was torn down one side and her shorts had damage as well. Her knee bled and ached. All she could taste was brine.

Now where were with Demarcus and SJ?

She crawled about a yard before Harry reappeared, scooped her up, and ported them to the church van in the parking lot. Demarcus sat next to SJ, who looked woozy but otherwise okay.

"What happened?" Demarcus caught her hand and helped her sit down on a curb. Harry scrambled over to check on SJ, worry etched across his face.

"I don't know. One minute we're running from you. The next

this water-witch is trying to drown us, or wash us to Nevada or something. After you left I knocked her back, but another guy showed up with some kind of sonic thing. He screamed and the worst sound ever came out. Worse than my dad trying to sing. It made me dizzy and nauseous, and gave me a ripping headache."

Come to think of it, she was still unsteady, and she couldn't really hear out of one ear. She tried to shake it off, but the motion made her symptoms worse.

Harry moved away from SJ, staring at Lily's left ear. "Dude, you've got blood coming out of this side."

That might explain things.

Lily tried to hold herself steady as she addressed her friend. "SJ, how are you? You took a beating there."

Sarah Jane stared off into the distance. Her skin was pale, more so than usual. "Huh? I guess okay. My head is killing me."

Pastor Sanchez ran up to the group. "Are you guys okay? What happened? Lily, you're a sight!"

Lily glanced down at her tattered clothes and blood-streaked leg.

"We got attacked. By a couple of people like us, if you get my drift." The pastor's eyes grew huge. "Harry took care of them. What did you do with them?"

"I ported over the water a mile down the shore and let go of them. I figured they could swim to shore."

Demarcus thumped Harry in the arm.

"Ow! Hey."

"Or maybe one of them can control water, so it's no big deal and they're on their way back here to take us on again. Dude, think."

Harry scowled. "You try taking them on next time. I bought us breathing room."

Pastor Sanchez raised his hands. "Knock it off, guys. We don't need infighting right now. But . . . Demarcus might have a point. Get your stuff and Harry, do your thing, however you do it. Get back to the church and I'll call John. I'll have him meet you to pray and figure things out."

"I'll have to hit a couple of waypoints at least on the trip back. With four it's definitely harder."

Lily reached over and rubbed SJ's shoulder. "Hey, I know you're not feeling well. Do you think you're up to healing my knee and ear? I think the trip with Harry could be awful if my balance is out of whack."

SJ bobbed her head. "Yeah, I think so. I can't seem to heal myself, which kind of sucks. But let me try for you."

Her hands wrapped around Lily's knee. The skin ached with the touch, but in a moment the swelling receded and the pain resolved. Then SJ touched her ear and the ringing stopped. Lily's world leveled out. What a gift.

"Thanks, girl. You're awesome." Lily gave SJ a hug and whispered her own prayer of healing for her friend.

Pastor Sanchez did a three-sixty to make sure the coast was clear. "Okay, Harry, get these guys home. I'll tell the group that you had to leave early. Take care, and be blessed."

They all took hands and blinked away.

The two teens returned to the conference room. Their heads hung low as they entered.

"What do you have to say about your failure?"

Kashvi kept her head bowed. "I'm sorry, sir. We got distracted with taking down the light-wielder and didn't account for the teleporter."

Aasif raised his head up defiantly. "I do not think we need to be shamed. We almost defeated twice our number. This was just the beginning."

Roberto could only watch the terrified teens react to what the Hoshek was doing to control them. His consciousness couldn't break through the stranglehold the creature had over his mind and body. He could only mentally weep at what was being done in his name.

The Hoshek held them in contempt for their weakness, but believed their abilities could make up for their perceived deficiencies. If they learned to fear failure enough.

Roberto stepped toward them, a puff of smoke escaping from his lips.

No! Stop!

Their bodies froze. Only their eyes moved as the Hoshek asserted his control over them. The widening of their pupils indicated their terror.

Chapter 17

Demarcus and Harry helped Sarah Jane down onto one of the orange couches in the youth room. Water dripped from her hair onto the furniture. Lily rummaged through their shared beach bag for towels so they could dry off better.

Demarcus placed his head in his hands. The episode in Santa Cruz was crazy. He had gotten cocky over the summer. It hadn't occurred to him that others would have powers, or would want to take them on, much less almost take them out. If only he'd been on the front lines of this fight . . .

A twinge in his leg reminded him of his mistake with the gang bangers as well. *Cocky and careless.*

Sarah Jane still looked groggy. A pretty good lump had developed above her right ear. At least her hair would cover it up. He guessed she had a concussion. Harry kept asking if she needed anything, an anxious look on his face.

Lily's blonde hair was ratted and strung out over the blue towel. Both girls had taken a pounding in the attack. At least Sarah Jane could heal Lily. He needed to be ready to protect the girls. A man shouldn't let a woman down.

A door slammed down the hall, and in a moment, John entered the room. He stooped a bit, a contrast to his usual good posture.

"How are you, children?" John scanned the four of them. His shoulders relaxed after examining things for a moment. "Bless the Lord. When Pastor Sanchez called, I came straight over. What happened?"

They took turns relating the confrontation with the two powered youth. Sarah Jane didn't have much to add—she couldn't remember anything after running away from Demarcus. John nodded with each key point. When Harry described how he dumped them back into the sea, John's brows furrowed, but he let everyone finish before he said anything.

"I knew you would face adversity, but I wasn't sure if this type of thing would happen." He stared off into the distance for a moment. "Moses parting the water. The children of Israel using trumpets to bring down the wall of Jericho. Amazing. Simply incredible."

Demarcus raised his hand. "Are you telling us those two are powered by the Lord as well? If that's so, why would they be attacking us? Wouldn't they be on our side?"

"'The gifts and callings of the Lord are irrevocable.' Our Father gives gifts to His children, but it is up to them what they do with it. There have been gifted people throughout history who used their talents for evil instead of good. Of course, our enemy likes to imitate and corrupt things, so that could be it as well."

John shook his head. "The battle is upon us. You four have been called to the fight, I'm afraid. I wish we had more time to prepare you."

Demarcus ran his hands through his dreads. "I've been thinking since our encounter today. We can have better tactics. I'm picturing Lily and me in the lead. She can provide cover with the light and offer ranged attacks. I'll rush in and hammer them up close. Harry can be porting in and out to confuse them and move Lily around. And if anything happens, SJ is backing us up."

"Wait, what? I'm support? Who took out the two of them today?" Harry argued.

"That was good, but we need to have a plan of attack. It just makes sense."

John knelt on the carpet. "No. You don't understand. This is exactly what I'm talking about."

"What do you mean?" Sarah Jane asked.

"You aren't prepared spiritually for this. Remember, the battle is the Lord's. Today you trust in your abilities and your plans. Plans are good, when you've sought him. This is spiritual warfare, and you have to train your mind differently. Submit to Jesus. He is your peace, even in the midst of conflict."

Demarcus started to counter, but dropped his hand down. Their mentor was right. They were very clumsy, and it wasn't due to tactics.

"You're right. What do we do?"

John pointed at the girls, who sat shivering on the couch. "The first thing would be to get these two home to change into warm clothes so that they don't look like they've been through war."

Sarah Jane nodded. "That would be appreciated."

"Then we pray. Why did these others attack you? What do they want? Why are they so hurt that they'd use their gifts for evil?" John's eyes glistened as he spoke.

Demarcus looked at each of his friends. They looked like they all were thinking the same thing. Love your enemy? Was there any way to reach those two and bring them to the light?

He wondered how to connect with two kids willing to attack without reason. Whatever their skewed motivation was, it reminded him of gang shootings in southern California. Young guys, creating damage, messing up their lives, with no end in sight. Somehow his mama had managed to keep him out of trouble, even with his father out of the picture.

What would it take to bring back two people who had already made their choice?

Chapter 18

Demarcus skidded to a stop, and the rapid deceleration whipped Lily's neck. They stood at the curb of her house. She felt her hair. Man, between the sea water tumble and the windblown look courtesy of Demarcus's run, it probably looked like her mom's pictures from the 80's.

"Okay, I'll get washed up and dressed really quick, and then I'll meet you back out here. Of course, if you're running me to church again, maybe I'll do a ponytail."

Demarcus narrowed one eye. "So, how long is this going to take you?"

"I don't have super speed, so fifteen minutes. Make it twenty."

"Riii-ght. A girl getting ready that fast can happen."

A challenge, then? She'd show him. "You go and get us some In-N-Out burgers. If I'm done before twenty minutes, you buy. If you beat me, then I'll spring for it."

Demarcus winked at her. "Do you want me to run backwards?"

She tried to give him a shove, but he dodged in a blink. *Okay, smart guy.* She pointed the opposite way. "Is that your mom driving up?"

His head turned. "Where?"

Lily took off for her front door. As she caught the door handle, a blast of air whooshed down the street. Seeing him dash about didn't get old.

She ripped the door open and ran right into her father, Jack.

"Lily! What are you doing?"

"Uh, hi, Dad. What's up?"

He pointed outside. "I'll ask you again, what are you doing?"

Why was he like this? "I just got dropped off from the youth group service project."

He ushered her inside and shut the door. "Wasn't it supposed to last until after dinner? It's 4:30."

Oh yeah. For some reason she didn't think explaining her near drowning at the hands of a crazy girl with mad water powers would work.

"It's okay, Dad. Some of us came home early. Sarah Jane . . . wasn't feeling well."

"And who dropped you off? Was it that boy in dreadlocks?"

"His name is Demarcus, and yes, he dropped me off."

"Well, where was his car? Is he old enough to drive solo? And why are you in your bare feet with torn up clothes?"

Snap. She looked down at her ragged outfit. Those were her favorite shorts too. "Dad, that's part of the reason I came home. I slipped on some rocks and my clothes ripped. But I need to get in the shower. We're going to pray together in a little bit, so I need a quick change."

Jack strode over toward his home office. "Come with me, young lady. I need to show you something."

She knew better than to argue with that tone of voice. Out of the corner of her eye, she caught Kelly standing in the kitchen, her eyes down and focused on cooking.

Lily had a bad feeling about this.

Her dad sat at the computer and slowly tapped out his password. Ugh. He was so slow. She always wanted to do it for him. How did he manage to work in the tech industry and be such a bad typist?

The screen changed and his email program was up. He clicked on a message, then opened an attachment.

A blurry picture at nighttime. It was on a city street.

Oh no.

There was a group circled around a male with dreadlocks lying on the sidewalk. A blonde girl had her back to the camera. A girl wearing cotton polka dot pajamas.

Lily's pajamas from the night Demarcus was shot.

Chapter 19

"**D**ad, I can explain."

Jack Beausoliel turned in his leather office chair. He pinched the bridge of his nose, but Lily saw a fine tremor in his hand.

This. Was. Not. Good.

"I don't know what to say, Kitten. When you came back from the Launch Conference, you were a different girl. You started being happy again. Life was coming back to this house. I didn't know where the religion came from, but if it was helping you, I was all for it.

"I've tried to be supportive and encourage you spending time with your new friends. But sneaking out at night? In your pajamas!"

Blood rushed to Lily's cheeks and tears welled up in her eyes. "Daddy, I know it looks bad. It's not what you think. My friend needed help. We were there and came right back."

"How?" He waved his hands in the air. "Did you call a ride share? Take a helicopter? This was the last time Sarah Jane spent the night here, right?"

"Yes, but—"

"Don't give me a 'but.' How did you manage to sneak out, go to San Francisco, and make it back in time for Kelly to bring you a snack? This doesn't make sense."

Lily leaned in and put her hand on his leg. "Dad, I'm not doing bad things. I'm not snorting drugs or having sex. I was helping someone in need. Isn't that worth something?"

He stood abruptly, displacing Lily's hand and pacing the room.

"Lily, you took the death of your mom and brother very hard. And I know that when I met Kelly, it was too soon for you and threw our family into even more upheaval. I'm sorry. Life gave me another chance at companionship, and I took it. Here I thought you had rounded a corner, but now I can't get a straight answer out of you. Maybe it was better when you only dressed in black—at least then you stayed in your room and I knew where you were at night."

Her chest tightened. It was better when she was depressed and locked away? Her tears broke loose and dripped down her face. "If that's how you feel, then maybe I should go." She spun on her heels and stormed toward the door.

A strong hand caught her arm. "You're not going anywhere. Until I get answers about that email, you're staying in your room. Do you hear me?"

This couldn't be happening. She'd never seen him so mad at her before.

"Dad, please, I have to be somewhere. We are doing good, church stuff. I have to be there."

"Get upstairs. You're grounded from your friends and church until further notice."

Lily yanked her arm away, ran up the stairs into her room, and slammed the door. How could he do this?

A blinding flash of light filled her room as she unleashed her anger.

Chapter 20

Demarcus slowed in front of Lily's place. The two-story house faced the street with large windows, so that Demarcus could see the fancy artwork that hung in the entryway from the street. Immaculate landscaping framed a wide cement walkway to the front porch. Two decorative columns guarded the front door. Yeah, Lily's house showed his up big time. Another reason why any thoughts of being something more with her were crazy. They lived in different worlds.

No sign of her. He knew she wouldn't beat him. Now, should he wait until she came out or go to the door? Mr. Beausoliel had been nice enough the one time he'd met him, but it was a quick introduction when she was dropped off at church. Might be better to wait and have her meet him outside. Maybe her dad wouldn't like him dropping by unannounced.

The smell of fries wafted out of the bags and made his mouth water. *C'mon, girl. The food's getting cold!*

A flash of light erupted from a side window toward the back

of the house. It could only be Lily, but why would she be using her power like that in her home?

He dialed her number. The ring tone played while he waited, a song called "Lights" by Ellie Goulding. How appropriate.

The line clicked on. "Demarcus?" Her voice cracked. *What was wrong?*

"Lily, are you okay? I've got the food outside, but I saw light flashing from a window in your house."

"I'm not hungry. I'll . . . I'll pay you back. Sorry."

It sounded like she had been crying. "Hey, what's up?"

"I'm grounded. I can't go anywhere."

"Why are you grounded?"

"I don't know what happened, but somehow my father got an email with a blurry picture of us the night you got shot. Unfortunately, my pajamas stood out, so he knew it was me. He's furious."

Demarcus's appetite vanished. "I'm so sorry. If I hadn't been an idiot, none of this would have happened. Would it help if I talked to him?"

"No. He's beyond. Maybe later I can talk to him, but he said I can't be with you guys or go to church for now. Demarcus, what am I going to do? Do I tell him about our gifts?" Her voice trembled, making him strain to hear over the connection.

"Don't do that. I'll go back to the church and talk to John. We'll pray and he'll help us figure things out. It will be all right, so don't sweat it. Your dad probably just needs to vent."

"Demarcus, I've never seen him so mad. I don't know."

Her final words planted a seed of doubt. Would this break up the Anointed?

Demarcus arrived at a back alley a block away from the church. Harry should be back with Sarah Jane by now. They really needed this time together, though it wouldn't be the same without Lily.

A lump formed in his throat. Thoughts of her twinkling blue eyes danced in his mind. He enjoyed her company so much that he took her for granted. But they were the Anointed. Of course, they would stick together.

God, why would you let this happen? Help Lily's dad to see the light. He chuckled at the accidental pun.

He finished the walk to the church. Recent events had made it clear that he needed to be more inconspicuous to avoid revealing his talent. Probably not the best idea to suddenly zoom up to his intended location. The doors swung open and his footsteps echoed in the empty foyer.

John knelt on the floor as Harry got Sarah Jane some water to drink. She looked better after putting on a sun dress and cleaning up, but she was squinting as she looked up at him. He guessed the light was bothering her concussion.

"Hey, where's Lily?" Sarah Jane asked.

Demarcus slumped into a banana chair in the corner. "Her dad grounded her. I talked to her on the phone from her room. There was something about him getting a picture of us the night I was shot. He's all mad that she was in the city in her pajamas—which I can get. But he basically grounded her from us."

Both Harry and Sarah Jane looked stunned. John's face drooped.

"What's going on? We're attacked, Lily gets grounded. John,

this is crazy. I don't understand." Sarah Jane wiped away a tear as she spoke.

The atmosphere in the room deflated, like a punctured ball. Demarcus looked at the different flags strung around the room. It would be hard to make a difference in the world if their own parents turned against them.

John sat straighter and motioned for them to join him on the floor. They formed a circle, an intimate gathering.

"We don't know what's going on with Lily's family. I can tell you that we are in a tremendous battle. I think it is just dawning on you all how much the enemy wants to resist the works of the Light. Our Lord gave you these gifts to be a blessing to others. However, it was never to make life easy."

Harry drew with his finger along the carpet as John spoke. "So is Satan using Lily's dad?"

"It's not like that. The enemy will use confusion and deceit against us. It's very important that you all hold yourselves to a standard like Paul suggested to Timothy, when he told him to not let anyone look down on him due to his youth. Live with integrity. We all make mistakes, but bring them to Jesus. He is the center of all we're doing, and if we focus on him instead of the petty distractions of the enemy, all will be well."

John led them in a time of prayer. Demarcus was used to it with Mama, but praying out loud was still new to Harry and Sarah Jane. They all took their turns and poured out their hearts. Demarcus didn't have any answers on their new adversaries or Lily's issues, but peace warmed his heart and drew away some of the tension built up from the day.

They stood, with John taking a moment to get upright. "This

old body doesn't cooperate as well as it once did. Be thankful for youth, my friends," he said with a laugh. "I think you should all go home for now. The rest of the youth group might wonder why you're praying with an old man when you could have been having fun. Keep praying for Lily, but know that things are in His hands."

Demarcus waved good-bye as John drove Sarah Jane home. He thought it best to have an adult from church deliver her with her concussion. Harry didn't need rides anymore, so he blinked away. Demarcus had no problem in getting himself back from the church. If traffic cooperated, he would be there in a few minutes.

The shadows of the alleyway behind the church he used as his take-off point grew darker as it got closer to sunset. A stray cat sprinted behind a dumpster for cover. Demarcus crinkled his nose—the scent of the garbage should protect the animal from any predator.

He was ready to dash off when he got a text. Hopefully it was an update from Lily. He pulled out his phone, ready to tap out a reply.

The message on the screen plunged a knife into his gut and slowly twisted. He staggered to the side of the building to support himself. This couldn't be happening.

"Demarcus, we need to talk. I'm Tony Carter, and I'm your father."

Chapter 21

The house rested in the midnight darkness. Nothing stirred as Lily carefully opened her door and scanned for any activity.

The master bedroom door was closed at the end of the hall. She wouldn't have to pass it to make the stairs. Lily slipped out of her room and tried her best ninja impersonation as she slinked down to the main floor.

Lily blinked a few times as she surveyed the living room on the way to Dad's office. Her eyes were sensing different things than they had before. Tonight she could see radiation coming off of the flat screen TV. She noticed their cat, Jiara, lying by the couch, lighting up in the center of her body like a bright red pulsing flame, with oranges and yellows flowing on her outline.

She could see outside of the visible spectrum of light? Her fingers squeezed her eyeballs for a moment, but nothing changed when she opened her eyelids. Okay, she now seemed to have . . . night vision?

As cool as that was, she had a mission. She crept to the office and shut the door behind her. Dad's computer was in sleep mode, with some residual heat apparent in the tower. According to her research, heat signatures were in the infrared range. What else could this mean? It would take some getting used to.

Lily memorized the layout of the desk before proceeding. Then she flicked the mouse to get it out of stand-by mode. Her dad never shut down the computer all the way, which would save her time. She concentrated and tapped her temple until her vision kicked back to normal mode. Weird.

The password remained the same: Teresa. The ache in her gut returned as she typed her mother's name into the prompt box.

Now who sent that email?

She pulled up his email program. He hadn't left anything open to make it easy. Her eyes scanned the list of senders. No names jumped out that she could recognize. The subject lines didn't offer any clues either. Would she have to search each email individually?

Think, girl. It just came in today, or he wouldn't have let her leave this morning. Lily found where the day's emails started. Six different messages had an attachment.

The third from the top had the picture. It was blurry, and it looked like it was taken from a distance, but there was no denying it. Demarcus lay on the ground, and Lily's back was clearly visible. Harry and Sarah Jane were looking down and weren't obvious. However, anyone that knew them as a group would be able to tell who it was.

The message of the email was cryptic. *A concerned friend pointed you out to me. If this were my daughter, I would want to know.* No signature.

She held the arrow cursor over the drop-down option for

senders. The name under "from" said Kim@baunderground.news. Wait, that was the girl from the web video. How did she get her dad's contact information?

As Lily tapped the mouse, the cursor dropped and pointed to the CC line. Her mouth dropped at what she read.

CC: fancymissaustin@hotlink.mail.

Missy Austin. Why was that witch sabotaging her?

Lily's vision flashed red. Her nails dug into her palms as she considered her rival stooping to such a level.

Out of her peripheral vision a shadow moved. She jumped out of the chair.

Jiara crouched at Lily's sudden movement. Oh, only the cat, not her parents. She lifted her hand to push a loose strand of hair away from her face. Her skin glowed with a growing luminescence.

Calm down, Lily. Turn off the light and cover up the snooping. Then there's time to figure out how to handle Missy.

Chapter 22

Someone called out, "Amen," behind him and it stirred Demarcus out of his thoughts. Pastor Sanchez moved around the stage, bringing an impassioned sermon. Too bad Demarcus couldn't tune in at all today.

After yesterday Demarcus needed illumination more than ever, but he could not concentrate. He had hoped that Lily would somehow be at church today, but her sunny smile was nowhere to be found. Even if she had been there, the bombshell of the text still would have tied his insides in knots.

Last night Mama knew something was off because he didn't want to eat. He should have told her about the message, but he was too stunned to say anything.

Harry and Sarah Jane both fidgeted with the bulletin. Sarah Jane doodled waves across the top of the paper, while Harry folded it in various directions. John had checked on them before the service started, but now was in his usual place in the pastor's office, interceding for the congregation. He never stayed in the main service, but Pastor Sanchez thanked him each Sunday for his support.

Demarcus inspected one of his dreads, then switched to picking at a scab on his knee. His brain couldn't decide which to focus on: the attack from yesterday, Lily's problems, or the text.

Why would his father be trying to get a hold of him now, after all this time? Was it truly him? How would this man get his number anyway? The jerk had abandoned Mama before Demarcus was born, after promising to take care of them and do right by her. Then Mama and Demarcus had almost died during childbirth.

The pain in Mama's eyes whenever she talked about it had sealed his anger at the man who had abandoned them a long time ago. A real man wouldn't do that, and Demarcus hadn't considered Tony Carter his dad for years.

The music started and everyone stood up, again startling Demarcus from his stewing. He joined the crowd to avoid sticking out, but the rising strains of piano and guitar couldn't shake him from his growing funk.

Pastor Sanchez's voice rose over the chords when the volume dropped. "We have a choice, people. We can let a circumstance or a person have control over us when we hold on to anger, disappointment, or fear. The power of forgiveness can break that control. Give forgiveness a chance to work a miracle for you this week." Then he blessed everyone as they left.

A hand slapped his shoulder. Harry leaned forward to catch Demarcus's eye. "Hey, bro. What's going on? You're out of it today."

"Man, I was thinking about yesterday. I'll be fine." That was the truth, right?

"Are you going to be there for our group tonight?"

He should. Confessing what ate at him would do him good. Right after he found some answers. "I should be there, but I have something I need to take care of first."

Harry furrowed his brows. "Is there anything I can help with?"

"I'll let you know, bro, okay?" Demarcus clapped Harry's back as he left the sanctuary. He ducked past Pastor Sanchez to avoid a conversation. It was time to get home and talk with his mom.

The Ford Taurus pulled into the driveway and Mary Bartlett stepped out of the vehicle. Demarcus opened the front door and stepped out past the lemon tree to give her a hug. "Hey, Mama. How was your church?"

Her big smile crossed her face, accentuating her full cheeks. "Oh, my boy. It was so good to be in the house of the Lord. But I'm glad to see you. You're so busy with school and your youth group, I don't see you as much anymore."

He nodded. The bad thing about their group was that it pulled him away from the church his mama attended. She had already found a congregation that she enjoyed, so they went their separate ways on Sunday morning. The amount of knowledge and wisdom he gleaned from John was worth it, but he did miss their trips to church.

Mama walked into the house and made a beeline for the kitchen. She poured some of her homemade lemonade for both of them. Tart and sweet, it was the perfect relief from his thirst.

"What's wrong, sweetheart?"

"I hadn't said anything."

"Oh, silly boy. A mother knows when her boy is hurting. Is there a problem with that cute blonde girl from youth group?"

"Mama! I'm just friends with Lily."

"Mm-hmm." She wagged her finger. "And you think I was born yesterday? Again, I know things."

Demarcus plopped on the couch and kicked his shoes off before putting his feet up on a footstool. "I am bummed because Lily's grounded right now, but we're like a brother and sister. That's not my problem anyway."

"Is it school then? How are classes going?" Mama picked up his shoes to put them neatly alongside the couch, like she always did. Her nose crinkled. "I swear, boy, how come you keep ending up with tar smell on your shoes? Do you go out of your way to find fresh asphalt?"

He shrugged, hoping to avoid more questions. It was probably time for new shoes soon.

"School is fine. I get my homework done during study period." Having the ability to read and write with super speed didn't hurt. It was pretty easy to keep up anymore. But school wasn't the subject he wanted to discuss right now.

"Mama, I have a few questions about my father."

Her body stiffened. Pain flickered across her face before she sat back and cleared her throat. "What do you want to know?"

"What was the last thing he said to you?"

A hangnail on her finger caught her attention before she answered.

"Why on earth are you asking about him?"

The true answer had to wait for a minute. "Mama, I need to

know some things. I'm a man now, and I deserve to hear about him."

Her teeth clenched for a moment. "Neither of us knew the Lord when I got pregnant with you. Tony tried to set his mind right, to psych himself up for having a baby. But when I got bedridden with you the last six weeks, he got real skittish. After two weeks, I got a phone call where he said he was in Vegas to earn some extra money."

"And you never heard from him again?"

Mama's eyes glistened. "No, there was one other moment. He sent a note, asking if you were a boy or girl. I foolishly thought he'd come back once he knew we had a son, so I wrote back. After that, nothing."

The feelings inside his gut swirled with confusion and anger. On one hand, he was glad such a loser wasn't in their life, but on the other hand he wondered what would have happened if he did have a father growing up.

"Demarcus, why you asking me this? You haven't worried about this in a long time."

Should he tell her the truth? That's what he was going to do today. His foot tapped on the stool and the velocity started to get out of control. He'd better be careful there.

Demarcus felt a nudge inside to open up and be transparent. This involved his mother as well, and she was always his biggest cheerleader.

A cloud passed over the sun and the light in the roomed darkened a little. Maybe this wasn't the best time. He needed some information, and he wasn't sure where to start. *Mama, I'm a superhero, and my father contacted me out of the blue. What's for dinner?*

Demarcus hopped up and leaned over to kiss his mama on the forehead. "We've had some conversations in youth group about family. It got me thinking, that's all."

She caught him in her arms and pulled him into one of her bear hugs.

"Mama!"

"Oh, my boy, you're never too old for a hug. Just because you're sixteen doesn't mean I can't catch you. I'm glad you've found these good friends. Are you going to youth group later?"

He flailed his arms enough that she let him go. Mothers could be so embarrassing. "Yeah, I'm planning on going. I might leave early though. I might have an appointment for a school assignment."

His lemonade glass glistened with condensation when he snatched it up and drained it. "See you later, Mama."

He couldn't stand being around her with his lies. It would be better if he did more digging before bringing her grief anyway.

His bedroom door shut with a click as he pulled out his cell phone. He typed out a response.

"When and where?"

Chapter 23

"Lily, you have a visitor."

Her father's voice echoed up the stairwell and into her room. Who was he going to let her see? It couldn't be her Anointed friends, if she was grounded from them. A sigh escaped her lips, and she finished the last bite of gelato on her spoon. She clomped down the stairs and dropped her pint of Mocha Madness in the freezer before rounding the back hallway to the living room.

Dad sat on one couch. The sight of her visitor stopped her in her tracks.

John sat on the love seat, holding a cup of coffee, his kind eyes welcoming her into the conversation.

Her heart skipped a beat. If anyone could change her dad's mind, it was John. Lily entered the room and sat on the piano bench to create a triangle. She put one leg over the other and groaned inwardly as she realized her lounging outfit of frayed leggings and an Evanescence t-shirt wasn't the best wardrobe choice.

"Hello, Lily. How are you today?" John's formal tone never ceased to amuse her.

"Um, I'm fine. I, uh, didn't really clean up since I didn't go to church today."

John chuckled. "Don't worry, it does not bother me."

Her father sat ramrod straight, his face a hardened chunk of granite, daring anyone to chip away at his façade. "Kitten, John wanted to talk to us together."

"Okay."

John set his drink on the coffee table, next to the potted African violet Lily had picked out for Kelly for her birthday. "I'm very thankful that you agreed to meet with me today."

Her dad nodded, but that was the extent of it. It was going to be one of those discussions.

"I understand that Lily has earned some consequences due to her behavior." John spoke with a calm, even tone. He had such grace in every situation.

"That's right. I thought Lily's friends and involvement would be a good thing, but circumstances have changed."

Lily sat rigid, matching her father's body language. He wasn't giving any room here for negotiation.

"I understand that one particular event involved Lily being in a city location without your permission."

Dad held up a finger. "In her pajamas, I might add. She was supposed to be here with a friend having a sleepover."

John nodded. "Very inappropriate, I agree."

Wait, wasn't he supposed to be here to argue on her behalf? So far his tactics were backing up everything her dad was saying.

"Lily's never done anything like that in sixteen years, until she started hanging out with these friends. I was more than a little disappointed."

"You are her father, and you have every right to be. I understand."

Dad unfolded his arms and re-folded his hands in his lap. "I'm glad to hear that, but I don't think you came here to give your approval on my daughter's discipline. What's your angle?"

John scratched his temple. "Angle? I apologize, I wanted to talk about Lily, not about geometry."

Lily held up her hands to intercede before her dad could react. "Dad, John's originally from Greece. Some of our sayings don't always translate."

"Okay. What's your purpose in coming today?"

"I have been helping with the youth group since June, around the time that Lily started coming. I can report that she has been a delight to have around, and that she has shown a lot of growth in just a few months. Would you agree?"

Dad's face twitched. Ooh, he wanted to say something contrary, but John nailed it. "Yes, I would say overall she's doing well. Ever since I signed her up for the Launch Conference."

"How has she changed?"

Her dad glanced at her. Wow, John was going for the honesty challenge. "Uh, she was very depressed from the loss of her mother and brother over a year ago. We couldn't really get her out of the house other than school. Since Lily's been going to church, she's been getting out and being social again."

John rubbed his beard. "If I may, sir. Your daughter has greatly improved her disposition since we started working with her, and when she makes one mistake, although a serious one, you forbid her from participating in the helpful activity?"

Checkmate.

Dad fumbled for a response, starting to speak a couple times and then halting, before he got his next thought out. "Yes, it helped. But being unsupervised with her friends led to a huge problem. Would you like your only daughter being in the city, in a dangerous area, at night while in her pajamas?"

Maybe she was too optimistic.

John's eyes searched her father's face. "You make my point for me, sir. I would suggest, humbly, that your daughter is improving while working with the church and even the youth group. But she and her friends need supervision."

Dad thought, then nodded in assent.

"My request, then, would be that if you would let Lily participate in youth group activities and church, then I would personally help in supervising the group. I pledge to you my sincere promise that I will monitor the youth as if they were my own. And if I am not available to supervise, then Lily shall not participate in that event."

Wait a second. Was this a victory or not?

His posture relaxed and her dad dropped his head into his hands. "Perhaps I was too severe and hasty in my judgment." He ran a hand through his hair and looked up at John. "I agree with your idea. If you are directly involved, then Lily may attend. She can work on earning my trust back through this, and hopefully it will continue to help her."

John turned to her. "Is this acceptable to you, my dear?"

Lily's head spun from the quick turn of events. Dad relented? At least partially. It wasn't ideal, but she could live with it for now. "Yeah, that's okay. How long do I have to have John's supervision?"

Dad chuckled, but with an edge to it. "Don't push it, Kitten. What you did was still outrageous, but I'm willing to work with you on this."

She walked over to him and hugged his neck. "Thanks, Daddy. You won't regret it."

He whispered in her ear. "I'd better not. I don't know what I'd do if I lost you as well."

Lily gave John a hug as well. "Thank you for coming and helping us."

They relaxed and John took up his coffee cup again. "If it is settled, then I am planning to take the youth back to Applied Sciences. They made an impression on the researcher there, and he would like to work with them more, if that's all right with you."

"Okay, but she needs to be home by 10. It's a school night."

Lily's heaviness lifted like the fog over the San Francisco Bay when the sun came out. This could work. But as John said his goodbyes and walked down the front sidewalk, the thought of the surf pounding her body and the hate in that strange girl's eyes broke through her relief. They were in a battle. Lily wondered how an old man would be able to protect them. As wise as John was, it may take all of their gifts to be victorious.

Chapter 24

The viewpoint on the screen fluttered to life, and Simon tapped keys in a fury to lock in the signal for the video and audio. An empty energy drink can flew off the desk when he whipped his mouse around. The encounter had to go according to plan. He was getting closer to his target.

"Rosa, can you hear me?" He spoke into his wireless headset. His mind focused on the smart watch on his intern's wrist. It produced the Wi-Fi that allowed him to connect to her Flare prototype glasses, but it also was a direct transceiver for his power to maintain influence over her.

The nineteen-year-old was clever and gifted in her own way, but she was also volatile. Easy to influence, but hard to control.

"I can hear you. I'm at the café. She's not here yet."

"Okay. The connection is holding now. As I monitor things, I'll keep you updated."

"Fine. Now get out of my ear so I can enjoy my caramel macchiato in peace."

Simon reached for another energy drink, feeling around

carefully since his vision was everything that Rosa was seeing, albeit blurry. His fingers brushed the aluminum container. He grabbed the drink and took a long swig.

While he waited, he ran fingers through his unruly wavy hair. It was longer than he'd kept it in a long time. As a billionaire CEO he'd kept it shorter and styled to help him be more respectable to the corporate powers that chafed at having such a young hotshot in their midst.

Until he could reclaim his sight, a haircut was low priority.

Suddenly his visual field swung to one side, then another, disorienting him. Not controlling his own visual input was disconcerting. "Rosa, why are you moving your head so much?"

The sarcasm dripped from her voice. "What, I can't shake my head out a little bit? Sheesh."

Simon held his fingers from tapping out a command that would retaliate against Rosa. He'd feel it too.

Now the view shifted to the door. The brightness from outside kept him from identifying the new customer. The backlight washed out the image. Rosa stood.

Was this her?

The weaker prototype Rosa wore had less definition than his cutting-edge device. Even as the person came closer, he couldn't make out details. He'd have to rely on audio.

The newcomer addressed his intern. "Are you Rosa?"

"Yes. And you're Missy, right?"

"Yeah. I recognize you from the conference. You were part of the special group that worked with Simon, weren't you?"

"I was," Rosa said. "Thanks for meeting me. Want a drink? On me."

Missy went to the counter to order. Simon's fingers flew over the keys. It would really help to have better definition. Wait, they had Missy's email address. He could use her smart phone to triangulate the signal and improve reception. After she had her drink, she joined Rosa at the table.

The image clarified. A pretty face wearing a nasty snarl. "Why should I talk to you? I wasn't good enough for your elite group."

Simon focused all his power through the connection to Rosa. He couldn't have her fiery temper blow this encounter. He didn't anticipate such attitude from this Missy Austin.

"Obviously mistakes were made at the conference." Simon's words came through Rosa's lips. "The point now is that we have a mutual interest in Ji-young Kim's report on the strange happenings going on in the Bay Area."

Missy pointed a finger right in the face of his puppet. "What do you know about that?"

"Enough. You go to school with one of the girls in that report, don't you?"

Disgust colored her face. "Ugh. Don't mention Lily Beausoliel to me. There's something seriously up with her."

"Why is it such a big deal to you?"

"She expects everyone to pity her. Then she bamboozled Simon at the conference. I don't think Lily's a victim at all. She plays people."

Interesting comment. Simon grinned, maybe the first time he'd done that in a month. So there was a jealousy slant to be had here. "How so?" he had Rosa reply.

"Lily came to our school playing the tragic backstory. My brother was interested in her, but she broke his heart. When I confronted her, she claimed she was overwhelmed. Even when I had gone out of my way to help her. I was so done with her."

"Why do you think she fooled Simon?"

Missy leaned back with a huff. "Who knows? It's not like she's all that cute. She has weird friends. But I got her good. I found her dad's email address and gave that to Ms. Kim, who sent a picture off that video to him—that was delish. I wish I could have seen her face."

The teen sitting before Rosa was tall and could be considered attractive, but what an ugly spirit. Simon had his own anger toward Lily, but this girl was almost pathological. Maybe it wasn't the best idea to use her.

Well, it was best to line up a bunch of threads and cut them off if they weren't needed.

Rosa slipped a micro SD card over to Missy. "We think you're right about this Beausoliel girl, incidentally. She's been in a couple of places where strange things have happened, like the attack in Japantown, as well as the accident at the conference. My employer would like you to put this in your phone and take any pictures that you think would be helpful. We'll analyze them for any anomalies."

The girl took a drink from her iced coffee before taking the memory unit. "Okay. I'll do it. Wait, what's in it for me?"

Simon was tired of this girl. He forced Rosa to grasp Missy's arm. The concentration made his head hurt, but he was able to use Rosa as a conduit for his influence to take hold.

Rosa's strong grip made Missy grimace. Simon overrode the pain caused by the harsh move. The girl's pupils dilated for a moment, then returned to normal. He'd gotten through to her.

"I'll send you whatever I get." Her fingers fumbled with her phone until she could slip the card into her Android.

Now Simon had another device to control and use to pick up anything he could on Lily. And her friends.

Chapter 25

The glass building shimmered in the falling sunlight. Lily hadn't noticed last time how many pinecones littered the parking lot of Applied Sciences. The numerous trees left their mark this time of year. Squirrels darted away from the approaching group and dashed up the bark of a nearby pine.

Lily inhaled a deep breath, thankful to be back with the Anointed in some fashion. The compromise between John and her dad grated a little. She didn't really ask to go to San Francisco in her pajamas to help Demarcus. Harry's panic move created the issue and it wasn't fair.

Still, better this than explaining to her father that they were basically superheroes. He probably wasn't ready for that.

For now, she wouldn't miss church or group meetings anymore. It would be nice to hang out as friends again. When he picked her up, John had encouraged her to be a good steward of her activity. Then, he believed, her dad would relent on the rest of the punishment.

The group entered the foyer and checked in with a different

guard. Steve, the friendly engineer, once again took them up to meet Ratchet. She wondered if he ever came out of his lab.

As they walked down the hall, Lily noticed Demarcus dragging behind the rest of the group. Um, that never happened. What was up with him? His cheerful demeanor kept everyone else going.

She dropped her notebook and stooped to pick it up, timing it to catch up with Demarcus. "Hey you, what did I miss yesterday?"

His eyes widened and he jerked back. Weird. You'd think she had zapped him with a live wire or something. "What do you mean?"

"Uh, at church? What did Pastor Sanchez talk about during the sermon? How was youth group?"

The tension in Demarcus showed in his tight lips and darting eyes. "I, uh, I'm not sure what the sermon was about. I forgot about a big homework project for the weekend and it kept my mind occupied. In fact, I couldn't go to youth group because I had to finish."

Uh huh. Liar.

She caught his arm as they reached the lab door. "What's wrong?"

His eyes searched hers, but they were interrupted by the swoosh of the lab doors and the jubilant cry of Ratchet. "You guys come in. Hurry! I can't wait to show you what I've come up with."

Demarcus tipped his head toward the lab, his dreads flipping around in the process. "C'mon. I'll tell you later."

That would have to do. He slipped into the room ahead of her.

The lab didn't have the gleam it did at their first visit. The entryway smelled of some kind of smoky residue. A greenish powder dusted the far corner. Scorch marks on the wall over by the spectrometer completed the new decorations. Lily squinted to examine the burns. Pretty sure that wasn't her fault.

Pastor Sanchez and John moved out of the way. Ratchet wheeled around the lab for a moment, unable to contain his excitement. An excited puppy, waiting to play with his master.

"Who should go first? I can't decide." He clapped his hands together. Was this for real? She looked around to see how many empty coffee cups were lying around. It had to be caffeine overload.

Harry stood closest to the work station, so Ratchet tagged him first. "Can I just say, I could run tests on you all day. The physics of what you're doing—mind-bending! Maybe if you have a day off of school . . ."

John cleared his throat, loudly.

"Right. So you're limited by your knowledge or memory of a location, right?"

"Pretty much. Like when we came back from San Francisco one night. I have a range of about twenty-five miles and I had to recall specific areas on the trip to get back to Palo Alto." Harry scratched the back of his neck, a sheepish look on his face when he glanced at the girls.

"Right. But what if you knew a location by something else? I mean, you could teleport all over the place to learn areas, or make it a priority to travel everywhere. But what if you could dial it in?"

Harry narrowed his eyes. "What do you mean?"

A tap on the counter caused a drawer to slide open. Ratchet produced a wristwatch-sized device. "How about a GPS unit?"

Everyone's jaw dropped. Seriously? Lily couldn't believe the tricks the scientist had hidden away.

"This should help you extend your range and make sure you

land safely. If you've got farther to go, it will take you a minute to punch in where you want to go, but it's programmed to find the back of buildings, empty spaces, things like that to keep you inconspicuous."

The GPS had a sleek look with a buffed aluminum frame. Ratchet held it out to Harry, whose wide eyes showed his amazement. It was a way cool item for him to have, but the thought of another wearable device like that creeped Lily out.

The sound of her bones popping when Rosa crushed Lily's Alturas Wi-Fi band while she was wearing it echoed in her ears, and the memory of the pain gave her a passing wave of nausea.

Ratchet rolled over to SJ and took her hand. "I've got something special for you, dear. I've been told if you understand what's going on with someone, you do better with your healing. Is that right?"

SJ nodded. "It seems so. If I can focus on it specifically, I think it helps."

Ratchet pumped his fist. "Yes! I've got an experimental scanner that can read and diagnose emergency conditions. Think a QR code scanner, but with something actually useful to do. It won't treat, but that's where you come in."

He rolled himself to a cabinet where he pulled out a few different gadgets, most with loose wires hanging out. One even sparked as he tossed it aside.

His prize held in the air, Ratchet came back to SJ. The device looked like the latest iPhone, with a smooth glass top and brushed metal backing. She took the scanner and turned it around. "Wow, it looks . . . cool?"

"Cool, that's all you can say? Oh, I guess a demonstration would be nice." The eccentric scientist turned the camera-type lens toward himself and tapped a button on the screen. "Cheese! Sorry, it doesn't actually take selfies."

Lily could appreciate a fine infrared beam emanating from the device and running up and down Ratchet. When it finished, a music tone started playing.

Pastor Sanchez shook his head. "Really? Game show theme music?"

"Why not?"

After a few seconds the music stopped. Ratchet handed the device to SJ. "What does it say?"

Her mouth opened, then closed in silence. Finally, she spoke. "Are you sure you want me to blurt this out?"

Ratchet smiled, the lines at his eyes crinkling up. "Dear, it won't come as a great surprise."

"It says you've had your spinal cord transected at the T10-11 level, causing paraplegia."

"See? Nothing you didn't already know."

SJ's tried to cover her grin with her hand. "It also says you have a significant case of toenail fungus."

Lily and the others couldn't help but laugh. He snatched it from her hand. "Well, I'm not trying to hide that either. Even though I won't wear sandals. I'll adjust the settings to leave out the minor conditions."

A few taps and he handed it back to her.

"Thanks, Ratchet. It's awesome."

"I've got one other thing for you specifically. Voila!" He pulled out two more wrist bracelets. He's giving out fitness trackers now?

"Wow. Thanks again. Um, what are they?"

He clipped the bracelets on both wrists. "They're a new kind of personal protective equipment for health care workers. Instead of wasting gloves, these produce a low-level field that vaporizes any foreign organic material. Click right here." He pointed to a slight depression in the band.

"That will be helpful," SJ said grimacing. "I remember the blood on me from Demarcus."

Demarcus ducked his head down at the comment. Lily thought of the way her stepmom had freaked out over the nail polish on the bedspread, not realizing what was underneath it.

"And if you tap it twice, it will turn into a kinetic barrier that will give your punches some . . . well, punch. I thought if you're going to be in dangerous situations, it would be good to have some defensive capability."

"Ooh, Sarah Jane's going to bring the hurt." Demarcus air boxed, shuffling his feet and doing a little dodging.

"I don't want to hurt anyone, but it probably would be handy just in case."

Lily couldn't honestly see her tender-hearted friend roughing someone up. But, lately stranger things had happened.

SJ double tapped the buttons and turned her hands slowly. Some energy signature followed the contour of SJ's hands, a criss-cross beam that made a fine glove around them.

Lily leaned over to Demarcus. "Can you see the energy gloves?"

Demarcus squinted. "I don't see anything."

That's what Lily thought—another example of her being able to see other spectrums. She should talk to Ratchet about it, but he was too excited right now to focus.

Speaking of excitement, Ratchet rubbed his hands together with a gleam in his eye and a broad smile.

"Okay, who's next?"

Chapter 26

Now Ratchet fished in a low cabinet. "I think I stuck these down here for our speedster." He sat back up with an orange shoebox. "Sorry, these aren't a particular name brand. Well, not after my modifications."

Lily watched as Demarcus eagerly took the offering. She knew how many shoes he'd gone through in the last six months. This would be something he'd really dig. Ratchet pulled out a blue tennis shoe with white flame highlights.

"Sweet. I always need more running shoes," Demarcus said.

A belly laugh erupted from Ratchet. "If these work like I think, they'll be the last pair you need. Frictionless surfaces on the soles. They'll give you good traction, but never wear through."

"This is sick! I can't believe it. Mama will be happy. So will my bank account. Thanks, Ratchet."

Ratchet did a head slap. "I really wonder what it will take for you guys to know that the surface is never all there is with me. Do you guys know what a non-Newtonian fluid is?"

Lily and SJ squinted in unison at each other. No idea. Demarcus cocked an eyebrow, but Harry excitedly waved his hand.

"Dude, we're not in class," Demarcus teased.

"I saw it on *Science Bros*, the new show testing all these crazy things. It's a liquid that can be solid as well. The host walked on it."

Ratchet rolled up to Harry and gave him a high five. "I knew I liked this kid. If you click your heels, the shoes will emit a low-level field that will change any liquid into a temporary non-Newtonian state."

Demarcus held up a finger. "Wait, does that mean . . ."

"That you can run on water? Oh yeah."

Demarcus pumped his fist and plopped into a chair to slip on the new shoes.

"At least it should work in theory. I got a hamster to run on top of a fish tank full of water. You're a little heavier than a hamster. You should try it out before going crazy with it."

Ratchet turned to find SJ with her hand on his shoulder, her eyes closed. A tear ran down her cheek.

"My dear, what's wrong?" he asked.

SJ wiped her face. "I was praying for your spinal cord to be healed. I—I wanted to the first time we met you, but now that I know how to pray . . ." She dropped her head, her fists clenched in frustration. "But I feel almost as if something is blocking it from happening. I don't know why."

John came up behind her and gently pulled her hand away, then clasped it with both of his. "Oh, my compassionate Sarah Jane. You have quite the heart for others, don't you? But sometimes God has a purpose in our trials."

A soft weeping began as SJ cupped her face. "I hate it when I can't help. I feel useless."

Ratchet rolled in front of her and took her hand. "Don't you worry about ol' Ratchet, okay? I had a car wreck when I was a freshman in college. Made a big mistake drinking and driving, and this is what happened. But the Lord gave me a wake-up call through it. I found him and got serious about life and studying. I would probably be working in a bowling alley, polishing balls, if not for my injury. So truly, I'm okay with where I am. But thank you. I'm honored that you care enough to do something."

Lily had to fight back tears at the scene. Demarcus and Harry ducked their heads as well. "What's wrong, boys?" she asked.

"Just some dust in my eye, that's all," Harry quipped.

SJ and Ratchet shared a long hug, then she pulled back and asked for a Kleenex.

"Why don't you try your organic barriers?" Ratchet asked.

SJ stuck out her tongue. "Um, no thank you. I don't want to blow my nose in my hands."

"Oh yeah, it wouldn't be foreign material, since it's keyed to your DNA signature." Ratchet pointed to a tissue box and wheeled over to Lily.

"Now to you, Miss Lily. I think you'll like this." He rolled over to a large freestanding cabinet and rummaged through it.

The guy had no system of organization, did he? Maybe it was his creative brain.

"Eureka!"

Before she knew it, Ratchet had wheeled up and handed her a thick black vinyl case. Lily had a thrill vibrate through her. It was kinda like Christmas. As long as they weren't wristbands. She opened it up and lifted a pair of stretchy blue gloves. Cool . . .

"Try them on."

Lily slipped them on. The soft texture soothed her hand. They felt truly like they were made for her. As she flexed her fingers, she noticed a raised area on the palms and the tip of each index finger.

"What do they do?"

"I heard you've been studying optics on your own time. Very admirable, by the way. The fingertips are focusers. Made with an ytterbium crystal of my own design, they'll let you be much more precise. You can do things from read the data on a laser disc to cut steel with them." He glanced at his ruined computer. "Please be careful with the last part."

Wow. This guy was a Swiss-Army-knife of awesome.

He pointed to a piece of four-inch-thick steel held between two clamps. "Try it out. I promise you won't get any refraction this time."

Lily pointed her finger and focused on the beam she wanted. Every time she used her power it tingled afterwards in her fingers and hand. The gloves collected the tingling right in her fingertip. A slight twitch was all that was required, and a thin stream of red lashed from the glove and into the steel.

Touchy trigger on that one.

She tried again and tried to reign things in. The laser cut through the steel as she carefully drew a pattern in the metal. When she completed her design, she gave a wider blast in the center of the hole and a heart-shaped cut-out fell onto the desk.

"Impressive. Most impressive." Ratchet gave her a thumbs-up. "Now for the palm attachment. Remember how you made the colorful designs in the air, like your own neon signs? That gave me an idea."

Ratchet wheeled over to a separate console. "It will take some practice and a different approach to how you concentrate. But I think I've set this up so you can project holograms. And I'm not talking about the blue light thing that R2-D2 did. I'm talking full projections, things that can look real. Fake-out-your-parents real."

Demarcus had lost his earlier moping. "Get out. Are you for real, man? This is getting crazy." He hopped around, pumping his fists.

It sounded pretty sweet. Except she had no idea how to do it. "So how does it work? It is a jump from my light designs to a full . . . hologram."

The scientist kept his fingers flying over the keyboard. "You should be able to take an image you recall in your mind and recreate it with light. With practice, you could make it move. The problem is audio. Unless you have a secret talent for throwing your voice, the hologram can't reproduce sound."

Ratchet turned around to face Lily. "I'm going to have to work on that." A megawatt grin flashed on his face. What couldn't he do?

"Okay. Think of an image. Focus on something you care about deeply. That should give you the best definition and clarity for what you're doing."

What should she pick? Lily exhaled, trying to clear her mind. Let her heart speak.

The palms of her gloves warmed, and the skin beneath tingled. It must be working. She thrust her hands out, scrunching her brow. Ripples appeared next to Ratchet. Browns, blacks, and blues swirled together. Something was happening. Okay mind, focus on what you want to see.

A picture jumped into her mind and she gasped.

The ripples coalesced into a form. The rest of the team gasped as well.

Ratchet let out a low whistle. "Now that's what I'm talking about."

A lifelike apparition of Demarcus, clad in the same blue jersey and silver shorts as the real article, stood next to the treadmill, his eyes staring ahead. That was . . . unexpected.

Or was it?

Scattered giggles came from everyone. The Demarcus hologram looked around at everyone. Huh. That wasn't too difficult.

Demarcus walked over to it, looked it up and down. "Dang, girl, this is like looking into a mirror. How did you do this?"

A bead of sweat broke out on her forehead. "Um, I'm not totally sure. I tried to focus on something . . . easy to visualize. I guess since Demarcus was right here, that was the simplest. But there's something to the gloves. What did you do there, Ratchet?"

"Do you want the technical or simple version?"

Harry asked for the technical, while the rest responded in unison. "Simple."

Harry folded his arms and frowned.

Ratchet rolled his eyes. "Fine. I was hoping someone wanted a challenge. Basically, I used Lily's brain as a computer producing the image, and the gloves turned into a projector. The gloves do microcalculations at a rate of 15 gigahertz to make something so complex."

It felt complex. Lily's arms started to shake, and her

concentration drained the longer she held the image. She only made maybe ten more seconds before the image flickered. Then holo-Demarcus crumbled into oblivion, fading into virtual dust. Energy jolted through her arms, causing pain to radiate to her neck. Her legs wobbled. Maybe sitting down would be a good idea.

She plopped on her butt. In the middle of the floor.

John came over and knelt down by her. "Are you all right? What happened?"

Her head felt like she'd stuck her finger in a light socket. Thoughts jumbled and words didn't want to form.

"I plenty feel quirky."

Ratchet scratched his head. "There must be a feedback problem. It does take a lot of processing power to manage something so intense. Maybe if I cycled the refresh rate slower . . ."

SJ touched his shoulder. "But Dr. Ratchet, she's not feeling well. What do we do for her now?"

Lily raised a hand to say she was okay. But why did her finger poke herself in the eye? Ow. "Frangnabit."

SJ left Ratchet and sat next to Lily. She placed her hands on each side of Lily's head and started praying. Her words lifted up to the heavens, and John joined in with his foreign tongue.

What was the big deal? She only couldn't speak or really move right. "Bleff. Me no oyster."

The world started to spin. This wasn't fun anymore. "Ahhhh," was all she could get out. Ratchet typed furiously at his keyboard. SJ and John kept praying, while Demarcus and Harry stood in front of her, eyes wide.

It would be all right. If she could just sleep for a moment. Her eyes fluttered closed.

"No! Don't do it. Stay with us, Lily." A voice from somewhere jerked her eyes back open for a moment. What was the worry? She needed a little nap.

Her head slumped back, too heavy to hold. A noodle. She'd been turned into a noodle. There was a vague sense of panic around her, but her eyes didn't want to open.

Suddenly another shock kicked in from the gloves. Her hands chilled, and the ice climbed up her arms and made her body tremble. It felt like a mental ice bath.

Her eyes kicked open with a rush. "Whoa. What was that?" Goosebumps stood up all along her arms. SJ hugged her and John breathed a huge sigh.

For a minute she felt like a gas station burrito being warmed up. Finally, SJ let go, and Ratchet leaned forward in his wheelchair, scanning her with his device for SJ.

"What happened?"

Lily had a funny taste in her mouth. A salty, sour taste lingered along her tongue. This kept getting stranger. "I don't know. I had the thought that I'd been noodle-fied. My brain was working, but the words didn't come out right and I couldn't control my body. It felt like sleep sounded really good."

The scanner squawked. Ratchet tapped it a few times, then smacked it once on the side. "I guess everything's not perfect. It says you have rheumatic fever. Do you have a temperature?"

She felt her forehead. "If anything, I'm chilled now."

"All right. I'll play with the code and the settings. Maybe don't try to use the hologram function until I get back to you. I'm pretty sure it's a feedback problem. I think it overloaded your speech and motor centers for a few minutes. I set a reverse cycle back through the gloves and it appeared to reset you."

Demarcus sat next to her. "So what's a frangnabit, anyway?" Heat rushed to her cheeks. She had made a fool of herself in front of everyone. What could go wrong next?

His arm reached around her shoulder for a side hug. "I'm glad you're okay." Brown eyes searched her face, and her cheeks warmed at the attention.

Her body shivered, not due to chill, but for a different reason. Oh, there was a problem developing, but it had nothing to do with mental feedback or the spectrum of light.

Sigh.

Chapter 27

Another day at school. Demarcus hoped he had learned something, but he couldn't say what. English, science, and math had all dragged and the clock was his nemesis. He wished he could be out testing his sweet new sneakers from last night. Or spending time with the Anointed.

Hanging out with Lily.

But a time approached that Demarcus had both wished for and dreaded all his life. He was going to meet his father.

He passed a couple of buddies on the way out the door. Matthew gave him a high-five for the Cowboys' victory from Sunday. Everything had been weighing on him so much he didn't even realize he'd missed the game.

Something that had never happened before the Anointed came along.

The breeze rustled the leaves on the trees lining the walkway to the street. The fresh air cleared his head as he took a left and walked away from the buses. He used to take them last year, but things were much faster on his own. He had a quiet route down where he wandered a few blocks away from school and caught an alley that gave him room to take off. Once he got going, the path home meandered compared to the bus, but he beat it by a half hour.

Today Demarcus would travel in a similar direction but pass his house by a few miles. The meeting spot with Tony Carter was at an out-of-the-way park that had seen better days. Few kids spent time there, and it should provide plenty of privacy for whatever happened today.

Demarcus fished his phone out of his pocket to check the time: 3:20. He'd make it in a few minutes with the crazy path he'd planned. He had time to walk a bit first for some peace and quiet with God.

Lord, you know my heart is pounding, and my head wants to crush in on itself. I can't believe that I'm doing this. I need Your grace and peace so I don't punch the guy out. Uh, sorry about the last part. Help me have the words to speak. Your will be done. And again, help me keep cool no matter what.

Oh, and don't let him see my gift.

The thoughts that bounced around in his head kept him from hearing the screams right away. But finally, they broke through and he realized a woman sounded hysterical a block away.

Did he have time to do something? Only a few minutes had passed. Yeah, he had time.

Demarcus followed the sound, careful to keep his wits about him. He didn't have Harry as back-up if he wandered into trouble again.

The screams intensified, matched by cussing and sounds of a scuffle. Demarcus glanced around him. There were a couple of people and several cars around. Not the moment to turn on the jets. He jogged as slow as he could to a parking lot at the end of a block.

At the back of the lot two guys were locked together in some kind of wrestling match. One wore a red headband, torn jeans, and a t-shirt, while the other guy had a basketball jersey and shorts. A girl, probably around Demarcus's age, stood back by a car, crying for them to stop. Tears created dark lines from her thick eyeliner down her cheeks.

The dudes separated, and the basketball guy backed up a couple of steps. "Man, just leave us alone. We ain't doin' nothin' to hurt you."

Headband stuck a finger toward the girl. "She is supposed to be goin' out with me. So stay away from my property."

The girl tried to argue the point, but Headband shuffled forward a step and swung a haymaker at Basketball. The dude's attention had been on his girlfriend, so the blow landed square and dropped him to the ground.

With his opponent down, he started kicking him in the gut. "Vince, you going to kill him," the girl screamed.

That was it.

Demarcus dropped his bag and shot over to Vince. He caught the jerk's shoulder and let his momentum spin Vince to the ground.

Vince looked up, his mouth wide but eyes aflame with anger. "You just made a huge mistake. This ain't your business."

"Leave them alone, and I won't make it my business. But you won't like it if you mess with me."

The thug didn't wait to talk it out more. He dove at Demarcus with a fierce tackle. It was quick enough that Demarcus was almost caught by surprise.

Almost.

He sidestepped the move and let Vince sprawl out on the asphalt once again. Stopping the guy without giving away his speed was going to be interesting. He turned to the girl. "Watch out. I won't let him hurt you."

"Look out!"

Pain rocked his head. He staggered back, lights flashing in his peripheral vision. What happened?

Vince swung again with a metal pole he'd found somewhere. Demarcus ducked back, barely avoiding another blow, but his head rang from the first impact. Liquid trickled down the side of his head. A finger came away red when he touched it.

The pole came at him again, and Demarcus tripped over a cement parking divider in the process of dodging it. Vince rushed at him with a snarl on his face, along with scrapes from his fall. Demarcus had to roll against a rusting Dodge Charger to miss the next attack.

Okay man, this guy was a serious scrapper. It wasn't some playground tussle. Demarcus pulled himself up with the car for support. His mind didn't want to connect with his legs like normal. His reflexes were sluggish.

Vince roared with his next thrust. Demarcus slid to the side and glass shattered with the impact. His chance for a counter-attack. While the pole was partially blocked by the car's interior, he swung for the guy's nose. Soft flesh crunched under his fist and Vince howled in pain and rage.

The guy didn't back down, though. He managed a kick that

made Demarcus stumble when he tried to flank. That left Vince an opening to score a blow to Demarcus's abdomen. He doubled over from the pain.

Vince freed the pole from the car and teed up like a baseball player swinging for the fences.

If only Demarcus had stayed put.

Time to finish this guy. Despite the throb in his head and ache in his midsection, Demarcus whirled behind Vince when he swung. The pole smashed against the car. Vince swore with surprise, right before getting his head pushed down against the car's roof.

He tried a backhand, but Demarcus darted around and threw a couple of punches as fast as he could. Vince's head bucked back and forth. He slammed against the car. One more blow to the midsection caused him to crumple to the ground.

Demarcus took a step back, panting. That wasn't fun. His head still hurt terribly, and his neck had started to spasm as well. At least Vince stayed down, groaning softly.

The girl stared wide-eyed at him, her mouth agape. Oh yeah, that's why he got in the fight. Trying to be a hero. "Are you okay? How's your boyfriend?"

She shook her head slightly. "How did you move so fast?"

Shoot. "I've practiced a lot."

"No. All of a sudden, Vince's head bounced around and he slammed into the car. It's like you were a blur."

Demarcus tried to take a deep breath, but his stomach complained. "The point is, are you guys okay? Do you need any more help?"

The girl wandered back to Basketball, who was trying to sit up.

"I don't know who you are, but we're getting out of here. This is too weird. And Vince, when he comes around, we got problems."

"Look, I'm only trying to help . . ."

She threw a hand up. "Save it, freak. We getting outta here."

An alarm beeped on his phone. Snap, he only had five minutes to make it to his meeting place. Well, she didn't want him around anyway.

His body aching, he jogged to the edge of the parking lot and unleashed his speed.

Chapter 28

The blur of run-down houses slowed. Demarcus dropped to a human speed, walking the last two blocks to the park. He normally didn't breathe hard after a run, but the fight had taken something out of him.

His mind buzzed with the repercussions of that battle. That girl feared him after he stepped in and helped. How about a little thanks, lady? Maybe being a knight in shining armor didn't always come with gratitude.

The edge of the park approached. Demarcus turned to walk across the dry, yellowed grass. The California drought didn't allow for green lawns. The old, creaky swing set hung solemnly, waiting for a child to take a chance on it. Farther on, a plastic climbing and sliding toy had faded paint and chipped edges.

Didn't look like a place for a lot of fun.

In the back corner were a couple of trees. Standing between them was a dark-skinned man with a shaved head and a familiar look about him.

Here goes nothing. Lord, have mercy.

Demarcus walked past the playground equipment, keeping his head up. The man caught sight of him and took a few wary steps forward. He regarded Demarcus, looking him up and down.

"You Demarcus?"

Hearing the voice of his father chilled his blood. He never thought this would happen. "Yes, I am. And you're Tony Carter?"

A single nod.

"Uh, hey." Why did he agree to do this?

"Wow. You're my son. Man, it's just . . . a lot to take in."

That was the truth. Tony had the same eyes as him. His nose, bent at an angle, was smaller. Demarcus got Mama's flat, broad nose instead. Lines extended from Tony's eyes, and pockmarks dotted his cheeks. A couple of tattoos peeked out from under a tight t-shirt.

Tony cleared his throat. "I can see your mother in you. That's a good thing."

Anger rippled through Demarcus. The dude shouldn't be bringing his mother into this. He couldn't be bothered to stick around. He sucked in a deep breath. *Calm down. You're on edge from that fight.*

"So, uh, why did you want to see me now?"

His father stood rigid, not betraying any emotion. "I've been away a long time. I know that. But why wouldn't a father want to see his kid?"

Now? He wants to see me now, of all times?

"My mistakes are big, man. I know. And your mom and I were young. It was scary, the thought of having a child. I screwed up when I panicked in Vegas. Seeing you, shoot . . ." Tony shook his head, his eyes down.

Demarcus's gut roiled. He couldn't believe he was finally talking to his father. And it took all his self-control not to tear into the guy for bailing on Mama. His fists clenched and unclenched, his fingers stiff from hitting Vince a few minutes ago.

"So why did you leave my mother to fend for herself with a baby on the way?" No sense going through the pointless pleasantries.

Tony's pupils constricted. "I told you. I was a scared kid. I went to Vegas, started the lowest grunt job on a construction site, and got in over my head."

His body language softened. "But I'm here now because I want to own my mistake. My story's same as a lot of people. I got caught in the wrong crowd. Drugs, jail. All of it. Typical thug life.

"But I met people that have helped me out. I did my time, paid off debts, and got back to southern California. But then I found you weren't there. After a while I found a lead and managed to get some time to come up here."

The words scratched Demarcus's emotions like broken glass. The druggie dad. Jail bait. His mama had always taught him to do good, and growing up in church kept him grounded. But a motivation had always secretly been to avoid being the kind of man he feared his father was.

And it had all come true.

Demarcus shook his head, trying to take it all in. The movement made pain radiate from his cut on his head. He absent-mindedly reached to rub the area. Dried blood came off and he wiped it on his shorts.

"Wait, is that blood on your head?"

"Yeah, it is."

Tony rubbed a fist. "Man, my boy's getting into it on the day I ask to see him. That ain't the way you should be goin', you know? It's gonna get you in trouble. Take it from me."

Did he seriously say that?

Fire scorched behind Demarcus's eyes. His muscles trembled from the adrenaline pumping through his body. "Dude, you did not just go there. You're in my life for all of five minutes, and you're trying to lecture me?"

His father held his hands up. "Whoa, sport. I'm pointing out that you don't want to make my same mistakes by getting in trouble."

"Screw you. Did you know how I got this cut? I saved a guy from getting beaten to death. I'm as far from being like you as I can be. At least I know not to bail on a woman. This is messed up." Demarcus jabbed a finger toward Tony. "I don't know how you found me, but I don't want anything to do with you. Stay away from me, and you'd better stay away from my mother."

Dust kicked up as he turned to go. Bile rose in his throat with each step.

A hand caught his shoulder. "Hey, don't walk away from me. I'm your father."

Demarcus twirled and shoved as hard as he could on Tony's chest, making him stagger back. "You're not my father. A father cares for a son, for his wife. Unfortunately, you helped make me, but that's all I ever want from you."

He cut back and started jogging back the way he came. Footsteps pounded after him. "Demarcus, I'm trying to make things right."

His speed picked up until Tony Carter's voice faded in the distance. He ran until he hit a nearby church. He skidded to a stop, gravel kicking up into the air, so he could catch his breath. Not from exertion, but from the sobs that threatened to choke him.

Roberto's phone rang. His mind, floating in the darkness, took a moment to register what the sound was. Sealing himself off from the Hoshek to maintain this fragment of independence took all his concentration. The force controlling him didn't seem to focus on things like technology, and Roberto wasn't going to remind it to answer a phone call.

The Hoshek finally recognized the sound and fumbled with the phone.

"Hello?" his voice answered.

"It's me."

Ah, the prodigal father. "Did you meet with him?"

A grunt on the other line. "Yeah. And it didn't go well. I hope you're happy."

The Hoshek had no concept of happiness. But Roberto noted a sense of pleasure from the creature because its plans were furthered.

"You will be well-compensated for your time," the Hoshek said.

A pause. "Whatever. I don't know if what you're offering is worth it now. I don't think he ever wants to see me again."

"You didn't seem conflicted when we contacted you."

A curse. "Well, you try seeing your kid for the first time. And I don't know what his mother feeds him, but that boy can move. I hope he goes out for football."

"If you'd like to consider this a donation to my cause . . ."

The sound of something hitting metal echoed through the

phone. "No, I need the green. One question though. Why the interest in my son?"

"We want to see what he will do, and you seemed to be the perfect motivation. I will stay in touch. We may need you again soon."

"What, are you some kind of scout?"

Roberto couldn't fully access what the Hoshek was planning, or the influence it had from the Archai. So he had no clue what the Hoshek meant by his answer.

"You might say that."

Chapter 29

Lily plopped on her new bedspread. Kelly hadn't even tried to clean the previous one, which suited Lily fine. No evidence to reveal the blood that Demarcus had brought in. That night had brought enough trouble.

She sighed. A non-Anointed night. Since their time at Applied Sciences had gone so long, Dad thought it good for her to stay in tonight. So here she sat, nothing to do. Her computer screen swirled with colors matching the music beats playing through the speakers. Her phone sat on her bed stand. SJ was out with her family and couldn't text. She didn't know where Demarcus was. He wasn't responding. Harry was out too.

So she had nothing to do.

The gloves! She had wondered about them throughout the day. She had gone to bed last night chilled from Ratchet's remedy, and her brain remained shrouded in fog for half the day. It had taken a quadruple-shot Irish cream mocha to break her stupor. But all the cool things she could do with the gloves—her mind kept playing with the possibilities.

She wouldn't mess with the hologram part again. Nothing was worth it. But what could she do with the other part of it? The fingertip thingy.

Cutting a hole through her wall was out of the question. What else did Ratchet say she could do?

Laser beams: check.

Holograms: check, but on hold.

Oh yeah, she could read the information off of disks.

How was that going to help the Anointed? Well, she wouldn't get anywhere if she didn't at least try it.

She scampered down the stairs. Kelly waved from the kitchen. Something with garlic scented the air and made Lily's mouth water. "Smells good, Kelly!"

"Thanks. It will be ready in a little while."

Her stepmother loved to cook. Some day Lily should try and learn from her. But not today. She needed some old-fashioned technology, and that meant her dad's computer desk.

Her dad had a meeting tonight, so hacking into his stuff again would be easy. No ninja tricks. Just wandering into his study.

Sure enough, the first drawer had several CDs. Most weren't labeled. *Geez, Dad, if you're going to keep this stuff around, why isn't it labeled?*

She didn't want to try some random disk that likely didn't have much of anything on it. Lily poked around a little deeper in the drawer. Toward the back a manila mailer with a torn edge looked inviting. Sure enough, a crystal case with a CD was inside. Care had been taken to protect this information, whatever it was.

The cat dodged out of the way when she ran back upstairs. *Stay out of the way, Jiara. I've got some investigating to do.* If Ratchet's gloves had any other side effects, it would be best to be alone.

Or not, if last night was any indication. Kelly would come get her for dinner soon if she passed out or anything.

Lily sat at her desk and opened the CD drive. She had told her dad she needed a new laptop, but his insistence that she was fine turned out lucky—her old one still took CDs. A quick check of her phone to make sure no messages from any of the Anointed gang . . .

Nope. Playing sleuth was the best use of her time.

The folders of the disk opened up on the drive. She wanted to see what was there first and compare it to whatever she could manage with her gloves.

A few documents came up. Nothing exciting. Lily tapped the eject button and pulled the CD out. The case with her new gloves sat on her bed. She leaned back and grabbed it. The gloves had a sheen to them. They looked like they'd be stiff, but the material really stretched and felt relaxed against her skin.

Stylish, comfortable, and they'll make you a master hacker.

Ratchet had said this trick was about the fingertip. She turned the disk to the underside and aimed at the silver material. There was data on here. She just had to figure out how to access it.

How did a CD drive work? The light pointed at one place, and the disk spun.

Lily remembered how fast light was, and the tingle in her finger grew. Her emitter didn't have to shine on one spot. She focused her beam on the edge and it raced around the perimeter.

Oh. OH.

Information flashed in her mind. Like words streaming on a

scroll along the bottom of a TV screen. She could feel her eyes ticking back and forth, thinking they had to move to keep up with the screen.

But she could pick out bits of data wherever she wanted.

Lily aimed again, this time circling ever closer to the middle of the disk. Her mind read the information like it was up on her monitor. But holy cow, did it come fast. She raced through the folders she had seen on her computer.

She stopped at an encrypted folder, one that hadn't shown up when she looked a minute ago.

She concentrated to make her beam even more precise, and like tumblers in a lock, the encryption fell away. All right! She *was* a hacker. Harry would be mad jealous. Take that, Doctor Whoever.

Lily's celebration came to a halt at the words, "Autopsy report of Teresa Beausoliel."

The disk tumbled from her hand. Tears welled as she cupped her mouth in shock. Shut up. This was the report about her mother's death?

She couldn't read that. She already knew what happened, anyway. Her mother had mixed her medications wrong and basically overdosed, killing herself and Luke in the process. Grief washed over Lily like twilight on a cloudy night, stirring a darkness she'd managed to avoid over the last couple of months.

But she had to see it for herself.

Trembling, she picked up the disk and blew any dust off. The laser from her finger was hard to control with her tremor. Data jumbled in her head like Scrabble tiles thrown across the floor. *Calm down. girl. You can do this.*

After a few calming breaths, she focused again. The report

made her nauseous. It detailed the trauma to her mother's body. Bleeding in the brain was listed as the probable cause of death. Lily wanted to toss the disk out the window and blast it with her laser, but she had come this far. She had to read the rest.

The autopsy continued in clinical detail. Lily thanked God for that part. She didn't know the real-life terms of what had happened.

Here it was. The toxicology report.

"No organic conditions or chemicals causes contributed to the accident."

What? That . . . couldn't be.

It made the newspaper. It went through her school. Lily's mom drove under the influence and killed herself and Lily's brother, Luke.

Her stomach fought to keep acid down. But there had to be more answers here. Lily concentrated harder. She peeled back every piece of code she could in the report, but it didn't seem like a forgery. What then? What about a level up?

She mentally did a back button to read the encryption. There. It was hard to make out, but bits of code stood out like little place markers showing how this report had been locked down so no one could find it. They pointed to a different report that had been placed in the original's stead.

Lily couldn't find the replacement on the disk, so she went back to the markers. Tiny little squiggles teased the bottom of some of the letters. Come on, optics is all about light getting back to the receiver to be interpreted. She bore down, straining her eyes to make out what it said.

The trail. She found a thread that led out of this program. And it left a clue as to where it came from.

Somehow, Alturas had hacked her mother's autopsy report and locked it away. Her mother hadn't messed up with medication in depression or suicide. Lily wanted to burn a hole through the ceiling. A face came to mind at who would be behind this. Simon Mazor.

Chapter 30

The stone kept skipping down the road until Demarcus couldn't see it anymore. Dusk shifted to darkness quickly in September. It didn't make a lot of sense to be out on a school night with nothing to do. But Demarcus wasn't ready to go home.

Mama wasn't necessarily happy with his text that something had come up after school he had to work on, but she didn't insist he come home, thankfully. A few hours after his confrontation with Tony, and his blood threatened to boil at every thought of the horrible encounter.

Who was he to judge Demarcus? The man admitted to drugs and jail time. His actions regarding Mama spoke louder than a scream. Then to show up and act like he could chastise Demarcus for a supposed fight?

Whatever.

He heard the sound of wheels on cement. When he had texted Harry, it was a surprise to learn he wasn't far from Demarcus's location.

The skate park loomed ahead. One of the large overhead lights had blown out, casting a shadow across part of the ramp structure—the hardest part, which had contributed to this place dying off when it got dark.

Apparently that was perfect for Harry, who leapt into the air in front of Demarcus.

Cool. His buddy had gotten over the fear that had first paralyzed him in trying to use his gift. Controlling his porting gave him a whole new world, and Harry lived like a new man.

But Demarcus wouldn't have pegged him for a skater. Harry and his board soared on the other side of the bowl, gaining greater height.

Uh, dude. Too high!

Demarcus stood frozen while Harry twisted in the air. He must have lost control. No way was he going to land this jump. Demarcus sped over to the spot of impact to try and catch him.

Except he caught nothing but air.

Harry appeared right next to him, the board under his feet, as he zoomed across the bowl to the other side.

"What are you doing? Trying to get killed?" Harry called out on his way up the other side. Instead of finishing another trick, he ported back to the edge of the ramp, standing and holding his board.

"I was coming to save you from a nasty slam."

Laughing, Harry hopped back down the ramp and shuffled over to Demarcus. "That's the point. I come here when it's deserted. If I'm in a weird position or falling, I don't panic any more. I've got it down where I can almost automatically port to a safe position."

Demarcus let out a low whistle. "Dude, that's almost messed up. But awesome."

Harry ran a hand through his growing shag. "Oh, I took a few good hits early on. It's been worth it though. Do you want to try it out?"

"Not real—"

Before he could finish his answer, Harry snatched Demarcus's arm and the two of them appeared at the height of the spotlights.

Plummeting toward the ground.

Demarcus's stomach bottomed out with the fall. They rushed toward the cement. "What are you—"

"Doing?" Harry finished.

With solid ground under his feet, Demarcus felt like he could kill Harry right now.

"See what I mean? That was no sweat."

Demarcus gave him the stink eye. "You'll be sweating when I catch you." He reached for Harry's shirt, but all he got was air. Again.

His friend appeared at the end of the skate park. "Dude. I don't think that will happen." The mocking tone begged for Demarcus to make him eat the words.

It took two seconds to get over there, but Harry blipped back to his original spot. Okay, his friend's tactic was pretty good. What if Demarcus used some strategy?

Demarcus started toward the same area, but cut right back. And ran Harry over.

The two of them tumbled down the side of the bowl. Demarcus tried to protect his head, but that resulted in an elbow smashing against the hard ground. Harry moaned as he skidded to a stop.

"What was that for?"

Demarcus sat up and held his arm. "I guess you can be caught. You've got to be more unpredictable."

Harry rolled from his back so he could push up with his arms. A nasty road rash dribbled blood from a knee. "We've got to stop skidding across the pavement. It's bad for my health. Ow."

A reminder of their first meeting and discovering each of them had powers. That brought a welcome smile to Demarcus's face.

They limped over to a bench and sat down. Harry dabbed at his knee with the edge of his shorts, while Demarcus took inventory of his wounds. Head laceration, stiff neck, sore abs, and now a swollen elbow. At least his legs didn't hurt.

"So what are you doing out at night? When you texted to ask where I was, I didn't expect to see you out here," Harry said.

A lump dropped in Demarcus's stomach again. So much for the chuckles from using their powers.

"I . . . I met my father tonight."

Harry looked up from his first aid attempts. "Dude, are you serious? How did that happen? I didn't think you knew where he was."

Demarcus shivered. "I didn't, but Saturday night he texted me. Out of the blue, after our prayer time. So we met today," he whispered.

Harry's hand rested on his shoulder. "How did it go?"

Thoughts careened inside Demarcus's head. How to describe it? Demarcus told Harry about the fight with Vince and the girl's reaction.

"Then when I met my father, he thought I was some hood guy, since I had blood down the side of my head. Tried to get on my case about it. But he admitted that he was a loser. Jail. Drugs. I can't believe that he'd try to ride me."

The feelings that Demarcus had battled all evening broke through all his barriers he'd tried to raise. Hot tears welled up and spilled from his eyes. "I wish I'd never answered that text. I knew that my old man was a loser. All this time, if he couldn't help my mom, that told me what I needed. But I went to see for myself. And now I realize that he's a part of me. Part of that failure, being a punk—that's my legacy."

He wanted to drive his fist into Tony Carter's face.

Harry placed a hand on Demarcus' shoulder, while Demarcus seethed, his chest heaving with deep breaths. After a minute of trying to calm himself down, he felt the impulse to cause bodily harm to someone fall away. Head hanging low, he muttered a thanks to his friend.

After Demarcus could catch his breath, Harry caught his eye. "Listen to me. I get that it would be hard to see someone like this guy and take it as your destiny. That he defines you. But if we've learned anything from John, that's not the case. You know who you are.

"You're the guy willing to race through traffic to knock me out of the way when we had barely met a couple hours earlier. The one to risk your life saving the Alturas interns when Simon's building collapsed. And tonight, you put yourself on the line for strangers because you saw a guy getting the snot kicked out of him.

"So, stuff the lies from the enemy. Do you hear me? You are boss, and nothing this guy says or does should make a difference. Yeah, he may be your father. But only biologically. Your mom rocks, and you rock."

Demarcus shook his head to clear it. "Thanks, dude. You should be, like, a counselor." He slugged Harry's shoulder.

"Hey!" Harry grinned. "Maybe. But don't think you're off the hook. I'm still upset with you for my knee."

Is that how he wanted to play it? "Okay. I'll make it up to you. My treat at DQ. I'll race you there."

"Seriously? You know I can take you, anytime." Harry interlocked his fingers and cracked his knuckles.

"Only if you know which one I'm going to. See if you figure it out."

Harry started to complain, but Demarcus took off before he could finish his sentence. That should keep him hopping for a little while.

As he ran, his smile started to fade. Grateful as he was for the pep talk from his friend, a sliver of darkness embedded itself in Demarcus's heart regarding Tony Carter.

Chapter 31

L ily's fingers flew over the keys. She had to find out if he was out there somewhere.

Simon Mazor should have died on the last day of the Launch Conference. By her hands. The thought of him tumbling in the air after she destroyed the Source always made her break out in a cold sweat, nausea rising along with it. She hadn't intended to kill him—only to stop his plans to influence the world with his mind control powers.

But no body had been found.

John had noticed an impact crater that would be the size of a small body. The speculation in their group was that Rosa's strength had made her able to survive her own plunge—this one on purpose by Lily after Rosa had seemingly killed SJ.

Could there be some way that Simon had survived the explosion as well?

When he wasn't found, he had been assumed lost and had a huge obituary write-up in all of the Bay Area press. However, news of strange dealings within Alturas came from former aides.

Testimony from Kelsey exposed Simon's ability to manipulate. She had left the tech industry and became a social media manager for the San Francisco 49ers, far from research fields. Most of his top assistants had fled to other jobs and the Flare network had been shut down while investigators and lawyers pored over the allegations of what had happened at the conference.

That would prompt a glory hound like Simon to stay hidden.

The idea was crazy. He probably was burned up or crushed to a pulp with the explosion. A lost, evil man who had faced judgment.

But Lily really wanted some answers. And retribution.

If someone had killed her mother and brother, she had the ability to make them pay.

Lily massaged her temples. *Settle down, girl.* That wasn't the right attitude, her mind kept arguing. But emotion overruled that point every time.

Unfortunately, she had no idea how to make her new laser ability work over the Internet. Google was her best weapon, and nothing she'd found held much promise so far.

Sure, the conspiracy freaks had a number of posts on the whole episode at Launch. Some of them hit pretty close to the target. "Alturas created superhumans with covert research, and the accident was a cover-up," one article's summary read, making Lily chuckle darkly. If only they knew the truth.

Her search hadn't found a smoking gun yet. In fact, she didn't have much of a case at all. Authorities speculated some on the fact that no one found Simon's body. The Alturas Collective acted like their president and CEO had perished and tried to salvage something out of his former billion-dollar empire.

What really happened to Simon Mazor?

A cold plate of pasta sat next to her, hardly touched. Maybe she should try to eat again. Kelly had been disappointed when Lily took dinner to her room, but when she saw the tear streaks on Lily's face, she relented.

Her poor stepmother had inherited a mess. When was she going to have a normal stepdaughter?

The creamy garlic taste didn't soothe Lily's raw ache inside. She set the plate down after one bite, and she flopped back on her bed. Who was she kidding? This was crazy. Simon was gone, and she didn't expect to get any answers from anyone at Alturas about the accident.

Ugh. Garlic and revenge didn't go together.

A ping sounded from her laptop.

She sat up and stretched her arms high above her head to loosen her back. As she brought them down, a rainbow arced between her hands.

Okay girl, remember that God loves you and has given you an incredible gift. Don't go into the darkness again.

The chair bounced with her impact. The notification hadn't come from any social media sites. But there was a green exclamation mark in the lower right of her screen from her search alerts. With everything that had happened the last two days, she hadn't even bothered to check for anything new.

The bite she had swallowed threatened to come back up. The alert was set to register new postings from Ji-young Kim.

The pointer hovered over the symbol. With gritted teeth, Lily clicked the mouse and the notification filled her screen. Just as she feared. A new post from Ms. Kim.

Wait a second. Lily relaxed her tense shoulders. She and

her friends had been far from San Francisco. The lady probably reported on multiple hoaxes and curiosities. It didn't have to be the Anointed every time. Feeling better, she clicked on the post. A new video. She grabbed her headphones as a precaution.

The video started in something that resembled a low-budget motel room. A few maps and charts decorated the wall, some with pins marking a location on a map of San Francisco and the surrounding areas.

"This is Ji-young Kim, reporting for the Bay Area Underground. New reports have surfaced of unusual activities, this time coming from Santa Cruz."

Oh, snap.

"Eyewitnesses report a large wave hitting near the pier, out of place with other reports of weather and surf conditions for the day. We also have exclusive access to a video shot by a local that reveals more paranormal activity."

This couldn't be happening. How could this woman be getting this information?

The video brought the terror of the moment back to Lily in a rush. A shaky image from a distance focused on the tail end of the wave. No light was apparent—it must have been after Lily and SJ tumbled back. The water pushed up the shore farther than it should have for the tide.

The girl Kashvi could barely be made out walking from the ocean to land. The camera operator moved the view back and forth, not sure what to focus on. When it came back to Kashvi, she was on the ground. So it missed Demarcus rushing in and rescuing SJ.

Now a few quick light flashes showed by the water's edge. Lily's handiwork. The camera settled on their battle. Aasif approached from the north. She thought her ears still rang with a high-pitched sound on occasion. Hopefully it was only her imagination.

Then a white flash blinded the screen. Her distraction. Wow, that really worked well. A muttered curse came from a disembodied voice. The dude with the camera must not have appreciated it.

That made the view wobble a bit more. By the time he righted it, Kashvi and Aasif were walking forward.

Then a blip, and they were gone.

Ji-young came back on screen. "Let me slow that last part down for our viewers."

The beach came back, with Lily's two adversaries moving in slow motion. Suddenly a third figure appeared. The two jerked back slightly when he grabbed their clothes. And gone.

They caught Harry porting them away.

"As you can see, two people were just there, then a third appears, and all three disappear. The strange phenomena matches my eyewitness experience from last week when people disappeared in front of me. Then, add the unusual wave and weird beams of light, and we have more evidence of supernatural activity, right here in California."

The frame came back to Ji-young pointing at a Bay Area map. "We've had confirmed sightings in these locations."

The Alturas campus. Japantown. Santa Cruz.

"And we've had other unconfirmed reports and rumors. One is just coming in tonight from San Jose regarding a man moving super-humanly fast, attacking another person. I want to get to the bottom of this. Please report any unusual activities to our website to help me uncover the truth of these mysteries that you won't find covered on the mainstream media.

"This is Ji-young Kim from the Bay Area Underground News, thanking you for your vigilance."

Lily felt the blood drain from her face as she closed the laptop screen. Everywhere they went lately, this girl was finding out about their activities. She'd seen all of them in action. Somehow they had the bad luck of a random guy catching their battle with the other kids with powers.

How were they going to uncover the truth behind the other teens if Ji-young hovered over their shoulders as a threat to expose them?

One last thought hit her. A speedster in San Jose attacking someone? What was Demarcus up to tonight?

Or was there someone else just like him out there?

Lily shot him a text to see what he was up to, then watched the video again. Ji-young Kim was right on top of them. Like it or not, they'd have to find a way to throw her off.

Chapter 32

Only Roberto's shallow breathing broke the chamber's silence. The Archai wanted an update on the various attacks on the Anointed. The air was stifling inside the smooth jade walls in the back of a shop in Chinatown—apparently a property of one of the Archai, Master Fen.

The ghostly silhouettes of the Four rippled onto the green reflective surfaces. Adeniji, Fen, Cezar, and Violette appeared as shimmering apparitions. Roberto gulped. He'd never seen the Four, the mysterious sages that led the Archai. Now that he'd been eavesdropping on the Hoshek's spiritual connection with these leaders, he understood his whole expedition was only one part of their plan to overthrow the world order.

The beast within rumbled against his human fear. The Hoshek was primal and powerful, but Roberto only knew terror at what he'd become, huddling in a corner of his subconscious.

"What is your progress?" The warm baritone of the African belied his ruthless nature.

Roberto bowed. "Masters, I am honored to come before you. I have done much since we last spoke."

A hush came from the Frenchwoman. "Enough with the posturing. Make it plain. It won't be hidden from us anyway."

"Certainly." If there was one on the Council the Hoshek would like to kill with his bare hands, it would be Violette. "I have found other broken subjects from a willing source to counteract the gifts of the Anointed youth. They have already inflected doubt and damage upon the team and their morale.

"I have also been tightening a noose around them, preparing to expose them. Every time they use their gifts in public, I feed the information to a woman who is more than willing to trumpet it everywhere. It is making the group anxious about using their abilities."

"What of the interference of the girl that worked with Simon? What was her name?" Cezar asked.

"Yes, Rosa Gonzales has been spotted visiting with a rival of the girl who bends light. I do not see it as interference, but as an opportunity. I will be watching to see how I can manipulate that situation as well."

Fen kept her head bowed the whole time. When she looked up, her eyes appeared only as voids, and the utter blackness chilled Roberto's mind even more. "These are mere tokens. We have one true threat that can stand against us. The others can be turned or eliminated. What about the elder?"

Roberto lowered his head, but his chest heaved with the beast inside fuming at the mention of the servant of the Light. "I am working on planting the seeds of betrayal in his charges. When they react against the ways of the Kingdom in anger and hatred, I am building up something that will shake them all. And I believe it will break the elder, if not destroy him completely."

In his secret heart, the one place deep inside he'd kept from the monster and the Four, Roberto wondered if in some way instead the Light could free him from this curse.

The Four appraised one another. Roberto could feel the mental pulses passing him by, a faint touch against his awareness without revealing the information carried. His eyes narrowed with disgust at their lofty ways.

Adeniji took the lead. "This has promise, our apprentice. Proceed with this plan. To surround the elder with such a trap is impressive. But beware, there are forces we cannot fully control. You must have patience but move swiftly when the time comes. Do not be afraid to strike. This is not a time for subtlety. That recent failure has been made clear."

Roberto could sense the contempt for Simon Mazor, who had been so oblivious to think that he was the only one favored by the Four, when all along they were marshalling different avenues to achieve supremacy. Since Simon's way of controlling people through suggestion and tricks of technology didn't work, it was time for something more direct from the Hoshek.

Fear and trembling. And good old-fashioned domination.

"If we couldn't manipulate the light, then we will do the opposite," Adeniji said with a smile. "We will come at them with Darkness."

Chapter 33

"**G**irl, are you okay, or are you just trying to not sleep anymore? You look like a hot mess."

Lily dropped her backpack in front of her locker. Way to make a friend feel good. She slumped against the edge of the locker and checked her reflection in the mirror. Well, Clara wasn't wrong. Grey circles hung under her eyes, and her pale complexion peered back.

Sleep wasn't a regular companion the last few days.

"I am a hot mess. I haven't been sleeping well. Things have . . . gotten complicated lately. So, thanks for noticing." Lily tried to grin, but the effort was too much.

Clara cocked her head to the side. "Are you ready for your media project today?"

What? Oh crap. Between getting their gear and the revelations from last night, the project was the last thing on her mind.

"What am I going to do, Clara? I'm not ready." She could read disks without a computer, but that probably wasn't what Mr. Hardt meant when he said "alternative media."

Her friend took her hand. "Are you sure you're okay? Missing assignments isn't like you. And you haven't called me in a few days. You hardly return my texts. What is going on?" Clara dropped her eyes to the ground. "Your new friends are cooler than me, aren't they?"

Lily's emotions reeled. How much more craziness could she endure? Now her best friend at school was insecure?

"Of course, they're not cooler than you. You rock, and you've been my rock when I've needed you. It's just that since I've gotten involved with church, they're in the youth group and we've had a lot going on lately."

Lily slumped to the ground and pulled her knees in close.

Clara knelt down next to her. "Then why don't you include me? Is it being afraid to ask me to a church thing?"

The church aspect was a small part of it. But mainly it wasn't a true youth group. Sorry, members are limited to those with super powers. What can you do? A weird image of kids auditioning to be part of the Anointed danced through her mind.

Wouldn't John love that?

"It's definitely not because they wouldn't like you," Lily said. "They're very cool, and they'd totally hang with you. It's just been tricky because we all met at the Launch Conference and we've related on that experience. But I need to bring you to one of our things. Maybe this weekend. I'll see what's going on."

Clara stood and reached out a hand to pull her up. "Sure. It's not like either of us have dates for homecoming."

Lily stood and banged her head into the next locker over. She had totally forgotten the dance was coming up. Yet another thing she couldn't keep up with. "So what am I going to do for media? I guess I could beg for an extension."

"I don't know. Two other kids tried and he got on them. I think he means it this time. What were you going to do before?"

Lily ran a hand through her hair, sending blonde waves falling down her shoulders. "I had an idea with optics, but I totally spaced on finishing things up."

Fishing through her purse, Clara pulled out her phone. "We've got twenty minutes before the bell rings. Can we whip up anything before class?"

That could work. Lily grinned at the thought of killing two birds with one stone. "I've got an idea. You can help me, and I'll share a secret with you too."

Clara clapped her hands together. "Ooh. That sounds dope. Where should we go?"

Lily tapped her teeth as she thought. "The wrestling room. No one's using it this time of year, and it will be nice and dark."

One side of Clara's lips turned down. "Are you sure about that?"

A smile broke out on Lily's face. "I'm sure."

The door creaked open and the sound reverberated through the empty room.

"Eww. It smells like boys and sweaty socks." Clara pinched her nose.

Lily felt for the light switch, even though she didn't need it. The lights would just be on for a minute.

"Okay, this is what we're going to do. We're going to experiment with different types of light and how they can change a picture's mood and character. We'll have to work quickly."

A confused look formed on Clara's face. "How are we going to do that? The overhead lights are a dull fluorescent. Do you have an app on your phone?"

"Not really." Butterflies threatened to break out of her stomach. Lily hadn't revealed her secret to anyone close to her yet. "I, um, found out something about myself at the conference." A memory hit her and she chuckled. "Actually, I think I first learned about it the day in drama class last May when you were almost crushed by the stage light."

Clara ducked playfully. "None of those here, right? That was a close call."

Why hadn't Lily thought of it before? The tingling in her hands after the light missed Clara should have clued her in. The canister hadn't missed crushing Clara. Lily had knocked it out of the way with her power. That was the first time she'd had that sensation. It had slipped her mind.

"You remember how I said I didn't know why I was picked to go to the conference? Well, it turns out I have a gift."

"They made you take tests there to find out?"

"Not exactly. Let me show you."

Lily stepped into the middle of the room. She held her hands out and the ceiling lights dimmed, throwing the whole area into darkness.

"Lily, are you there? I think there's been a power outage. What happened to the lights?"

The photons continued to stream out of the lights, but they

obeyed Lily now. Lily let her skin begin to glow, increasing in intensity.

Clara yelled. "What's happening? You're glowing! Are you —radioactive?"

"I'm not radioactive." Lily made a little diamond of light that floated over to rest above Clara's head, illuminating the area around her friend. "I've got a gift from God. I can manipulate light. That's what I've been keeping secret from you since then. But I don't want to have a barrier between us anymore."

The light created a glossy reflection off of Clara's brown hair. She held her hands up to try and grab the beacon. Lily made it float a little higher.

"This is freaky. I . . . I don't know what to say!"

"Well, I've got two thoughts. Number one, please keep this our secret. No one at school knows. Heck, not even my dad knows. And number two, we've got to take some pictures in a hurry for media class."

Chapter 34

Mr. Hardt pointed to the screen. "Impressive photo-manipulation, Ms. Beausoliel. By using light in different ways, it brings out many different aspects of your lovely subject. It must have taken a while to get all the equipment together to make this work."

Clara started to giggle, but Lily flicked the back of her shoulder. "It wasn't too bad, Mr. Hardt."

The instructor moved on to the next student's project, and Lily had a moment to consider her next hurdle: Missy Austin. Missy had missed the last two days for some school club trip, but today she was back and leering at Lily every chance she got.

Why did Missy have to send that email to Ji-young, and where did she get it anyway?

Lily's temper heated up several degrees every time she caught Missy's eye. Whatever was going on, Missy wasn't going to let up until Lily gave in and confronted her.

When the bell rang, the students shuffled out into the hall.

Clara turned toward their lockers, but Lily had a different objective. She went the other way to chase down Missy.

The scheming, raven-haired witch sashayed down the hall, as if she knew she was being followed. "What's the matter, little miss perfect?" Missy called out in a sing-song voice. "Did your 'woe-is-me' act run out with your daddy?"

Lily ran up a couple of steps to catch up with Missy, grabbed her arm, and pushed her into the girls' bathroom.

"What the heck is your problem, Austin? Why are you trying to make my life miserable?"

Missy shook her arm away and smoothed her blue school blazer. "You're miserable, you phony. You broke my brother's heart and moved on like he was nothing to you. All you focus on is yourself. You made it into Simon's special group, probably by manipulating him with your tears. And now you're acting all innocent when you're running around San Francisco in your pajamas.

"Maybe you just needed to be exposed."

Lily bit her lip during the stupid tirade to keep from screaming. "What are you talking about? Do you even hear yourself? You're jealous. Yeah, your brother and I liked each other, but I didn't mean to hurt him. I tried to apologize, but dealing with my mother and brother's death was hard. So hard."

Missy waved a hand dismissively. "See, there you go again. Always blaming your actions on your sucky life. Well, you can't live that way forever."

This was incredible. "You can't be serious." Lily said. "You know what? Simon Mazor wasn't all he was cracked up to be. Did you know that what happened at the conference was his fault? He was a megalomaniac that was trying to use all of us—"

"You're insane. Do you even hear yourself?" Missy shouted.

Lily couldn't help but be grateful Missy had interrupted her before she could blab anything more.

Missy was nearing hysterical. "I'm sick of your self-righteous act, pretending to be friends with Clara to make yourself feel good. All the other girls in school see it. You've got mommy issues and you blame everyone else."

That was it. Lily took one more step up to Missy and used a forearm to pin her to the wall. "My mom didn't do anything. She was murdered, and don't you bring her up again." A tingling rushed to Lily's fist. Rage boiled inside her, and all she wanted to do was to hurt Missy somehow. Missy's eyes grew wide as she tried to push Lily off, to no avail.

The door opened and Clara wrapped her arms around Lily's midsection, pulling her back. "Okay, no fights here. Besides, this one's not worth it."

Missy huffed and stomped out of the bathroom.

No way. She wasn't getting off that easy. Lily waited a moment, then turned to Clara. "Just one more thing." She pushed the door open and strode into the hallway.

"Seriously, the girl's not worth detention. Forget about her," Clara said, following her.

"I'm not going to hit her." Lily caught sight of Missy heading upstairs. Perfect. She wouldn't see what was coming.

Lily slipped a glove out of her pocket and onto her hand. She ducked just behind the wall next to the stairs, then leaned out for a peek. Missy had almost reached the top of the stairs, and had no clue she'd been followed.

Perfect.

Three quick zaps, and Lily hustled to class, stowing the glove away. She caught up with Clara who looked around, confused. "Why are you hurrying?"

A screech sounded from the stairwell. "What happened to my skirt?" A flap of material floated down to their hallway. The checkered pattern matched their skirt uniform perfectly.

Lily grabbed Clara's hand. "They don't make things like they used to. C'mon. We're going to be late for class." Missy's crying and other kids' laughter echoed down the stairs and hall as Lily led Clara toward their next class.

A grin occupied Lily's face the whole way, and a dark seed planted itself inside her heart at how good it felt to punk her nemesis.

Chapter 35

The car stopped near the condemned building. Simon popped a gummy bear in his mouth. The color didn't matter anymore—his superstition about different colors bringing luck had been a fool's thought. His glasses had glitched on the way over, no thanks to Rosa's stop-and-go driving. Probably a loose connection. He could only see blobs of varying shades of grey.

Simon felt around for the door handle, swung his feet out and stood up carefully, using his hands to avoid hitting his head. Rosa came around and took his arm. The direct connection allowed him to overpower her mind with calm and control. At least now she would act predictably for the next task. He just hoped that what he required had survived the destruction.

The smell of the Alturas campus flooded his mind with memories. The fall air brought a crispness tainted with sorrow. Flare had launched in September three years ago now, which enabled students to dive into his new social media network. Then it really did catch fire, and Alturas became the darling of Silicon Valley. He recalled the day after it went live, tossing a football around in the grassy square next to his barely framed executive building. He could almost feel the pigskin in his hands.

So much was lost at that conference. But if what he sought remained intact, he could begin to reclaim his destiny.

His toe caught the edge of the sidewalk and he stumbled. If only he could manage to get there! He used his other hand to flick the side of his glasses. Maybe an inelegant solution to his problem. But no, it wouldn't kick back in to give him some definition for his sight.

Rosa slowed down. "We're at the edge of the warning tape. There's just a pile of rubble."

Okay, stay calm. Losing his temper wouldn't help now. She didn't know the secret plans like he did.

"Are we at the front of the building?"

"Yes. On the edge of the sidewalk in front of all the mess."

"Right. Let's go around to the back corner." He gestured with his free hand. They stepped off the cement to the soft grass. The smooth, manicured lawn had given way to a thick mat of dry, crunchy blades under his feet. Simon thanked his lack of sight for at least letting him miss what had happened to his dream facility.

They slowed again. "Here we are. Now what?" Rosa asked.

"Can you see the edge of the foundation?"

"*Sí.*"

"Great. Start from there and walk fifteen paces due east. Do you see a rock near the walkway?"

Her feet tromped for a moment. "Yes. It is a marker for a historical site. They let you build on one?"

"Not exactly. That's what it looks like, but can you lift it up?" The block was heavy for him.

"Please. You're joking, right?" The sound of a heavy object thumped nearby.

"Do you see the metal ring?"

"Yes. Should I knock?" The sarcasm in her voice showed her irritation at his questions. If only she didn't have to act as his eyes.

"No. Pull up on it and it should open a hatch with a ladder in it."

He heard a scraping sound, followed by dirt dropping into an open space. It amazed Simon how his ears and nose had compensated for his lack of sight. He held his hand out for Rosa to guide him.

"Is the tunnel passable?"

"I think so. Do you want me to go down and get something? Check it out?"

He shook his head, facing the nebulous shadow in front of him. "No, I'm the one that has to do it. I just need you to stay here and get me when I'm done."

"I'm not exactly inconspicuous here. What am I supposed to do?"

Simon shrugged. "I don't know. Act like a college student and stare at your phone. You can do that, right?"

She didn't answer verbally, but he picked up on the huff she gave as she guided him to the opening. He knelt down on the grass and lowered his feet onto the rungs of the ladder. Feeling carefully with each step, he lowered himself down the hatch.

His feet finally hit the dirt-encrusted cement of the bottom. Simon turned and used his hands to find the narrow walls of the passageway. He shuffled forward, his shoes kicking bits of rock and dirt out of the way. The stale air and dust tickled his nose, the dank scent strong from months without ventilation.

In his mind he counted the steps. It should normally be twenty, but with his halting gait it took almost forty before his outstretched hand bumped against the back of the chamber. It hadn't collapsed. Now if his back door still worked.

Simon groped until he found a latch. He tugged and nothing happened. No, it couldn't be jammed. Not after he had come so far. The metal latch resisted his pull, but something finally gave. A click sounded and the door pulled back. Gravel tumbled from somewhere and tinkled on the floor of the small room.

He slid into the chamber. The back portion nearest the foundation bulged into the already cramped space. The collapse of the building nearly took this with it. He shut the door and felt the smooth surface of the jade. His mind could picture the deep verdant of the specially crafted stone.

Simon dropped his head and began to offer the words that would activate the signal. He kept repeating them until his mouth dried and he longed for a drink. Would they even respond? All he could do was keep offering the words. Words that pledged his fealty to the Archai.

A ripple emanated in the claustrophobic space. Simon couldn't see details of what happened with the jade, but the darkness became somewhat brighter. They had answered.

"Who can access this?" A feminine voice this time? His usual master didn't have time for him, apparently.

"Simon Mazor. I've come to beg for forgiveness for my failure at the conference. For messing up the transference."

Silence. Was he cut off so soon?

"You aren't dead after all. This intrigues us. You had been cut off from our connection." The voice registered definite surprise.

That's why no one had reached out to inquire about him. His tether had been severed?

"I was injured badly, but I have mostly recovered. And I want to prove my worth to the Archai once again." Simon hoped the desperation didn't carry through his voice.

The voice scoffed. "The Archai can't afford to be forgiving with such monumental failures. We have moved on with other operatives. You were never the only plan."

Fear washed over him. There were others out there? But he knew important information. Would he be a security risk now that they knew he was alive? *Focus, man. Show them what you have to offer.*

"I understand. But I see that this group of youth that I uncovered at the Launch Conference is active. How are you dealing with them?"

"We have our ways. They will be dealt with at the time that we choose." Every word dripped with the dismissive tone.

"I've worked out how to track them. I know their habits and I've learned that they've managed to upgrade their abilities."

No response. They were thinking about this revelation.

"How do you know?"

His heart skipped. Time to seal the deal. "I have other abilities besides my influence. I've marshalled all my resources into tracking these teens. I mean to prove my continued usefulness to the Archai."

If he prayed, this would be a time for it. Agonizing seconds ticked by. His ears picked up the trickle of dirt falling against the edge of the door. Sweat beaded on his brow, the tickling sensation of each drop running down his face driving him mad. But he had to stand strong.

"Very well. You may yet have use to us, Mazor. Give us the information. We need to understand how the youth are potentially upgrading things. That could be an unexpected variable."

Simon didn't realize how long he'd held his breath. A long puff let the air out.

"But know this: your failure weighs heavily on how things proceed. Do not fail us again. Mercy does not get us closer to our goals."

The signal died before he could say anything more.

Chapter 36

Demarcus felt like limping into the youth room. His legs didn't hurt, but emotionally a wound festered inside him. Thankfully John had called a special meeting of the Anointed. They weren't supposed to meet until Friday, but something was up. All Demarcus knew was, he needed it.

His head still throbbed if he tried to move too fast. Maybe Sarah Jane could help him out.

Then there was Lily. She texted him a few times last night, but he couldn't face baring his soul again. He knew she'd be very understanding. Too much had happened to rehash it one more time. Hopefully she wasn't upset about it.

The orange couch was open, and he dropped on it like dead weight. *Poof.* A ton of sparkly stuff filled the air and floated down around him. He checked his hand. Glitter?

Harry appeared behind the couch. "Did it work? Oh man, did it!" He doubled up laughing and fell to the floor.

Little bits stuck to Demarcus's lips. He tried to blow them off as best he could while sitting up and shaking his body off. "Dude. What did you do?"

It took a minute for Harry to stop laughing enough to talk. "I put a bag of glitter attached to a hose under the cushion. See?" He pointed to a plastic tube just protruding from between the seat cushion and the back of the couch. "I didn't think you'd lie down like you did. That was epic!"

Not what he needed. He wasn't going to get glitter out of his dreads for a week. Well, maybe there was one thing he could try. Demarcus focused on shaking his body as fast as he could. His body vibrated. *Faster!*

A new glitter cloud drifted across the room. Harry sputtered as it passed over him. Now they both looked like they'd showered in the stuff. And the room was covered with little sparkles.

"Nice, dude. Look at this mess."

Sarah Jane walked in and stopped, her eyes wide. "What happened here? Did a unicorn vomit?"

Demarcus stuck a thumb in Harry's direction. "Dork happened. Thought it would be funny to prank me."

"I wasn't targeting you, just whoever would sit there. And you landed with all your force on it."

Sarah Jane put her hands on her hips and cocked a knee. "Great. Who's going to clean this up? Or are we all going to look like the preschoolers' craft class at Vacation Bible School?"

The boys looked at each other. You could tell she had a younger brother, because Mother Bear had come out. Harry asked, "Is anyone else here?"

"Pastor Sanchez let me in as he was leaving. Said to have John lock up when we're done, so I assume we're all alone," Sarah Jane said. Demarcus thought he noticed a lingering look and smile from her towards Harry. Were there feelings brewing between them?

"I'll get supplies. You quickly do the vacuuming," Harry said, pointing back at Demarcus.

"Hey, just because I'm fast doesn't mean the vacuum is. And . . . he's gone." Harry had vanished to the supply room in the middle of the sentence. "Do I do that?" Demarcus asked. "Take off in the middle of a conversation?"

Sarah Jane nodded. "You both do. It's annoying."

Harry ported over the vacuum and other cleaning supplies, and in a few minutes most of the big clumps of glitter were gone. It would be a while before every trace disappeared.

The suction from the hose clamped down on the vinyl couch cushion when John and Lily arrived.

"Cleaning up glitter? Did I miss gluing macaroni to a painted soup can?" Her soft laugh warmed Demarcus's heart. Man, it was good to see her. And she looked great in a blue-and-yellow checkered button up and skinny khakis. Her hair was in a loose braid slung over one shoulder.

Take a chill pill. She's a friend. Nothing more.

"Okay, everyone. Time to get started." John motioned for them to join the circle. Sarah Jane pointed Lily's attention to Demarcus's dreads, and the two giggled at his shiny new hair-do. Great.

Weariness lined John's eyes. He had a strength that impressed, a vitality that outdid his appearance. But Demarcus wondered if he was burdened with something. Was it the confrontation from Saturday at the beach? Man, that felt like a long time ago with everything that had happened.

John led them in a time of praise. It felt good to Demarcus to get his eyes on God and to hear the others sing and speak praises. But it didn't fully dispel the heaviness of his heart. The nagging memory of his attempt to help against Vince and his bitterness toward his visit with his father kept him from fully opening up.

After a time of silence when they all reflected on things, John cleared his throat and caught everyone's attention. "I wanted to check with you children. My spirit has been burdened, and I am worried about how everyone is doing. I believe the enemy wants to attack you all. It is important that we stay humble with one another. We'll all be in different places. Some strong, some weak. But we are a body together. When one of you hurts, we all do.

"So please, if there's something going on, then let's share with one another." With that, he spread his hands open in an invitation. Spill your guts on the carpet. Confession time.

Lily looked around at the group. She had been subdued today. How was she doing with her father? Demarcus hoped that her grounding would end soon. It would be fun to hang out, just the two of them.

Heat flared in his cheeks as he thought about it. Hopefully the lighting wouldn't let people see him blush.

Lily finally spoke up. "I'm definitely worried. A new video surfaced by Ji-young Kim. She found footage from someone who'd filmed our battle at Santa Cruz. Do we have a stalker?"

She pulled out her phone and streamed the video. It looked like it caught Lily and Harry in the act, but the distance was too far to make out any identities. It reminded Demarcus to be cautious with his gift. Who knew when someone watched, or even recorded, what they were doing?

John closed his eyes in prayer. The four waited expectantly. Lily fidgeted with the tip of her braid.

John's eyes fluttered open. "Yes, I believe it is an attack. Definitely more than a random occurrence. All of you need to use discretion when faced with using your gifts. I do not believe it is wise to be exposed to the world right now. You have lives, school, and family. The pressure would be too much."

Harry elbowed Demarcus. "See, we need the secret identities and code names."

John didn't smile. "You boys, this is serious. It is not comic book material here. I need you to realize this."

Ugh. A little lighthearted fun wouldn't kill anyone. Demarcus appreciated the running joke, although he knew Lily would never let Harry give her a code name.

"How is school going for everyone? Are you keeping up with your studies?"

A bunch of nods followed from everyone. Demarcus had the advantage of being able to go faster, so his homework hadn't been an issue.

"And families? How are you doing with them?"

Everyone looked to Lily. "Dad's fine so far with this. In fact, I think he's softening fairly quickly. I hope he'll let me off the chaperone bit before too long. No offense, John."

He raised his eyebrows. "Why would I be offended?"

Demarcus said everything was fine with his mom. Which was true. It just wasn't the whole truth. Sarah Jane and Harry reported things going well with them. Sarah Jane had the best grade in her biology class so far. The girls' extra studying was paying off.

John sighed. "Okay. I still have a sense that all is not well. Again, please be open with us all, or with me if you feel you need privacy. We must stay unified. I don't want unconfessed sin or unknown issues to surprise us at the wrong time."

Lily raised her hand. "I do have a, um, question. I've been told at church that God doesn't give us more than we can handle. If that's true, He must think I can handle a whole lot. But I don't know if I can."

John's soft chuckle soothed the anxiety in the question. "No, that is a misconception of the words of Paul. That is why we must read the Word carefully. It never says He won't give us more than we can handle. The whole point is that we can't handle things. It says he won't let us be tempted greater than what we can bear.

"But life in general is more than we can handle. My daily breath is from him. So, we need to remember that it is not through us, but through His Spirit empowering us that we can carry on."

They shared for another half hour, talking about spiritual discipline—things like praying, studying, worship. Then John received a call from Pastor Sanchez and excused himself to take it.

As Demarcus stretched his leg, Lily slid up next him. "Hey you. Are you sure you're all right?"

How did she know?

"I'm fine. I guess. Why do you ask?"

She smiled. "You're very distracted. And you got a little irritated with John about the code names earlier. That's not like you."

Huh. She paid that much attention? "It's been a hard couple of days. I didn't mean to ignore your texts, so I hope you're not mad."

"I'm not mad, but I am worried about you. Can you tell me?"

Demarcus tipped his head to motion them off to the side.

"Yeah, I want to, but I don't want a lecture from John right now, you know?"

She put a hand on his arm. "Got it." Man, her blue eyes sparkled.

"I had a crazy day yesterday. I got in a fight with a guy beating up someone else. I took care of him, but got knocked in the head pretty good. I think I got a concussion."

"Let's get SJ over here to pray for you."

"No, not now. I'm okay for now. And if John hears, he'll be upset. The weird thing was, the girl that I helped in stopping her boyfriend from getting beat up too bad, she was upset with me. I thought I was helping."

"People are weird."

"That's just the first thing. The second thing is worse."

Demarcus swallowed. Okay, if he trusted Lily, then he could share about his confrontation with his father.

She looked up at him, her eyelashes framing her eyes to make them pop. Okay, dude, just spit it out.

John pushed open the door in a hurry. "Pastor Sanchez said there's been a situation. Applied Sciences is under attack."

Chapter 37

Lily's hands went to her mouth in shock. "Under attack? What do they mean?" The group huddled around John. Her heart stuck in her throat at the news.

"Ratchet called him and said that strange things were happening at his building, and then a loud explosion happened, and Ratchet cried out that they were under attack. It was just a few minutes ago, so I called 911 to report it to the authorities."

Demarcus raised his hands in frustration. "Man, why didn't you get us first thing? If this is related to other gifted people, he's going to need us!"

"But the last thing he said was to tell the Anointed to stay away. Don't you see? They are trying to draw you out to attack you. Unfortunately, somehow Applied Sciences became a pawn."

Demarcus looked around at Lily and the others. "We've got to go help. Harry, get us over there."

Of course. If Ratchet was in trouble because of them, they had to do something. But John tried to interrupt their circle of hands so Harry could port them.

"Please, don't do this. It's what the enemy wants. You're not ready."

Lily couldn't imagine how they could do anything different. She felt ready. Her powers were a responsibility.

For a split second, burning off the back of Missy's skirt snuck into her head. Not very responsible to humiliate her, even if she deserved it. Her neck warmed at the realization of what she had done.

"I'm sorry, John. I love you, but we've got to do what's right. Are you guys with me?" Demarcus asked.

They all nodded.

Harry clasped hands with Demarcus and SJ, and Lily completed the circle. Demarcus looked at John. "We'll be careful, but we need to go if we're going to help. Stay here. We don't want you to get hurt."

John's gaze fell as he and the youth room disappeared around them.

Smoke billowed out from the Applied Sciences building when they appeared on site. Shattered glass from the front entrance way littered the parking lot. Pools of water gathered in the foyer.

A slight wave of nausea made Lily shudder. When Harry had to move all of them, his power had a stronger side effect of queasiness. At least it wasn't as bad as the first time he teleported her.

Demarcus pulled them together. "Let me do a quick perimeter check. Lily and Sarah Jane, stay close to protect each other. Harry, wait just a second, then we'll make a plan."

Before anyone could negotiate Demarcus zipped around the building. Lily put her gloves on so she could use a focused laser if need be. "Don't forget your glasses, gang. If I go supernova, I don't want you affected."

Harry and SJ slipped their glasses on when Demarcus returned. "Oh, good idea." His were on before Lily could remind him. "There isn't anyone doing damage outside. Let's go in."

The four moved to the ruined glass doors, Lily careful with her steps because of her sandals. She wasn't dressed for battle. SJ put her bracelets on. Lily gave her a thumbs-up. Good thing she was prepared. Lily had wondered if she'd ever use them.

The glass got worse as they crossed the threshold into the building. Demarcus picked Lily up without warning. "Hey!"

"Girl, look at your footwear. Let a man help a lady out."

Heat rushed to her face again, as she felt the strength in his arms holding her out of harm's way. She didn't want to be babied, but it didn't feel bad, all the same.

A security guard sat slouched against the corner behind his station. SJ ran forward and pulled out her scanner. Blood trickled from his nose and ear, and he had black eyes on both sides.

SJ gasped at the readout. "He has a fracture in the base of his skull. He's in critical condition!" She dropped her tools and laid hands on him, starting to pray furiously. A conduit sparked above them, dropping the entrance area into darkness. Lily started to glow to illuminate things for them.

Demarcus pointed toward the stairs. "I'll go find Ratchet and see how he is."

She snagged his arm. "No way. We need to buddy up. What if

you're all alone and get hurt?" Lily shuddered, remembering the feeling of being outnumbered by the two powered teens.

Sweat trickled from SJ's brow as the guard moaned softly. Harry looked around at the circumstances. "I probably shouldn't be porting in here if there's damage. I don't know what I'll end up in. Here, I'll call Demarcus and leave my phone on speaker. Answer the call and do the same. I'll stay here with Sarah Jane until we can move on. But if you need help, just holler and I'm there. If you're there I'll be safe enough."

"Good plan." Demarcus switched so he was holding Lily's hand now and led the way over some strewn ceiling tiles and down the hall.

A high-pitched noise sounded like it came through the ceiling. "Aasif—the boy with the sonic powers. Watch out for him. One of his screams made me feel like I just got off the worst roller coaster ever."

Demarcus grinned. "Good thing I like roller coasters."

They pushed forward to the stairs. Another person lay unmoving just around the corner. Steve, the engineer they'd met before. Lily checked his pulse. It felt fine, but he must be knocked out. "SJ, there's someone unconscious by the stairs," she said, talking at Demarcus's phone.

A muffled reply came back. "Okay. We'll be there in a second. This guy is starting to come around."

Cool. Demarcus dashed halfway up the stairs before remembering Lily wasn't as fast as he was. He stopped at the landing and motioned for her to hurry up.

"You know, nothing is faster than light. I just haven't figured out how to travel by it yet."

Ratchet's office was on the third floor. They entered the second floor to see what it looked like. Glass was broken out of a few doors, but nothing major had happened here. The next floor must be where the action was.

They crept out onto the third floor. Lily brought the lights down. Hopefully they'd think it was the power causing the problem. What about seeing in different spectrums? She had forgotten about that.

She thought about the order of wavelengths. Visual light only took a small slice of the whole spectrum of light. UV rays were shorter, and infrared was longer. She pictured sliding to the longer wavelengths, and normal colors disappeared. Demarcus radiated as bright red almost to his skin, with an orange outline surrounding him.

"Hang on a second. I'm scanning infrared to look for heat signatures."

"What? You can do that? That is so wicked." She couldn't tell the details of the expression on his face, but she could make out his wide-open grin by the temperature variance.

Stepping carefully to avoid debris, Demarcus led the way. Lily flipped back and forth from the visual spectrum to infrared, but made sure to follow his foot placement as a precaution. The hallway led past the manufacturing labs. Again, the glass had been shattered, but most of it lay inside the previously sterile labs for semiconductor work. The machinery closest to the window had been knocked back haphazardly. The damage here would probably cost the company millions.

A water line leaked, the cooler water a blue trickle in her alternate vision. A few hot sparks of red came from damaged equipment or power lines. Thankfully, she didn't find any signs of people's heat signatures in the chaos.

Another noise pierced the air, this time making them both clench their teeth. Lily's body reacted to the memory of her insides going all queasy. They had to take Aasif out quickly. He was too unpredictable.

They maneuvered around a fallen beam, heading toward the corner where Ratchet's lab had its only entrance. A few brighter hot spots came from in there. Fire? Lily squinted, trying to push away the habits of seeing only in the visual spectrum. The wall in front of her thinned out, becoming ghostly and transparent. There! A crumpled form on the ground. A body for sure, but still very warm. Another red silhouette shimmered in the corner. One of the attackers? Only one way to find out.

"Let's go. There's someone on the ground—probably Ratchet, and it looks like one of the teens is guarding him or waiting for us."

Demarcus held his hand out. "Be careful. I don't want to see you get hurt."

Lily winked. "The same to you, buddy." She shuffled toward the door, trying to avoid debris. Her back slid against the wall as she neared the corner. The sliding door stuck halfway out into the opening, bent back at a strange angle. It must have been forced open.

Demarcus signaled that he would dash to the opposite side of the doorway. Then in a flash, he was. They both leaned in. Lily held her hands like a gun, feeling strange, but also like a secret agent or something at the same time. Demarcus nodded at her. Go time.

The smoke in the room made it hard to see, and her light would just reflect off it. She switched to infrared and cut into the room right behind Demarcus, both of them crouched down. The hot spot in the corner was just a fire—a mannequin that was burning. She led them around the long counter/work station and saw Ratchet sprawled on the ground. His wheelchair lay crumpled behind him.

Demarcus appeared next to him in a second. Lily scooted down to him as well. Blinking, she switched to normal vision. Thank goodness it was getting easier. She had a feeling she was going to need to push her gift to the limits tonight.

Ratchet's eyes fluttered and he groaned. Blood dripped from a gash on his forehead and matted his hair. His wrist was bent at a funny angle. Wait, that wasn't his wrist. His forearm! "Is that a bone sticking out from his arm?" Bile rose in her throat.

Demarcus leaned down to Ratchet's ear. "Dude, can you hear me?"

Ratchet turned his head toward the sound and coughed a couple of times.

"Hey, it's okay. We're here now. Sarah Jane's here. We'll get you taken care of, man." Demarcus held up his phone. "Harry, where are you guys?"

The phone squawked with a static burst, making the reply hard to pick out. "We've moved on from the main guard. Sarah Jane's healed him, and we're with the next guy down."

"Hurry up to Ratchet's lab. He's in a bad spot. Get up here as soon as you can."

"Will do."

The smoke swirled above them, making it hard to breathe. Lily coughed and wished she could do something about it. "We need to get him out of here. We're all going to suffocate."

"I thought we shouldn't move someone with trauma. What if his neck is broken or something?"

Ratchet's hand fumbled at Demarcus's collar before he caught a dread and pulled him down. His voice came as a hoarse whisper. "The sprinklers aren't on. It's a trap. They want you to find me. Get out." More coughing wracked his body and his face locked in a grimace before he slumped down, his hand dropping.

Demarcus stood and held his arms out. "Maybe if I whip my arms around real fast it will blow the smoke."

What was so important about the sprinklers? Lily knew they should be going off with the flames. What if Ratchet had tampered with them? But she remembered a presentation one time. Sprinklers only go off in the section where the fire is, not around the whole building. So this room at least should be getting sprayed.

Unless . . .

Lily grabbed Demarcus's leg. "Get down!"

He looked back at her. "What are you doing?"

A pipe shuddered above them. Water trickled from one sprinkler head farther back, then to the one above them.

The nozzle blew off and pinged off of Demarcus's head. "Ow!"

Water poured out like a jet stream and hit Demarcus in the shoulder, knocking him down. Lily aimed her hand at the stream and tried another solar flare. Instead of a shield, she tried to boil off the water as it poured out. The water vaporized into steam at the point of contact, but some water spilled onto her, and the superheated liquid burned her cheeks.

"Ahh! That isn't working."

Demarcus tried to stand, but the water turned into a coil and whipped around, catching him in the chest and sending him flying back into the treadmill. He crumpled in a heap.

No! This wasn't supposed to happen.

Ratchet seemed safe where he was, but the water snaked around, searching for another victim. Likely her. Lily scrambled on hands and knees over to the other side of the workstation to get a better look out the doors and down the hall. The water snapped right behind her as she turned the corner. She tried to make herself as flat against the metal cabinet as possible, to be a smaller target.

At least the fire died down with the water now in the room, but that meant the low light made it harder to see. Lily blinked over to her infrared mode. The water rippled in cool blue hues. Demarcus started to rise up on the other side of the counter. Where were Harry and SJ? They would be heading into the trap as well.

She peeked beyond the counter to risk a glimpse down the hall. There! The water-witch strode down the hallway, making her way toward the lab. But her color wasn't bright red. Her temperature was a lot lower than it should be, but it was clearly a human figure.

Another blink, and Lily created a light orb and flung it out the door to illuminate things. The glowing ball floated down the corridor. Streams of water smacked at it, but only refracted the light.

Kashvi stood halfway down the hall, near an open door. What was going on with her? A blue force field of some kind formed around her body, and a squirt of whatever it was shot from her covering to take out the light. Oh, she'd put water around her body as a shield. Clever girl.

But would it stand up to a plasma blast?

A beam of white light shot out of Lily's palms. It hit dead

center in Kashvi's abdomen, but the water just rippled. What? How would Lily beat her and protect everyone this time?

Now that she knew why her opponent had the weird heat signature, Lily drew all the light in the corridor and room down to blackness and switched to her infrared. If nothing else, it put Kashvi at a disadvantage.

"Lily, are you in here? I can't see anything." Oh yeah, Demarcus needed to see as well.

"Are you okay?" she whispered, trying to hide her location.

"Bruised and battered, but I'm not out of the fight, not by a long shot. Point me in the right direction."

"Hang on a second, let me take the lead. Kashvi's in the hallway straight ahead."

It looked like Kashvi was casting about to find her way. Water seeped along the floor, streaming toward Lily's position.

"Watch out for the water!" After warning Demarcus, she hustled over behind the door to hold a new position. If that water touched her, could Kashvi sense it? On the other hand, if Lily shot another light blast, that would give away her position for sure.

She noticed the ceiling in the hallway was still intact.

A sloshing sound approached as Kashvi pushed the water out, away from herself, searching. She kept advancing, her water shield now extending out to the wall to give her something to sense. This girl was good.

But what about this?

Lily switched her vision back and flooded everything with light. The brightness increased exponentially, hopefully to disorient the girl. Then she aimed for the ceiling near Kashvi's position and cut three long strips into the tile. Almost a full rectangle.

"Give it up, Anointed one. My master wants you gone, and that's what's going to happen." Her voice came out flat, forced. Was she under control, like something Simon would do?

That could wait. Lily dropped the brightness down to normal levels. Now all she needed was Kashvi to come a little closer.

"Why doesn't he face us himself? Is he too scared, so he has to send his minions?" Lily dared a peek over her metal cover. Just then, a trickle of water ran over her toes.

Shoot. It had to be now!

Lily felt the water wrap around her foot and climb her leg. Hanging on to the door with one hand, she cut the last section of the roof. The watery grip started to pull her out, forcing Lily to hang on with both hands.

A crack reverberated and a section of the roof collapsed over Kashvi. The girl screeched as she tumbled down with the debris, and the wet snare around Lily's leg released.

The water retreated around Kashvi and pulled her back toward an open door down the hall. She used it as a bubble to carry her into the room for cover.

"Demarcus! She went into the office on the left. Let's go."

Demarcus dashed past her, and she ran over at her top speed. Just when she reached the door, glass shattered, spraying shrapnel across the room. Demarcus dove for cover. Kashvi was partially encased in ice for protection.

Oh great. She really is some kind of water bender.

Lily tried another plasma blast. At this close range it made Kashvi stagger back. Her pupils grew large at being confronted by both of them. Lily held a hand up, letting it go a brilliant red for effect. "Stop this and stand down now."

Kashvi started to bow low. Demarcus moved to stand right over her, and Lily waited a couple feet away. At last they could get answers.

Then water whipped out in an arc at their feet and both of them slammed to the ground. Lily's shoulder took the brunt of the blow, forcing an involuntary cry.

The water bubble around Kashvi flowed out the window, carrying her out as well. The girl called out as she dropped from the building, "Do it, Aasif!"

Um, what was that supposed to mean?

Demarcus stood at the window. "Lily, we might have a problem." The building started shaking. Was this the San Andreas Fault?

The blast of sound waves followed, and suddenly she knew that it wasn't an earthquake. "Aasif's the sonic guy and he's screaming at the building, right?" she hollered over the din.

"Yup, pretty much. He's going to bring this part of the building down!"

They had to warn Harry and SJ, and get Ratchet out of here. Demarcus zipped by, her hair fluttering in his wake. She pushed herself up with her left arm and lurched down the hall, the vibrations of the floor worsening by the second.

Ratchet's lab had things flying in the air. At least the fire had been put out by the release of water. A scorched plastic scent stung Lily's nose and throat. Demarcus knelt by Ratchet and he tried to pull the man upright.

She pushed past a cracked monitor on the floor and a tipped robot arm. Then she turned and fired a plasma blast to knock open a clear path for them. Ratchet groaned as they pulled him upright. Blood from the wound on his arm streamed down Demarcus's chest. His legs dangled, dead weight that dragged with every painfully slow step.

The poor guy's head lolled around. Lily struggled to keep him steady with the shaking, and her shoulder throbbed with every beat of her heart. Demarcus yelled for Harry, but nothing came through his phone.

Something metal gashed the side of Lily's foot and she couldn't stifle a cry. They tripped, but Demarcus bounced into the metal workbench, which kept them from tumbling into a heap. The cut stung, but Lily pushed the pain aside. If they didn't get out of here, the whole side of the building might collapse.

They reached the doorway. Lily gulped for air, and even Demarcus sounded winded. Okay, down the right to the stairwell.

"We've got this. It isn't so crowded in the hallway." Demarcus started pulling again and she reluctantly pushed on. Then a sound of crushing and snapping came from the lab. Lily glanced back in horror to see the outside wall of the lab pull away and plummet to the ground below. A crack in the floor snaked through the doorway to where they stood.

"Ahh! Go! Go! Go!" She tugged with all her strength, but they couldn't move very fast. The floor shifted and they all hit the wall. A moan came from Ratchet's mouth at the jarring contact.

The ceiling above them trembled and slumped in. They were going to be buried under rubble.

"Demarcus!" Harry's voice came from the stairwell. She turned to look, but he ported in front of them. "I've got you all, let's go."

No time to argue. The rest of the lab falling to the next floor was the last thing Lily saw before they appeared under some trees across the street. Several dazed people sat or laid on the grass while SJ knelt by one person with a foot twisted the wrong way.

Lily and Demarcus carefully set Ratchet down as best they could. She checked his pulse. It didn't feel very strong. "SJ, we need you!"

Sirens wailed from down the street and red emergency lights flashed everywhere. Fire trucks, squad cars, and ambulances raced from different directions to converge on Applied Sciences. What was going to happen when they confronted Aasif and Kashvi?

Lily realized the thrumming of the sonic shout had quit. Normal city noises, along with the sirens, were the only things she could make out. Their adversaries had retreated. So, it was a tie, then?

Ratchet sputtered and coughed as SJ scooted next to him. "Oh wow, he's beat up bad." Her words poured out and his body settled peacefully, but new shouts interrupted her flow. Paramedics ran into the grassy area, looking for victims to triage.

Harry leaned in close. "Guys, I wonder if we shouldn't get out of here. There's going to be a lot of questions. Most of the people I got out were doozy, but I'm not sure if we should stick around to see what happens when they point to us as the ones getting them out."

SJ's eyes grew wide. Lily could imagine what her thought must be. How could she leave Ratchet at this time? But the decision was made for them. A paramedic ran up with a gear bag. "Watch out. Let me see what's going on."

The four of them backed away. Lily limped on her injured foot and held her right arm close to her body. Demarcus looked like he'd done a cage match with a bear. As much as she hated to admit it, Harry had the right idea.

"I think a strategic retreat is the best idea, gang," Demarcus said.

Lily nodded, and SJ lowered her head in assent. "You're right. I can't heal him now," she said in a low voice.

They quietly turned and walked back toward a nearby parking lot. Lots of emergency services pulled into the area. Commands were barked and uniformed men and women scurried around to secure the scene. Lily felt the tears stream down her face as they joined hands and materialized in the youth room.

John knelt on the ground, his face in the carpet, his voice trembling with each impassioned plea. Lily's adrenaline had drained away, and all she could do was slump against the wall and slide to the floor. Demarcus joined her with a subtle groan as he hit the ground.

Their mentor turned and slowly stood up, lines of concern crisscrossing his face. "What happened? Are you all well?"

SJ explained what she and Harry did. The redhead breathed hard too, from porting so much. No one moved. Demarcus sat with his head tipped back, holding his side with each deep breath.

John sat down in front of Demarcus and Lily. "What about you two? How was Ratchet?"

What could they say? They'd been owned again?

"We found him in his lab right before he lost consciousness. He tried to warn us about the trap. The water girl tried to take us out, but when we beat her back, the boy almost took half the building down with his sonic scream. It was madness." Lily sighed.

She hadn't thought her junior year would entail epic battles to the death.

"I've been praying since you left. I didn't want you to go, but I believe that many lives may have been saved with you there. Thank you, Lord."

Sniffles came from SJ. "Ratchet is hurt really bad. I got to pray for him for a minute. I could sense some stabilization, but he's going to be in serious condition for a while. I feel terrible. The poor staff being attacked due to us. Is it worth others getting hurt?"

John motioned for her to sit next to him, and he caught her in a side hug. "Dear ones, remember that the enemy comes to steal, kill, and destroy. He wants to take your joy and confidence, destroy your faith, and take the lives of those the Father loves. We are in a battle. But even as you wage war against these two deceived children attacking those we love, remember two things:

"Our battle is not against flesh and blood. Always remember that. Even against this Kashvi and Aasif. Also, greater is He in us than he who is in the world. Our Lord will have His victory. Be assured of that."

A small stain of blood grew under Lily's foot. Exhaustion almost made her forget her injuries.

Harry handed SJ a Kleenex as she took a spot between Demarcus and Lily. "I need to stop being frightened, and starting using my gift properly," SJ said with resolve.

With that, she closed her eyes and laid hands on both of them. Lily closed her eyes, too, and relaxed as what felt like a warm solution of healing flowed through her body.

Of all their gifts, Lily was most thankful for her friend's compassionate touch.

Chapter 38

L ily held on to the handrail to avoid stumbling down the
staircase in her fatigue. No need to punish her healed body
with a fall. And no matter how hard SJ prayed, nothing
could heal her thoughts, her emotions. A raw hunger in her chest
ate away any chance of peace.

The television in the living room was on, which wasn't a normal
morning routine. She needed coffee in the worst way, but she took
a detour to see what the commotion was about. Anything to put
off getting ready for school. That was the last thing she wanted to
do today.

Dad sat on the couch, leaning forward with his own cup of joe,
a frown settled deep on his face. Lily shuffled in and flopped onto
the cushion next to him. "Whatcha watching?"

Oh.

The local news stations had converged on the partially destroyed
Applied Sciences building. The reporter motioned toward the
damage and her lips moved, but Lily didn't hear any of the words.

The report cut to footage from last night when all of the first responders scrambled to deal with the situation.

Lily's stomach was empty, but that didn't stop the bile from coming up. She barely made it to the small garbage can nearby to retch in. Her nose and mouth stung from the acid. Her dad rushed over and offered her a handkerchief to clean off.

"Kitten, are you okay?"

Her sobs rushed out. How could she keep doing this? School. The conflict with Missy. The mystery behind her mother's accident. Everything with the Anointed. Thoughts collided and careened inside her head. Nothing made sense, and the stress of having this great ability and all the trouble that had enveloped her life overwhelmed her.

Her dad held her and tried to soothe her, but his eyes were frantic with worry. "Lily, what is going on? What's so bad? My girl. Oh, my baby." He stroked her hair and spoke calming words, but the waves of emotion kept battering her self-control. Her body shook, her chest heaved with cries of anguish, and nothing could stem the flow.

After an eternity of tears, her despair was spent. Her lungs complained about a lack of oxygen. Her nose ran and she didn't care; at least the worst of it had passed. Lily leaned into her daddy's chest. He kept saying, "Shhh. I'm here."

Thankfully it was Kelly's day for a morning spin class and hanging out with friends. The two had time alone to deal with her misery.

"Hey Kitten, I think it's obvious you're not up for school today. Do you think you can tell me what's going on? Other than our issue over the weekend, I have no idea what would do this to you.

I hate seeing my little girl like this." His voice quivered with his last statement.

Oh, Daddy. You don't know what you're in for.

Lily couldn't decide what to do. She didn't know how he'd react when he found out about the Anointed. But it seemed equally crazy to keep him in the dark anymore.

"Can I get a drink?" she asked.

Dad scooted out from under her and ran to the kitchen for water. *Okay, Lord, what do I do now?*

He brought a glass of water and a wet washcloth to her on the couch. Did she look that bad? She guzzled the water and wiped her face off, clearing off tears and snot.

"How are you doing now?" he asked

For some reason a giggle bubbled up. "Are you sure you want the answer to that?"

Lily hugged a pillow close to her chest. Just like her mom used to, she realized. She closed her eyes tight, feeling a nudge to step off the cliff and trust the outcome to the Lord.

"Kitten, I want to know what's going on. I want to help you."

Fear twisted her guts into a knot. She tried to start a couple of times, but couldn't figure out what to tell first. *Steel yourself. You're not going to break down again.*

"Dad, things have changed a lot for me this year. The conference was huge."

Dad shook his head. "I can't believe I let them talk me into sending you. It was a major landmark for you, but you could have been killed there."

Heh. He had no idea.

"Yeah, there's that. But what I learned was incredible. Looking back, there were clues, but I couldn't see them until the conference. And . . . you're not going to believe what happened."

He let out a sigh. "Obviously something's up. I can handle it."

"The conference was about finding gifted youth. But not like smart, IQ, or talent. I'm talking . . . superpowers. Strength. Healing. Things like that."

Dad tilted his head and raised an eyebrow. Then he gave a soft chuckle. "I'm glad you're feeling like joking, but after such a meltdown, I need the truth."

"I'm not making anything up. I'm serious."

He massaged his scalp. "You can't be serious. Who's ever heard of that? Fifty kids with powers running around the Bay Area?"

"Well, there were only five of us at the conference. But there's been more since then."

His eyes widened. "Wait, you said 'us.' What are you trying to say?"

"Dad. Um, I have a special ability. I can manipulate light."

His eyebrows scrunched together and his mouth formed an "O." "Lily, what is going on? What on earth are you trying to say? This doesn't make any sense." His voice gained an edge. "This isn't funny if you're joking."

The room darkened. She used her ability to connect with the light from outside and stopped it at the window, as if she'd pulled shades down. Pitch blackness enveloped them.

"What is happening?"

Lily started to glow. She let the light infuse her hair and her eyes especially. Her dad recoiled at the light emanating from her. His fists clutched the couch cushions, so that he could hold himself upright.

She didn't want him to have a heart attack, so she toned it down. Now she raised a finger and created one of her simple light designs, a bird carrying a spark of light. She waved it free and it flew to the center of the room where it dropped the spark. When it hit the ground, the room sparkled. More illumination filled in the gaps until normal daytime returned.

Her eyes caught Dad's. The emotions cycled on his face. Confusion, fear, amazement.

A slight grin crept on to her lips. "Well, what do you think?"

The color drained from his face. Was he going to pass out? Lily leaned over to steady him. "Dad, are you okay?"

He nodded his head absently. "I think I need more coffee. What the . . . when did . . . I mean . . . Whoa."

His reaction reminded her of the day she first consciously learned about her power. Sure, it had started breaking out a little before that, but the way it tripped her out—she shouldn't expect anything else from her father.

"Are you okay, Kitten? Does it hurt you?"

She smiled. "I feel tingling after I use it, but otherwise it's like an extension of me. It feels so . . . natural."

He sat in silence for way too long. The pounding in her chest threatened to send her to her knees. "I'm sure you have questions."

Dad sputtered, trying to get words out. "Well, yeah. Who wouldn't? So, did they do something to you to cause this?"

"No. I actually used it once before the conference. It did happen to be the day I was invited to the Launch Conference. But Alturas had been screening for youth before this."

"You said others had this. Do you know them?"

"Uh, yeah. Why do you think we have so much mentoring from the youth group?"

His hand slapped his forehead. "The kids from church? So you're not really doing religious stuff?"

Lily shook her head. "No, we are. The gifts are from God, Dad. I know that will be hard to believe, but it's true. Some crazy things happened at the conference—that could take a book to tell it all. That's where we met John. He knew that God was gifting youth for a coming evil. 'The gifts and callings of God are irrevocable.' When he gives gifts, it's up to the recipients to use them for good or evil."

"I don't know what to say. Just . . . keep telling me stuff."

"There were five of us discovered at the conference. One girl went rogue. I don't know what happened to her. Then Demarcus, Harry, Sarah Jane, and I started working at church with John to use our powers and to be taught about God."

Dad gestured toward her room upstairs. "Sarah Jane, your friend who has spent the night? What can she do?"

"She's a healer."

He gulped. "Do I want to know the rest?"

Lily rubbed her sweaty palms on her shirt. This conversation was going surprising well, and she didn't want to derail it. "Actually, Dad, I can finally explain the San Francisco disaster. See, Demarcus has super speed. Harry can teleport. They were trying to find who was behind the attacks in Japantown. But Demarcus got shot in the leg—it hit an artery and he was in trouble. Harry panicked, teleported to our house that night, and took us there so SJ could heal him before we had time to think. Or change out of our pajamas. We didn't mean to go there. But she did save Demarcus's life."

Dad was running out of ways to look dumbfounded. Both hands pulled his hair back. "You're saying that you *teleported* to the city?"

Yeah, that probably was a crazy thing to hear out of the blue. "Sounds funny to say it. It makes me a little nauseous, but otherwise it's such a trip."

A hurt look appeared on his face. "So I lost it over a time when you were helping someone?"

Lily put her hand on Dad's. "It's okay. I get it. Who would think anything else? That we were only gone for five, ten minutes? No big, Dad."

"But the thing that upset me today—well, the tip of the iceberg—was seeing the news report about Applied Sciences."

"That's where your group, your super group, did those tours." He squinted, and she could tell he was trying to make sense of the outlandish things coming out. Could she blame him?

"Right. But again, that was a cover. One of the guys there is a brilliant mad scientist, seriously, and he made gear for us to help with things. But some other powered teens attacked the place last night. They attacked us the day at Santa Cruz also. There you go, another piece of the puzzle."

"Your outfit being torn up?"

"Bingo. So we went to help our friend. We rescued him. We actually saved a lot of people. But the other two must have gotten away. Things have just gotten so crazy lately, I couldn't handle it after seeing what happened there."

He took her hand. "Were you hurt?"

She couldn't lie about it now. She was too vulnerable. "Yes. Not badly, but I had a gash on my foot and my shoulder got slammed. But SJ healed us all. Unfortunately, the paramedics got there before she could do the same for our researcher friend. He's in the hospital today."

Dad leaned on his knees. "I had no idea. This is … simply incredible."

"Soooo. What do you think?"

He stood and paced the room. After a moment, he said, "I don't know what to think. There's nothing in the parenting manual about your daughter turning into a light display."

"Hey! I can do a lot more than that."

"I'm kidding. Trying to get a handle on things. Obviously, I'm not very excited about you being in harm's way. Do you have to put yourself in such danger?"

"It's scary, but I know that God is with us. Even last night, when things weren't going the best, I could feel something lifting me up."

"There you go with God again. Why would he give such things to a teenager? No offense, Kitten, but you've been in a bad place."

Lily rubbed her hands together. "I know. I think that's part of it. Because we've had hard times, we're open to him moving in our lives. It seems those that have it together don't feel they need as much. Trust me, after what I've seen, I know I need him."

Dad checked his watch, then walked across the room to get his phone. "Sorry, did you have an appointment that I kept you from?" Lily said.

"No. I figure your school needs to know that you're not coming.

Then I'll need to call in to work. I think we need a daddy-daughter date to figure out where we go from here."

"Thanks, Dad." He held out his arms, and she let his embrace take her. The scent of creamer on his breath reminded her of when he would let her steal sips of coffee without Mom knowing. This could have gone really badly, but thankfully he wasn't freaking out. Yet. Her heart swelled with praise to God. She had needed a victory today.

Kelly pushed through the front door. "Cyndi got called away, so we had to cut our time short." She stopped, taking in the scene. "What's that smell? And why isn't Lily at school?"

No hiding it—her stepmother would need to know too. "You might want to take a seat, Kelly. I've got a few things to share," Lily said.

Dad nodded. "Yes, take a seat. I promise. You'll need it."

Chapter 39

Demarcus walked through the sliding glass doors. Normally he'd wave his fingers like he was using the Force, but it didn't feel right tonight. Not when they were checking on Ratchet. The Palo Alto Hospital was one of the best in the country, so it was good that he could be here.

The day had dragged at school, and he might have bombed a quiz. All he could think about was getting back at those who had hurt his friend.

He approached the circular welcome desk.

"Demarcus! Over here." Lily and Sarah Jane waved from the waiting area.

John exited the gift shop with a bag. They joined up and headed to the elevators.

John put a hand on Demarcus's shoulder. "It was a hard time today, wasn't it?"

Their mentor had such wisdom. He had such a way of sensing things. "I made it through, that's what counts."

"Where is Harry?"

"He wanted to come, but he had a major project he has to finish for class. In his text he said to keep in touch. He could meet us if need be." Demarcus and Harry had figured out that if a location was tagged on social media, then Harry could use that as a shortcut with his GPS device from Ratchet. Handy in a pinch.

They entered the elevator and hit the button for the 6th floor. Ratchet was still in intensive care. Hopefully they would get to see him.

"Dear ones, be strong for Ratchet's sake. We don't want to cause undue attention to ourselves. And he is in good hands here."

Sarah Jane leaned against the side of elevator, her face tight with concern. How did it weigh on her to be in the hospital when she could help so many with a touch and a prayer? Demarcus nudged her with an elbow. "How you doing?"

She bit her lip. "I'm fine. You?" The short, clipped answer wasn't like her. But could he blame her?

"About the same. You know, worried about him."

"Yeah." Sarah Jane looked away.

At least Lily looked somewhat upbeat. He'd have to ask her how she managed that later, because the ding of arrival made them all stand straight. The silver doors slid open and the scent of disinfectant hit his nose. He'd never liked the smell of a hospital, and that didn't change now.

The nursing station stood guard over the intensive care unit. Sentinels in scrubs milled about, checking charts. John approached and offered a smile. "Excuse me. These students were in a mentor program with Dr. Lowry. They would really like to see him, if possible."

The woman with salt-and-pepper hair looked at the clock. "Cathy, is this a good time for room 616?"

Another nurse, a blonde woman with a warm smile, looked at a chart. "Just a few minutes. The doctor will be rounding soon."

Cathy led them around a bend. A lab tech passed with a tote full of tubes. Blood samples? Demarcus hated needles, so the thought sent shivers down his arms. Beeps from various machines pinged back and forth. How did medical people keep their head with all of this? The chaos boggled him. Scratch one field from his future plans. No medicine for him.

The nurse pushed a curtain back. Lily gasped. Demarcus steeled himself for what he'd see.

Ratchet lay on his gurney, tubes and wires connected everywhere. One tube protruded from his mouth, with some kind of guard to hold it in place. Demarcus had never seen the man not in motion before. Even in his wheelchair, he was a dynamo. It was strange to see him like this.

John addressed Cathy. "How is he?"

A laptop sat on a stand next to the bed. The screen had different lines and blips, with numbers keeping tab of his vital signs. She tapped a few buttons and checked the readout.

"He's in a coma. He's in serious condition, but stable right now. They'll decide how to proceed when the doctor comes."

Cathy backed off and let them gather around. John pulled something out of the bag and set it on the little stand by Ratchet's bed.

"You got him a get-well bear?" Demarcus asked.

John nodded. "Isn't it the tradition to wish sick ones well like this?"

A hint of a smile broke out on Demarcus's face, the first one all day.

Lily stood closest to the head of the bed. She leaned in to Ratchet's ear. "Hey, your gloves did well in field testing. I thought you'd like to know." Her eyes watered up, the tears magnifying the blue.

Demarcus held onto the rail on the side of the bed. One thing was for sure—he was done waiting around for things to happen. From now on, he would be vigilant in keeping his friends safe. The time had come to be proactive. How could they take the fight to those other kids and whoever was controlling them?

Ratchet's body started to move. His chest had been moving evenly with the machine attached to his tube, but now it started rising faster. His arms twitched. A monitor clanged with an urgent tone.

Cathy pushed through the curtain in an instant. "What's going on?" Her eyes passed over the different things on the screen. Numbers started to climb, and the wiggling line that kept going by sped up. "I'm going to have to ask you to leave. I think—it seems like he's coming out of his coma."

But the nurses didn't expect anything to change. The doctor hadn't even shown up. Demarcus and the rest started to back out, but then it hit him.

Sarah Jane held a hand on Ratchet's foot, the blanket pushed away to expose his skin. Her eyes scrunched closed, and her lips moved furiously as she whispered prayers of healing.

"Sorry, young lady, but I need you to move." Cathy motioned for her to leave. But Sarah Jane didn't move at all. She kept on, her voice gaining volume as well.

The nurse stepped over to her. "Please, I need you to leave the ICU. We need to get him stabilized."

Sarah Jane kept her hold on him, her prayers getting more insistent. John stepped over and put his hand on hers. "We need to trust him to God right now. It will be all right."

Ratchet's eyes started to flutter. Cathy pushed past them, calling out into the corridor. "Room 616 is awakening. We need to get him extubated. Page Dr. Totah." The nurse made her way to the head of the bed, pulling gloves on. She yelled at Sarah Jane. "Leave. Now!"

Demarcus gave a tug on Sarah Jane's arm. She resisted. "Come on. They need us to go."

Her eyes flashed open and she turned her head to stare him down. "No, can't you see? He needs me to heal him. This is going to take a long time otherwise—but I can do it now. Just leave me alone."

Cathy stared at the situation for a moment. Two other staff showed up at the curtain. "Jenny, help me with the patient. Blaine, call security and have this girl removed."

That was it. Demarcus caught Sarah Jane around the waist and twisted her away from the bed. John helped direct her out of the ICU even as she thrashed against their hold on her. "Let me go! I can do this."

Once they got out of the Intensive Care, with all eyes glued on to them, Lily came up and caught Sarah Jane's head, a gentle hand on each side of her face. "Girl, get a hold of yourself. You did help him, but you're also exposing us. Think about it. Is this the place to do this?"

Demarcus and John let go. Sarah Jane stomped a few paces

away and whirled back to them. "Of course, this is the place for it. Where else should I use my gift? Just to patch you guys up all the time?" Her words flew out laced with frustration. "I'm going. If Ratchet wakes up, tell him I said I hope they're taking care of him." She pushed past someone getting out of the elevator and disappeared behind the cold steel door.

The door to the stairs opened and a couple of security guards strode out and into the ICU. John motioned to the elevators. "Let's just move along and find a place to talk."

The ride down was silent torture. Other people in the elevator made Demarcus uncomfortable. He would have liked to stop the elevator in between floors like in the movies and just hash things out. When they reached the first floor and filtered out into the hallway. Sarah Jane was nowhere to be found in the main entrance.

The three of them walked in silence out to an area with a reflecting garden. The beautiful flowers and shrubbery did give the place a peaceful mood. Demarcus needed that right now. His thoughts roiled inside. Despite helping pull Sarah Jane away, he knew that she was right. Why should they be hiding their powers?

They sat on wooden benches. The aroma of bark lent an earthy scent to the air. Demarcus sat with arms crossed next to Lily, while John searched their faces.

"I know it must be hard to sit and allow God's will to continue. I believe Ratchet knew we are in a spiritual battle, and that he wouldn't want harm to come to you all for his sake."

Demarcus shook his head. "I dunno, John. I mean, why shouldn't Sarah Jane heal him? Why shouldn't she go to the cancer ward and help all those sick kids? Isn't the point of having these gifts helping people?"

"Certainly. But most of all, it is to do His will. If the Lord guides us, then we move. Sometimes the more difficult obedience is to be still."

It sounded good, but it didn't ring true. "Man, I heard a saying once. You don't ask a drowning man if he wants to be saved. So, should I wait for the Holy Spirit to tell me to save someone? That doesn't seem like the best plan."

John never rushed his replies, and his end of an argument never escalated. He always maintained a peaceful demeanor, which could be maddening at times. Like now.

"I have lived for many years. More than you would even guess. And I have had to stay my hand many times when it I could have charged in and done something. The heart breaks every time. So please do not take my pleas as being passive. Greater control, better wisdom, even deeper love comes from doing what the Lord asks—even when it tears against your very nature. David could have stopped King Saul twice from terrorizing him, but he stayed his hand to let God's will be done. If it's good enough for David, then we should consider that."

The other thing that sucked about arguing with John was he always could back his side up with the Bible. The thought of standing down in such a situation burned at Demarcus's core.

"I'll keep that in mind, but I've got to wrestle this for myself. Will you excuse me?"

Demarcus needed some time to think it out and not be lectured. He stood and left the garden before either John or Lily could offer another answer.

The crowd of people flowing in and out of the hospital meant Demarcus wouldn't have anywhere to take off and use his speed.

He headed for the bus stop. Maybe just going slow would give him time to think.

He reached the crosswalk when he heard his name. Lily came running up behind him, her blonde hair fluttering in the breeze. Seeing her coming after him seized his heart.

Demarcus realized how much he cared about Lily. How, he had to admit, he was drawn to her. And if she was in trouble, there was no way he could hold back.

Chapter 40

Demarcus stopped to let Lily catch up with him.

"Hey, where are you going?" she asked.

"I don't know. I just . . . I appreciate John, but this doesn't sit well with me, you know?"

She looked at the ground and kicked a rock with her tennis shoe. "Do you mind some company? Or, I don't know, we could talk things out together? I don't want to see you hurting and alone."

"What about Sarah Jane?"

"I'll connect with her in a bit. You're here right now. Do you want me to stick around?"

Yes, dummy. The answer is yes. "That's cool. I mean, yeah. You know what I'm going through. What about John?"

She waved back towards the garden. "I think he knows this is especially hard for us to get our minds around with what we can do."

"So where do you want to go?"

Lily pointed both hands and winked. "Nope, you get to make the call. I'm up for anything."

The bus he was going to take wouldn't be a great place to talk about powers and villains. "Let's just walk toward downtown and see where that takes us. Maybe to a yogurt place or something."

Her smile lit up the sidewalk, even without her gift. "Now you're talking."

They turned left and started down the sidewalk. It was strange not having the whole Anointed gang around them. Why was he more nervous to talk with her when the two of them were alone?

Oh, snap. What about the thing about being chaperoned by John? "Is this okay? Won't your dad be mad about you being out alone? Don't want you in trouble."

"Actually, I didn't get to tell any of you. My dad and me, we're good. I kinda had a meltdown this morning. I didn't even go to school because it was so bad. I saw the news reports on Applied Sciences and turned mental on him. He needed to know what was going on, so I . . . ended up telling him about the Anointed."

His eyes bugged out, a lump caught in his throat. "You did what?"

She froze, wringing the end of her scarf. "I didn't really have a choice. There was no way I could hide it anymore."

Demarcus wondered if he could bring Mama into the picture. Now he felt bad about keeping it from her. "You said things were good?"

She shrugged. "Turns out my dad can be understanding when your secret nighttime romp into San Francisco was to help save a friend's life." She elbowed him and skipped a couple of steps.

"Really? He's okay with what happened?"

"Yeah. He felt bad about the grounding even. I mean, he doesn't really want me out and about looking for trouble, but if people need something, then I think he gets that I've got a chance to help out."

"That's exactly what I'm talking about. How can we sit back when we've got opportunity to help people? Isn't that ministry anyway?"

Lily giggled at that. "Is there anyone in church who needs extra light? Maybe their lawn mowed, like, really fast?"

He felt the heat rise in his cheeks from her teasing. At least Lily was in a lighter mood now that she'd released the burden of hiding her secret from her family.

"But seriously, what are we going to do? Sit and wait to get ambushed by those guys again? Or wait until they set a trap? If they knew about Ratchet, then what about our families?" All of the tropes about superheroes bombarded his mind. Number one: make sure to always get the bad guys monologuing if possible.

Her lilting walk stopped. "I didn't think of that. How are they following us? If anything happened to Dad or Kelly . . ."

Demarcus clapped his hands in agreement. "Exactly what I'm talking about. When do we reach the point where we take the fight to them? Is there anything we can do to draw them out? Maybe a battle to our advantage?"

They resumed walking, passing a park with kids crawling all over a rock wall leading to a slide. Their squeals and laughs punctuated the traffic noise from the street. Lily looked like she wanted to speak, but they had to weave past a short Vietnamese woman pushing a cart along.

"This is so weird. Where would we set a trap? I don't know if that's really what we should do," Lily said.

"See, I think it's exactly what we need to do. Decide things on our terms, and not let them dictate the action. The best defense is a good offense. Because what if they hit us at church?"

The conversation stalled. The ramifications rolled around in Demarcus's head, and Lily was pondering it herself; he could tell from her twirling her hair. A warmth bubbled up in his chest. It was so cute when she did that.

After another block she cleared her throat. "Okay, so if we try to do something, how do we go about that? I don't think they left any calling cards. Maybe their location showed on Snapchat? A selfie on Instagram, hashtag destroy laboratory?"

He bumped her shoulder. "Nailed it. That's totally my plan. No, what if we did expose ourselves somehow? I mean, after last night's attack people know they're out there, but we aren't really known except for whatever looneys follow the Bay Area Underground."

Lily wagged her finger. "When I saw their video, it had a lot of hits. In fact, the Santa Cruz video was on their trending list."

"It's something to think about," Demarcus said. "We need to get together and come up with something. I mean, without John. He won't be down with it at all."

Her scrunched eyebrows made him hesitate. He didn't like the idea of leaving their mentor in the dark, but how would John ever agree to a confrontation?

She spent several moments eyeing him curiously. "Are you okay? Last night was super hard, but at church you were going to tell me about something. Seems like something else is up."

Demarcus took a deep breath. "Yeah, it's been an even crazier week for me. But hold that thought—I'll tell you over a frozen treat." He pointed to a shop on the other side of the street with a snowman holding a cone painted on the window.

"Deal."

They ran over with the crosswalk light ticking down and made it into the store. An ice castle mural decorated one wall with another cartoon snowman holding his stick arms open wide, ready for a hug. Someone was playing fast and loose with trademarks. They snagged a cup each and Demarcus thanked his job for giving him the cash he needed to pay for her dessert.

The sweet, tangy berry puckered his cheeks. Lily had gone for a double chocolate something with Oreos as a topping. She gave him a big grin right before chomping down on a giant spoonful. He opened wide for an even bigger bite when something bumped his hand and fro-yo went up his nose.

"Whoops! Clumsy me." She jogged down the block, leaving him sputtering over purplish yogurt and granola on his face.

Her laugh melted his resolve to return the favor as he caught up with her. "Sorry, I couldn't resist."

"Uh-huh. All I can say is, watch your back."

She sashayed a few steps in a teasing manner. "Score is two to zero in my favor, I believe."

"Yeah, you just got lucky with being attacked by a huge wave controlled by a freak. I was so going to drench you guys myself."

Her hand twitched. "Let's not go there. Okay, being serious. What's up this week?" She gulped with the bite she was taking. "Ow, brain freeze!"

Demarcus paused. It was now or never. "Well, I met my dad."

"Wait, did you say you met your dad?"

"He texted me on Saturday after everything was done at church. So I met with him on Tuesday after school."

Lily pinched the bridge of her nose. "Carry on."

"It didn't go so hot. Before I met him, I helped a guy that was getting the crap beat out of him. But that guy's girl got scared by my speed. Then because I was bleeding, my dad chewed my butt about scrapping. Like he has any place to say something. I can't believe I went."

"You were in a fight?"

"Mm-hm. The dude was tough, so I may have had to use my speed to help out. But he would have really hurt the other guy. I don't know why the girl freaked out."

"We're different. Any time people see something different there will be fear. The look my dad had on his face when I showed him my power—holy cow. I'd never seen such a look of confusion on his face."

Demarcus couldn't help a silly smile at Lily. "You're really wise, you know that?"

Did she blush now? "Well, if we're complimenting each other, I really like how steady you are for the group. I haven't had a lot of that in my life, so to see it in a guy is pretty cool."

His heart stutter stepped. "Um, thanks?"

She led them over to a bench and they both sat down. He had a tickle of something in his nose from her little stunt. But his belly wiggled at the banter they had just had. Was there something between them? What would that do to the Anointed?

Lily licked her spoon clean, then waved it in the air. "So what's your super-secret plan for getting the Corrupted?"

"Corrupted?"

"If we're the Anointed, and they seem to have someone controlling them, then I would say that they've been corrupted. And it's getting to be a pain to say 'those guys.'"

Made sense. "Well, we definitely need to avoid a place with a lot of water. And getting them away from people is top priority."

"No problem. We only live in an enormous metro area by the ocean and a huge bay."

"Hey, not helping. Let's see, did you see them use cell phones at all?"

Lily shook her head. "Not between near drowning and a building almost collapsing."

Demarcus dug into his yogurt, hoping for some inspiration from the frozen treat. Why couldn't it be easier to look up bad guys? His brain had been fried over the last couple of days for sure.

"Whatcha thinking?" Lily prodded him with her spoon.

"There's got to be a way to find them—or if nothing else, to force their hand. How can we get them on our terms?"

"Is there any way to convince John to go for this?"

He shook his head. "No, probably not. But he's not the one in the middle of the battle either. Last night, innocents got hurt. What happens if they try to take us at school? Or home?"

Lily stopped mid-bite. "Man, you know how to be a downer."

"We're in a battle. Even if we don't like it, it's the truth. I know John says it's spiritual, but those water whips last night felt pretty real." His cracked ribs had been healed by Sarah Jane, but he could almost imagine the ache in his chest from where he was hit after getting knocked back.

"It is crazy. We've got family issues. Homework. Insane people trying to kill us. And I thought junior high was bad."

They both cracked up. "Junior high was almost as bad. Slightly lower risk of death. But it was definitely higher on the wedgie scale," Demarcus said.

Lily rolled her eyes. "Must be a boy thing."

"You forgot a conspiracy nut job trying to expose us."

Her eyes widened. She thrust her empty spoon into his face. "That's it!"

"What? You're out of yogurt? I've got enough for another cup if you want."

She waved her hands in an "x" motion. "No, I'm not kidding. I think I know how we can attract their attention."

He raised an eyebrow. "Really?"

"We reach out to this Kim girl. Tell her what's going on. Maybe we can set a trap. Have her announce that she's going to film us and we'll reveal ourselves. We pick a safe place and boom, confront them when they show up." The excitement of her idea made her bounce up and down.

His lips pursed. "Do you really think that could work?"

"Why wouldn't it? They're able to get information about us somehow. I bet there's a connection. It wouldn't even have to expose us. I can mask things."

Demarcus held his hand up. "Hold up. Ratchet said no holograms until he's figured out the glove problem." The brain glitch she had was freaky. He didn't want to see that happen to her another time.

She laughed nervously. "No way, not doing that ever again. I'm thinking about just affecting light levels. I can darken things, or even oversaturate the light so she can't make us out. We've got Harry to port us in and out quickly. This could work."

The idea wasn't half bad. If she could conceal their identity, then what would be the risk? "They'd have confirmation that we're out there. It would bring more scrutiny."

She ran her spoon around the bottom of her cup for one more bite. "That might be the risk we have to take. How else can we expose the Corrupted?"

He had to admit, it was better than anything he could come up with. Offering themselves as bait. How could anything go wrong?

Demarcus felt his phone vibrate. He slid it out of his pocket enough to check who it was. Harry had finished his homework and wanted to know where they were. "Let's go find an empty alleyway or something."

"Ooh, how romantic." She winked at him. She probably didn't realize the flutter that her bit of teasing caused.

They wandered down a side street and found a back alley unoccupied. Demarcus texted the location to Harry, and in a minute, he appeared in front of them.

"Hey guys. Wait, you didn't get me any yogurt?"

Demarcus slugged his arm. "Dude, did we know you would be butting in?"

Harry rubbed the spot on his shoulder. "Sheesh, touchy. How was Ratchet?"

They explained his situation and what had happened with Sarah Jane getting worked up and taking off. "That might explain why she's not returning my texts. I hope she's okay."

Lily tossed her empty cup into a nearby garbage can Frisbee-style. Demarcus tried a fade away jumper, but the container clanged off the side of the rim and onto the ground. Sheepishly he picked it up and slammed it in.

"I think she just needs some space. I'll call her in a minute— you know, actually talk to her like a human being," Lily teased.

"We have fun texting," Harry said.

Demarcus interrupted the banter. "Dude, Lily had an idea for drawing out the ones attacking us. And she came up with a cool name for them: Corrupted."

She explained it again, and Harry's grin grew bigger with each detail. "Yes! This is awesome. I can scout out a location that would give us the advantage."

This could actually work. Harry's enthusiasm infected Demarcus, and the plan grew quickly. They'd have to talk to Sarah Jane and see what she thought.

"What about John? Should we tell him what we're up to?" Harry asked.

Lily spoke first. "Not yet. Let's see what we can figure out and decide then. We probably should—but then again, I don't want to go against him if he says no. That's a hard call."

Harry shrugged. "We're the ones under attack. I like the idea of going after them. Maybe we can get some answers."

Demarcus clapped his hands together. "I don't know about you, but I don't want to keep waiting and let them push us around or surprise us. What about this weekend?"

Lily checked her phone. "Saturday night is our Homecoming Dance, but I'm not going, so no loss for me."

"No one is taking you?" Harry said. Demarcus couldn't believe it. What kind of idiots went to her school?

Lily shrugged. "It's no big deal. There's not really anyone at my school that's into me. I'm only close to Clara. At least she got a date. I can live vicariously through her."

"Um, I've got a big project due Monday. Can we plan for Sunday? I'll be done by then." Harry said with a half-smile.

"Let's find our final member and get a consensus on this." Lily dialed Sarah Jane. "SJ. Where are you? Are you decent? Are you alone? Would you like some visitors to cheer you up?"

He chuckled at all the questions rapid fire. It took a minute for Sarah Jane to catch up. "Uh-huh. Okay. Sweet. We'll talk in a minute." She clicked her phone off. "SJ went to home after visiting Ratchet. The rest of the family is at Danny's school thing, so we can meet her there. She said it's safe to port right in."

Harry gulped. "Are you sure? The last time I ported into a girl's house I got into it pretty deep."

Lily gave him a shove. "What did I just say? No one's there, so I suggest we take advantage."

"Okay. Hang on, everyone." Harry grabbed their hands. A moment later they appeared in a garage.

"Harry." Lily put a hand on her hip.

"I was just making sure."

Another blink and they stood in front of the couch. Sarah Jane came out of the kitchen. "Lemonade?"

They all took a glass and sat down. Lily joined Sarah Jane at the love seat, while Demarcus sat next to Harry on the big couch. He bounced up when he felt something under him as he sat. An Iron Man figure, one of Danny's toys, had a hand sticking up, as if protecting himself from the giant coming to squash him. Demarcus pulled it out and tossed it in Harry's lap. "I know you've wanted one of these."

His eyes lit up. "Actually, I have. I mean, I wish I'd had this one when I was a kid." The great thing about Harry being a red head meant when he blushed, he looked like a tomato.

Lily waved a dismissive hand at the couch. "We'll leave the boys to their dolls."

Harry and Demarcus answered in stereo. "Action figures!"

"Whatever. So, are you feeling better about things at the hospital?"

Sarah Jane shrugged. "I guess I'm better. What good is my gift if I can't use it? Let me decide how to handle it. Then again, what if it didn't work? I'd be crushed."

"Well, hopefully Ratchet's feeling better since you prayed for him. It seemed like whatever was wrong, he came up a few notches."

Demarcus took a sip of his drink. It was a little sweet for his taste. Mama's lemonade would put hair on your chest.

Lily crossed her legs on the seat and leaned forward to put a hand on Sarah Jane. "We need to run something by you. Demarcus and I were talking, and we came up with a plan to try and draw out the other kids, the Corrupted."

Sarah Jane's eyes grew big, the green irises nearly glowing in intensity. "Are you kidding? Picking a fight? How would we even do that?"

Demarcus spoke up. "We thought if we talked to the Kim woman from Bay Area Underground and set up a time to meet her and 'reveal ourselves,'" he used air quotes, "she'd blab that all over and it would get their attention. We could pick a site that we'd scouted and that would be away from anyone who could be hurt. Then we finally have them on our terms."

Sarah Jane pointed at Demarcus. "That's a wild idea you came up with."

"Hey, it was mostly my idea," Lily answered with a pout.

"Okay, sorry. In that case, that's pretty wicked. Remind me not to get on your bad side."

Lily giggled. "Remind me to tell you about Missy Austin later."

He wondered what that was about. Demarcus knew that girl drove Lily crazy with being mean. He wished he could teach the girl some manners.

Sarah Jane took a sip and started thrumming her knee with her fingers. "I guess that could work. The idea of us knowing the layout and being prepared is good. But do you really think John will go for it?"

Everyone shook their heads at the same time. Demarcus coughed. "Yeah, I think the best answer is that we avoid telling him."

Sarah Jane sat up straight as if she'd been shocked. "I don't think that's a good idea. He's our mentor, watching out for us. How can he do that if we're hiding this from him?"

Lily answered, "What do you think will happen if we tell him? He'll plead for us not to, and he'll quote some awesome scripture and we'll be like, 'Oh, okay, we won't.' How do we say no to him? I mean, last night was the exception because it was an emergency, and he even admitted he was wrong there." Lily kept tugging at a strand of hair. Demarcus understood that meant she was talking herself into this plan too.

"That doesn't seem smart. What if we need help?" Sarah Jane countered.

Harry set the Iron Man figure down in a lotus pose. "If we tell him right before we go, send him a text or something, then we've technically told him, and someone knows in case we've got an issue. That solves things, right?"

Made sense to Demarcus. Ask for forgiveness instead of permission. Isn't that the saying?

Sarah Jane folded her arms. "I say we pray about it. Seems like a bad idea to make such plans without checking with God about them. And should we be trying to take them out? Maybe we need to reach out to them instead?"

"Okay, we'll all pray about it and confirm things tomorrow after school. We need to have time to set things up, so we can't take long." Lily was on top of things tonight. Maybe he could talk Mama into letting him take a mental health day tomorrow.

Harry raised his hand.

"Dude, we're not in class," Demarcus scoffed.

"I'm being polite. I've seen an area with abandoned warehouse buildings in Newark. I'll check those out as a possibility." Harry sounded excited to be doing reconnaissance.

"And I've got Bay Area Underground bookmarked. I'll track them, see if I can figure out how to reach Ji-young Kim," Lily replied.

"Guys, did you hear me?" Sarah Jane shot looks at all three of them. "You keep making plans. Didn't you hear what I said?"

Lily downed a big gulp of her lemonade, licking her lips. "Yeah. Like I said, we're pressed for time, so we need to be prepared just in case."

Sarah Jane looked at a clock next to her on an end table. "Speaking of that, my folks will be home soon from Danny's program. You guys better get out of here. Now be sure to really pray. We need to be smart about this."

They gathered in the middle of the room. Harry smiled at Sarah Jane. "Don't worry, babe. We'll be serious." As Sarah Jane blushed, Harry snatched up Demarcus's and Lily's hands and ported them back to the alley where they started.

"Babe?" Demarcus winked as he elbowed his friend.

"Yeah, so?"

"Um, maybe you could warn a girl next time. I still have my drink." Lily held up the glass.

"Right. Do you want me to take it back?"

"Please?"

Harry took the glass. "I'll be right back."

"Don't be long, I need—"

Harry vanished.

"To get back home. But yeah, thanks for not making me carry a glass around."

Demarcus felt his face flush. A thought had been brewing ever since Lily mentioned the dance. *Don't do it. You don't need to complicate things right now.*

"So . . . if you wanted to go to the dance . . . I'd take you, that is, if you didn't mind."

Lily gawked at him. "Did you just ask me out?"

Moron. "You don't have to. I just thought—"

She smiled brightly. "Yeah, that would be great."

"It's okay. It was a bad idea anyway. Wait, what?"

Her head cocked to the side. "First you ask me out, then you say it was a bad idea. Now I'm confused."

She said yes. And you are blowing it, idiot. "No, it's a good idea! I just worried you'd say no."

Those killer blues pierced his confusion. "I'd love to. It would be cool to do something normal. Except you'll have to tone down your wicked dance moves. I'm not as good as you."

Demarcus just gave a lopsided smile.

"Hey, let's take a picture. I need to let Clara know that I have a date as well. Your arm's longer, so you take it."

She handed him the phone. They knelt down and leaned in, smiling for the camera. The first shot had shadows dimming their faces. "I can fix that," she chirped with a grin.

Demarcus counted backwards from five. The picture this time looked great. A hue of sunlight shone from behind them. Lily especially looked like an angel with a halo, with the extra glint. "That's incredible."

Lily took the phone and tapped on the screen. "I guess my back-up plan could be a photographer. I wouldn't need to worry about lighting—it's all right here." She held up a finger.

She finished typing and held up the image. The Instagram photo was tagged for Clara to see, with #date, #light, #happy included at the bottom.

The air warped and Harry reappeared. "Sorry guys. I had to talk to Sarah Jane about something. Do you want me to take you home?"

Lily pointed to a smudge on his face. "Is that lipstick?"

His hand shot up to his cheek, while his face almost glowed with blushing. "What? I don't know how that got there."

She squinted at Harry. "Sure, buddy. Anyway, I would like a trip home. Apparently, I have to figure out what I'm wearing for Saturday night."

"What's Saturday night?"

Demarcus made the kill sign at his throat, but she didn't see it. "Demarcus asked me to the dance at my school."

Now he'd never hear the end of it. Harry turned and punched his shoulder. "You sly dog. Look at you."

Demarcus held up a fist. "Now take our hands, or you'll get a fist."

As they ported, Demarcus heard Harry mutter, "Not very Christian of you."

Chapter 41

Simon's monitor beeped, stirring him awake. He'd fallen asleep at his desk again? If he wasn't doing anything else, it made sense. He shook his head to clear the cobwebs and looked for the notification.

Ah, another hit on Lily Beausoliel's phone. The picture of her and the speedster popped up on his screen. It looked like they were on a date. He had to admit they were an attractive couple. He chuckled when he saw her tags. He'd used algorithms to analyze pictures that had been taken in the Bay Area to pick up on her light manipulation anyway, but when she tagged it "light," that made it all the easier.

His worm had done exactly what he wanted. By picking up on her unique light signature, he'd been able to track her phone's signal. Then it was simple getting into the rest of her friends' devices. Simon couldn't believe that the powered youth he'd discovered stayed good friends after the conference. Maybe that made sense. They understood each other.

Simon had never had that.

The attack on Applied Sciences by the other operatives was short-sighted. He had enjoyed the challenge of hacking into the secure servers there. Now that was out of the question. Whomever the Archai had gotten to do the damage—that impressed him. It had to be something supernatural. If he could get into the security system, he'd find out more. The FBI was investigating it, and he wasn't interested in jumping through government hoops to get to the material.

It wasn't a challenge to him. It just took time he'd rather use elsewhere.

Now, what to do with the new information about Lily? He needed to get Sarah Jane. They could just go over to her house and kidnap her. But he had to avoid interfering with the Archai's plans. They had something in mind. He was afraid they were out to destroy all of the gifted youth. That would be a shame, with their considerable potential.

Once the Archai made a move, his waiting would be over, and when it appeared that Sarah Jane was in imminent danger, he could strike. If he could make it look like she had been destroyed, he'd have unfettered access to her. It would eliminate the manhunt a kidnapping would trigger.

Simon ran his hands through his hair. How had he gotten to this point? He really had wanted to change the world for the better, and under the Archai's tutelage, the possibility dangled in front of him like . . . a carrot.

He was a donkey for thinking he was functioning on his own initiative. And now he couldn't imagine any other possibility. Yet, if he could regain his sight and restore his full abilities, he could prove to the Archai he was more than a glorified hacker.

For now, he needed to remain patient. Be ready to go when things built to a head. Simon reached for his glasses. The loose connection had been fixed, and he'd brainstormed another couple of tricks to improve clarity. Now he could see general objects and people fairly well. Enough not to stumble everywhere.

Yet not enough to use his influence. He had to be able to read their faces and customize his influence to connect with a person.

Another text box popped up. Ugh, that Austin girl. She whined to her friends about being humiliated at school. The girl hadn't even gone back since some confrontation with Lily. Somehow the light wielder had burned off the back side of Missy's skirt.

Proof to Simon that there was darkness inside all of that brightness.

The girl was very tiresome and trite with her texts and social media, but it provided one more surveillance opportunity. His cheeks burned at the thought. Six months ago, he wined and dined with pop stars, professional athletes, politicians, and movie moguls. Now, he watched his computer to follow a couple of teenaged girls around.

He sighed. If that weren't enough, he kept an eighteen-year-old under his grip to be his eyes and muscle. Rosa probably deserved something different. But there was so much anger in the girl. What kind of trouble would she get into if he weren't keeping her busy assisting him?

A new email pinged in his inbox. A message from the Archai. Nothing high security, or it wouldn't come over such mundane channels. The idea that such a mystical cabal would contact him through ordinary email amused him. But he couldn't access the chamber for discreet communications very often, so it had to do.

They wanted an update on the status of the "Anointed." The new term for these kids, apparently. All right, he'd play along, if it meant he would be ready to take what he needed when the opportunity struck.

Chapter 42

"**D**ude, so you and Sarah Jane are a thing?" Demarcus gave a sly smile to Harry while they rummaged through the discount store. He wanted to find something stylish for the dance that still fit in his limited budget. Mama couldn't stop gloating over being right about Lily. At least she advanced him some allowance, and he used the excuse of shopping to get away from the teasing.

Harry's eyes darted around, as if he wanted to teleport somewhere in a panic. "Is it obvious?"

Demarcus smacked his forehead. Harry was that clueless? "I'm not dumb. The lipstick on the cheek gave it away, but I'd been wondering for a while now."

A contented sigh was the answer. "She thanked me for being there for her, and before I knew it, she planted a kiss on my cheek. Then she dashed off to her room as her parents pulled up, and I was outta there."

"Good for you. Sarah Jane's super sweet. Just don't break her heart, or I think Lily will have something to say to you."

He let out a chuckle. "She might take out my appendix with a light blast."

Thumbing through some dress shirts, Demarcus nodded in agreement.

"Now it's your turn. How serious is this date with Lily?" Harry waggled his eyebrows as he wandered to the accessories and scanned the hooks for anything interesting. And low priced.

Demarcus considered the question. He'd realized how much he cared for her, but what did that mean? Things were complicated with being part of Anointed. They lived in different areas and went to different schools. How would these things impact their relationship? To the best of his knowledge, Lily thought of him as a friend.

The dance was an opportunity to give her a normal high school activity, away from the craziness of the last couple of weeks. That's all.

"You know, she's pretty cool. When she mentioned that the dance was almost here and no one had asked her out, I thought it would be nice to give her the chance to go." Did he sound authentic enough?

"Sure thing, boss."

"Can you believe the idiots at her school? Not one guy would ask out such a caring, thoughtful girl." Demarcus could rail against those boneheads, but it worked out for him. That realization brought heat to his cheeks.

A shirt caught his eye. He pulled it off the hanger and pulled it over his t-shirt, buttoning it up to the top. Looking in the mirror, it fit like ... well, not like a t-shirt. Missing out on sports over the last several months, between moving and his ankle injury, he hadn't really needed to dress up that fancy. He could get away with polos at church.

Harry came over with a sneaky look plastered on his face. "You said I could pick out one thing for you, right?"

Oh no. Demarcus was going to regret this.

Lily twirled the dress around, looking for approval. Clara just stuck her tongue out, her face scrunched.

"No? I love the red. What's wrong with it?" Lily asked.

Clara and Kelly looked at each other. "Girl, I tell you, stick with blue. It does wonders to your eyes. Not like you need help with them anyway." Clara rolled her own eyes at the last comment.

Kelly nodded. "You look good in anything sweetie, but blue is your color."

Okay, she wasn't going to win. Blue was one of her favorites, but wouldn't it be fun to rock red once in a while? "I get the picture. The next one I'm trying should make you happy."

Lily stepped back into the changing room and pulled off the red number. Her excitement for trying on dresses was dampened by a tumbling of deeper thoughts—in particular, the implications of Demarcus asking her out.

Was it a pity date? He had reacted when she said no one had asked her out, though that hadn't really bothered her. There weren't any guys at school that interested her. And after the insanity of the summer, her focus had been on the Anointed and her friends.

But was it more? She tried to think of any clues that could tip her off. Nothing stood out. Demarcus had always been a gentleman and good friend. She didn't get a vibe of him flirting or trying to impress her.

The blue dress slid up easily. The high neckline appealed to her. But it was the delicate beading, like crystals of the lightest blue that caught the light like prisms, that made it stand out. The peplum silhouette was different than anything she'd worn before, but it suited her well. It took her a second to catch the zipper and pull it snug. She wiggled a little to make sure she could dance in it.

Now the question was, what were her feelings about Demarcus? SJ had sent a few excited texts, and Clara had been all over the post of her and Demarcus, going on about how hot he was. He definitely was a handsome guy. He was fit and smart, funny and kind.

Lily sighed. Sure, his smile could light up things as well as her gift. But the circumstances didn't lend themselves to being something more.

That was it, then—Demarcus was a special friend. No matter if it was a pity date, she would relax and enjoy the night. They'd have enough on their plate on Sunday with their attempted ambush.

Lily padded on bare feet out to the chairs in front of the changing rooms. Kelly and Clara chatted away, unaware of her approach. "Ta-da," she said, posing with arms outstretched.

The two looked at her and went silent. That bad, huh?

Kelly put her hands to her mouth. "Oh, sweetie. That's beautiful on you."

Two thumbs up from Clara. "I told you. Total babe. Demarcus will need smelling salts when he gets a look at you. But you need one more thing." She reached under her chair and pulled out a shoebox. "I figured this would be the one, so I took the liberty of picking out the shoes you would need."

She handed the box over and Lily pulled the top off. Silver strap heels glistened in the light of the store. They were cute, but heels? Those weren't her thing. "Do I have to?"

Clara shot her a look. She didn't do that very often, but this meant business. Lily slipped her feet in and stood taller. At least it would help her reach Demarcus to dance with him.

Kelly clapped her hands. "Perfect."

"Do you think Dad will like it?"

Kelly winked. "He probably will argue the length. I think he said something about a 'nun's frock' when we left. But I'll vouch for it. You look too amazing to fuss about a hem line."

Lily examined her reflection in the mirror. The dress came to just above her knees. She smoothed it as she regarded her reflection, turning from side to side. She discovered it even had pockets, which convinced her this was *the* dress. The bling at the top sparkled. If she combined it with her illumination, she could really make it pop. Her balance was precarious, but they did complete the outfit, she had to admit.

"Are you sure the cost is all right, Kelly?"

She came up and put her hands on Lily's shoulders, looking into the mirror at their reflection together. "I'm certain. I'm excited for you. Your first formal dance."

Lily pushed a loose strand of hair away from her face. It looked good, and it should be a fun time. A dance on Saturday, then possibly a huge, supernatural confrontation on Sunday.

A typical weekend for a teenager, right?

Chapter 43

Lily set the table for six at breakfast Saturday morning. The Anointed were coming over for the first time since she'd told her dad and Kelly about their powers. She made him swear up and down that he'd play it chill and not come with a bunch of dad questions. He promised that he wouldn't, but she knew that it would be hard for him to totally behave.

Kelly was becoming cooler all the time. She wasn't Lily's mom, but her taking Lily to get the dress had meant a lot, and now she was determined to run interference on Dad about the powers stuff.

Of course, Kelly couldn't guarantee anything about interrogation about the dance. That was understandable, but it didn't mean Lily had to like it.

The smell of bacon wafted through the air. Kelly had asked what the boys would like to eat, and the answer was obvious. If the way to a guy's heart was the stomach, then this was the express lane. Dad pulled the lid off the frying pan and flipped each strip, the grease dancing on the sizzling skillet. At his side, Kelly kept the waffle maker turning out crispy confections.

Lily was anxious about how things would go down. They hadn't ever gotten together with anyone's family. Lily guessed that everyone wanted to see how her family reacted as a gauge for telling their own. Hopefully it would be a positive and not a disaster.

She laid out the syrup, butter, and peanut butter. Kelly insisted on the last one for her waffles. Strange, but nothing beat Harry's culinary habits. He had tried fish sticks and custard at the Launch Conference. Gross.

The doorbell chimed, melodic tones filtering through the bustle in the kitchen. Lily jogged to the door.

Demarcus stood with his hands behind his back. "Uh, hey. Thanks for having us."

"You're welcome. What's behind your back?"

Did he blush? "Well . . . it's for your parents."

Now Lily felt herself blushing. He really was considerate. "Okay, come on in."

Demarcus stepped through the threshold, glancing around nervously. Lily stifled a laugh. Here Demarcus was taller than her dad and probably outweighed him, but he shied away at the thought of meeting him. There really was something about dads and daughters.

Lily led him to the dining room. He walked up to the table and set a potted centerpiece in the middle. "Ta-da!" He stood back, beaming.

A windblown stem with a couple of leaves poked out of a wicker basket.

Lily blanched. "Um, why don't we deposit this in the garage and file it under 'good idea, but better luck next time'?"

His jaw dropped. "That's not what it looked like. What happened?" Awareness dawned on his face. "Snap. I happened, right?"

She nodded. "Yup. Now let's get it—"

Kelly walked in from the kitchen. "Hello there. You must be Demarcus."

Too late. The Charlie Brown version of a centerpiece drooped to the side. Kelly's eyes were drawn to the movement, and her voice caught for a moment.

"You . . . brought us an arrangement. That's so thoughtful."

Demarcus stuck his hand out. "I'm sorry Mrs. Beausoliel. I wanted to say thanks for opening your home and, well, I must have picked poorly."

Kelly picked up the weeping willow wannabe. "I really appreciate it. So thoughtful. I believe I have just the place for it." She headed for the side door.

His hand slid down his face. "Man, I blew it."

"No, it's the thought that counts, right? It wins you points, so don't worry if it decorates the garage."

The bell rang again. They returned to the oak door and pulled it open. Harry and SJ stood holding hands. SJ jumped in and hugged Lily. She leaned in to whisper to her ear. "Because of Demarcus asking you out, Harry's taking me to a restaurant tonight! Thank you!"

Lily couldn't help but laugh. "For what?"

"For getting him past his nerves. It got him thinking."

She should thank Demarcus, who was busy with a complicated high five routine with Harry that involved fist bumps and smacking elbows.

Footsteps sounded behind them. Lily turned to find Dad and Kelly hand in hand, a smile plastered on his face. She thought he was cool with everything, but his protective instinct was trying to burst out of him.

"Hello, kids. I'm Jack, and this is my wife, Kelly. It's an honor to have you all here. Come on in. Everything's ready."

Demarcus sniffed the air. "Is that bacon? Sweet." Kelly flashed a surreptitious wink at Lily. At least one thing was going right so far.

Lily led her friends up to her room. It was funny to think they'd all been in there already, even though today was the first time Demarcus and Harry had been through her front door. Dad had done well, considering. She could have sworn that Kelly kicked him once, for he'd started a question, got a pained look, and changed the subject. He encouraged everyone to share with their parents about what the Anointed was doing. The rest of them seemed relieved that Dad hadn't freaked out over everything.

The best part was when he asked Demarcus about his highest speed. A look that mixed fascination with pure horror crossed his face. He must have been thinking, "And you've run my daughter around?"

Lily pointed them in, leaving the door open like her dad wanted. Harry took a sip from his tea cup. Kelly had been thrilled to have a tea connoisseur at her table. Lily stuck with her coffee mug and a good Kona roast.

"It's a nice room. I couldn't really see it last time." Harry grinned at her.

"That's what you get for barging in. Next time I might burn your hair off."

Harry ducked and ran a hand through his hair. That made her laugh.

SJ plopped on the bed. "So what did everyone think?"

Demarcus shrugged. "Other than my disaster of an attempt at a gift, it was cool. The food was great."

"That's not what I meant. I meant, what about our prayer? What do you think we should do?" SJ said.

A somber mood fell over the room like a blanket. Lily took a swig from her mug. She honestly had been distracted by dance prep. The intention to pray had flitted around on the edge of her thoughts. She'd tossed a few brief prayers up now and then, but nothing in depth. It still made sense to confront things.

"I'm good with it. If we can get on top of this, we can get on with our lives," Lily said.

Harry nodded. "There's an abandoned car factory in Newark. It's far from an open water source, and we can control things better."

"But have you guys really prayed about it? I just don't know. It seems rash to me." SJ's eyes pleaded with them to reconsider.

Demarcus put his hand on her shoulder. "Look, I know it's scary to face the problem. But this is our chance to put an end to this."

SJ leaned back on the plush comforter, a long sigh escaping from her. "Okay, guys. I won't leave you hanging. But we've got to have a plan, and it's gotta be okay to get out of there if things go bad. I don't want any of you getting hurt. You realize, it gets tiring healing you guys. Not that I wouldn't, but it also upsets me seeing you get hurt."

They all nodded. Lily hadn't considered what it would mean for SJ, what it could take out of her. She gave SJ a hug, and that seemed to make her feel better.

"Let's begin part A of Operation: Entrapment." Lily spun in her computer chair and tapped out a few commands. "Here we go. I've got my camera ready to go. We'll record a message for Ji-young Kim, and I'll make the light so intense that all she'll see is faint outlines. Then we'll give our conditions and see if she takes the bait." Lily ran to the door and peeked in the hallway. No parents. They'd need the door shut for a minute to pull this off.

Harry was ready to port out of his skin in excitement.

Demarcus steeled his jaw. "Let's do this."

Lily jumped into her chair. The others had their sunglasses on, so she lit up the room and hit record. The monitor was almost washed out in white. Perfect.

"This is for Ji-young Kim. We hear that you've been looking for us. We're the Anointed, and we're ready to meet you. If you meet us at the Newark auto plant off of the highway tomorrow at 5 p.m., we'll give you an exclusive. But this is a one-time offer. If you don't take us up on it, we'll wait and give someone else the first real scoop on what we can do. Reply to confirm. That's . . . all."

She clicked stop. The luminosity returned to normal. She motioned to SJ, who opened the door again.

"I don't know if you stuck the ending." Harry said while tapping his cheek.

"Hey. It's my first time giving an ultimatum."

Demarcus slugged Harry's arm. "That's right, give the girl some slack."

"Ow. I'm just saying, maybe we should try it again."

Lily shrugged. "But I sent it already."

A ping sounded from her laptop. "That was fast," Harry said with eyes wide.

The email response sounded terse. "How do I know this isn't a hoax?" What, Lily didn't sound sincere enough?

SJ stepped over. "Here, let me write her back." She typed out, "We aren't nursing students, and you know who this is. If you want answers about that night in Japantown, then you'll be there."

Harry mimed an explosion. "Boom. That's our girl. Blow her up!"

Another message zinged back. "Okay, I'll be there with a cameraman. Will you promise an exclusive?"

A series of shrugs around the room confirmed that there wasn't anyone else they wanted to tell. "It's on, guys. Let's take a few minutes to pray and ask for covering," Lily said.

They moved to the side of her bed and sat cross-legged on the ground. Hopefully John would approve, once they finally told him. That way they didn't have to lie or confront him. It would have to happen.

Part 3

Chapter 44

The back of the school auditorium seemed like a strange place to make their appearance. But Lily appreciated that Harry was willing to be their transportation. Neither she nor Demarcus could drive yet, and travel by teleportation was so much handier anyway. Harry loved to use his gift, so it didn't put him out at all. He dropped them off and ported back to meet SJ for their dinner reservation.

Demarcus tugged at his maroon bowtie. He sure looked handsome with the blue button up shirt and the stylish neck wear. Harry had especially enjoyed the look, since he'd picked out the accessory. "Bow ties are cool," was his exact response, in his best British accent. Somehow that had to be related to his favorite show.

Lily sniffed at the flower on her wrist. A carnation was perfect. Roses were overrated. Carnations lasted for a while. She'd had an aunt who was a florist in Washington. Lily remembered careening along in the delivery van on Valentine's Day, helping Aunt Virginia to get all of her orders out on time.

The only thing that stood out was his footwear. Demarcus had his special sneakers from Ratchet on. "Are you sure that was the best thing to wear with your outfit?" she asked.

"It's too late now. But I think they look great, and Mama didn't mind. Trust me, I would have heard it from her if they didn't work."

Okay, if they were mother-approved, then it was probably fine. He offered an arm to her. "Shall we?"

A tickle fluttered in her chest. This was really happening. She brushed her curls behind her shoulder and took his arm. "You bet. Lead on, my handsome date."

Demarcus didn't know what to do with his mouth. His lips wanted to stay in a perma-grin, his pride at having such a beauty as his date bursting out. But the nerves of going to a strange school and situation made him jittery. He didn't want to make a fool of himself and embarrass Lily at all.

It probably looked like he was ready to cry.

They walked up to the auditorium doors. The crowd of kids in formal clothes milled about. Some chatted in different groups along the broad walkway, while others moved toward the dance doors. He and Lily stopped when a girl squealed and scooted over to them.

She had large brown eyes and scarring on her face. This must be Lily's friend Clara. The two girls hugged, while the guy trailing Clara gave Demarcus a shy nod. Demarcus took the initiative, offering his hand. "Hey, I'm Demarcus."

"Blake." The guy glanced around like they were under surveillance. At least Demarcus wasn't the only nervous one here.

Lily and Clara finished with their girly exchanges and made introductions. Demarcus flashed Clara his best smile, and she giggled as he bowed deeply. He wanted to make a good impression, but it was very possible he was overdoing it.

"Are you guys ready to go in?" Clara pointed to the dungeon. An intimidating gauntlet of chaperones waited to inspect them as they entered.

The auditorium's main lights were dimmed, with a few lights on stands shining a variety of colors on the dance floor. Nothing compared to what Lily could do, but Demarcus knew she couldn't show off here.

Clara and Lily chatted back and forth as they walked around the perimeter of the dance floor. The first stop was pictures. Lily explained that her stepmom had insisted on them, that Kelly had done enough styling on Lily's hair that she wanted a record of her work before it got messed up. He admired the loose falling curls of blonde hair tumbling over her shoulders.

The picture line moved briskly. Blake started to warm up a bit, and they were able to joke together. The pictures were fun. They took a normal picture with big smiles, then the photographer gave them mustaches on sticks and goofy glasses to take weird photos. That really made the girls laugh, and it helped loosen Demarcus up. He needed to remember why he had asked Lily here. They both needed some fun.

He noticed some looks at him and Lily while they wandered around the dance. Demarcus wondered if they were questioning who she was with—a strange kid from another school. At one point Lily caught his attention. "Don't worry about anyone's opinion. I'm happy to be here with you."

That made him stand straighter.

Pop music blared through the speakers, a beat pumping the crowd up. Kids slowly started moving with the rhythm, though several stood on the perimeter and watched. Demarcus felt the itch to break things out, but wasn't sure what Lily would think.

She elbowed him. "When are you going to show them what you can do? I remember your awesome moves at the conference."

"Will you join me?"

Her cheeks flushed. "I'll try to keep up."

Dancing would help him really break the ice. *Remember, fun.* He led the way to the dance floor toward the back, to give them a little space but not a lot of visibility.

A song with some funk started pounding. Clara wiggled around, obviously having fun, while Blake did the country two-step or something. Lily stood back and crossed her arms. He could read her body language.

Okay, sister. You asked for it.

He spun on his heels and started pumping his arms. The beat oozed into his muscles, giving him a flow with the music that echoed into his soul. Lily matched him in energy, even if it wasn't as stylish. If she had training, she'd do well. She had a natural grace, and they moved in sync, despite never dancing together before.

Clara cheered him on, and he did a few stutter moves that accentuated the chorus. Lily laughed and twirled around. She stumbled and he caught her as she fell toward him. "Stupid heels. I let Clara talk me into them," she chuckled over the music.

"Well, you look amazing."

Her blue eyes caught his gaze. Could she see how much he cared about her? Despite the rapid pulsing of the bass line, they started doing more of a slow dance as he held her in his arms. She leaned into him and put her head on his chest, the two of them swaying back and forth until the song ended.

Lily leaned up to his ear. "Thank you. You don't know how much I needed this. You make me feel special."

Demarcus grinned. Unfortunately, his mouth was too parched to give an answer. "You are special. Let me get you a drink and we'll talk about it."

They left Clara and Blake to groove to the next electronic number. Demarcus handed Lily a cup of punch and they both drank, emptying their cups and tossing them in the garbage. He soaked in the huge smile on her face. That was something he could strive for the rest of his days: making that smile come out.

Demarcus bent down to catch her ear, with the booming chords filling the auditorium. "I wonder how things are going for Sarah Jane and Harry?"

Lily started to answer, but she got jerked back suddenly. A dark-haired girl in a strapless red dress had pulled Lily around by her shoulder.

"Missy?" Lily gasped in surprise.

"You have a lot of nerve coming here, after what you did." This Missy practically snarled at Lily. She was flanked by two other girls with angry looks on their faces.

Lily took a small step back for space. "I don't know what you're talking about."

"Don't give me that. I don't know how you cut my skirt, but you made me look like a fool in front of everyone. Why do you think I haven't been at school the last couple of days? I was too embarrassed."

"You have no proof, so I don't know why you're coming and blaming me. But as far as being a fool, you do that fine all on your own."

Oh snap. Lily had a bit of a temper.

Demarcus started forward to get in the middle, but Lily's hand reached out and held him back.

Missy's hand lashed out and caught Lily across the cheek, a loud slap sounding as her head snapped to the side. Demarcus was shocked for a moment. She dared strike her in front of everyone?

Lily must have been surprised too. She held her cheek, her mouth gaping.

Missy gritted her teeth. "Your parents are going to hear from our lawyers. Well, your dad will anyway. Your mom was a lousy pill-popper. Probably like how you'll end up."

Oh, she didn't. Demarcus was ready to deposit this brat outside.

A bright flash came from Lily's side. *Oh no! Don't do it!*

Lily's hand, bright as a beacon, arced through the air and returned the favor on Missy's face. The girl staggered back, wailing.

"Oh my gosh. What did you do to me?" Her voice trembled and tears welled in her eyes. Her hand touched her cheek, but she immediately pulled it away. "Ouch. What was that?"

Demarcus's eyes widened at the sight. A cluster of blisters grew into welts on the mean girl's face. It looked like a bad sunburn.

Lily looked at her hand, bright in the darkened auditorium. "What did I do? I . . . I didn't mean to do that."

Missy screamed as a pattern of blisters grew in a handprint pattern on her cheek. Her two friends held her arms and started dragging her away. Missy shot daggers at Lily with her eyes.

"You're a freak. That's why Simon picked you," she yelled, her voice cracking.

A couple of adults came over and Missy broke down into loud sobs. Lily stood stunned, her hand glowing bright. Demarcus noticed a growing number of eyes fixed on them.

"Hey, turn out the lights, okay? Lily, you've got to turn your hand off."

Lily shook her head, breaking out of her numb expression. The hand faded to normal. "Oh, Demarcus. What did I do?"

"I don't know, but let's get out of here, okay? It seems like a good time to split." He put his hands on her shoulders and guided her through the crowd that stood gaping at either Lily or the hysterics Missy put on behind them. He could barely make out faint whispers of people wondering what had happened. He didn't know himself. All he could tell was that Missy's attack had provoked something that Lily didn't expect.

They pushed through the doors and hit the fresh air outside. Lily's breath quickened. She held her head as if she would pass out. Demarcus found a spot on a sloping cement wall for them to sit and collect themselves.

Lily fanned herself with a hand. "Demarcus. I did it again. I hurt someone with my power. I killed two people at the conference, and now I've done something crazy to Missy. God, why is this happening?"

Demarcus kept a hand on her shoulder, trying to think of a way to calm her down. "It's okay. Take some deep breaths. Don't go hyperventilating. It wasn't your fault. Missy came up unprovoked and hit you."

She dropped her head. "I wish. She was being awful to me the other day at school, before the attack on the lab. I zapped her skirt so that the back end came off and her butt was hanging out."

He didn't know what to say to that. "Uh, that sounds kinda harsh. But she didn't need to hit you."

"I fried her skin! Did you see that? It was like an instant second-degree sunburn, at least. I'm going to get suspended." Tears trickled down her face with the realization of the severity of the injury.

Demarcus heard gasps, and he looked back to see people pointing at them. Great, now everyone was yakking about her.

"Let's keep going. I'll get you some place quiet where we can talk about things. We'll figure something out."

At least she had stopped with the panicked breathing, but her shoulders gently shook with the sorrow engulfing her. Demarcus knew that, even if striking out in anger, Lily wasn't one to wish harm on a person. Even a brat like Missy.

They started walking out past the parking lot, where couples continued to arrive. He really wanted to scoop her in his arms and dash off somewhere private so she could settle down, but he had to bide his time. As they climbed the gentle slope of the sidewalk, Lily's phone trilled.

To his surprise, there was a small pocket built in under the folds of her skirt. Lily pulled her phone out and saw Sarah Jane's number. She sniffed a couple of times to gain composure and answered.

"Hey, what's going on?" Lily's face quickly transformed from sadness to shock, her eyes wide and her mouth hanging open. "You've got to be kidding me. Let me check something. I'll call you right back."

"What is it?"

Lily fumbled with her phone as she disconnected the call and pulled up another app. "SJ said there's been something happening down near Fisherman's Wharf. Strange things with water and sound."

His gut dropped. The Corrupted, active tonight? Seriously?

Lily pulled up her email and tapped on the first message. It was an alert link for the Bay Area Underground. She clicked the link and held the phone so they could both see what was going on.

A frightened Ji-young Kim stood near the water somewhere. Her face was contorted into a mask of fear, her hands trembling as she held her microphone. "This is a message for a group calling themselves the Anointed. I'm being held hostage near the Hyde Street Pier. If you don't come here within thirty minutes, then I will be killed and innocent people around here will be targets. Please, help me! You've done it before—I pray you get this message in time. Hurry!"

The video blinked with a time stamp: 7:45 p.m. Lily switched to her clock. It was 8:07. According to the threat, they only had eight minutes to get to Ji-young.

Demarcus looked at Lily. They had to move. No time to waste. "Call Harry and have him come get you. I'm going ahead to make sure we beat the deadline."

She caught his hand. "Even with your speed, you'll have trouble making it on the roads on a Saturday night."

"Then I'll have to trust Ratchet and take a short cut. Be careful. I'll meet you guys at Hyde Street Pier."

Chapter 45

Demarcus didn't care who was watching. He sprinted up to his top speed. Cars and pedestrians flew by in a blur. His senses flared, keeping up with his legs as they processed his surroundings. He dodged in and out of traffic as he headed toward the Dumbarton Bridge.

The Bayfront Expressway twinkled with cars traveling to the East Bay area. Demarcus hopped on it for a moment to get him toward the water's edge. But he didn't want the bridge.

A briny, swampy smell greeted him on the approach to the bay. This was it. He found an exit that led him toward Ravenswood Point. He stopped to get his bearings, then clicked his heels together.

The wetlands blurred by as he accelerated. This better work, or he was going to be very wet. And possibly in trouble if his momentum made him skip like a stone out into the bay.

The water's edge rushed closer. *Here goes nothing.*

A spray of mist pelted his face. But he wasn't sinking. Incredible!

He could run on water! Demarcus said a prayer of thanks for his gift and one for Ratchet's healing as he skimmed over the surface.

He kept the shore on his left and he looked for his next landmark. The Bay Bridge connecting San Francisco and Oakland glistened in the distance. Now that he knew his shoes worked, he focused all he could on pumping his muscles, lengthening his stride, and releasing as much power as he could with each step. The spray intensified in his wake. In only a couple of minutes he'd pass under the bridge.

A huge barge with shipping containers loomed just beyond. A tugboat sailed alongside it, guiding the behemoth to its port destination in Oakland. Demarcus zoomed under the bridge and past the ocean-going vessel. He veered more to the left. The piers of San Francisco zipped by. He tried to maintain enough distance that no one would pick out the teenager in dress clothes running on the water.

The shoreline turned left, which meant he was heading toward the opening of the bay and the open ocean. Now the Golden Gate was visible several miles away, and it grew larger with every step. But he needed to stop well before. The lights of the tourist areas on Pier 39 and Fisherman's Wharf drew him in like a moth. He didn't exactly know which one was Hyde, but this area would be a start.

Demarcus slowed his pace to pick out landmarks better. He passed a large marina and had to maneuver by a couple of ferries. That meant it should be close. There—a spray of water high in the air wiggled back and forth like a snake dancing on the ocean. That wasn't natural. It meant only one thing.

He pushed forward again, racing past a long wharf where some decommissioned navy ships docked. Then he saw the sailing ship moored next to a long pier. That was it! His memory kicked in. Hyde Street was where the trolleys picked up folks to head uphill into the city.

Jets of water shot into the air, announcing that he had found the right place.

Demarcus used his momentum to leap into the air, barely clearing the edge of the pier. That would have been painful if he'd crashed. He slashed through the screaming people on the pier and made for land. A large clock read 8:13. He'd made it with a couple of minutes to spare.

There was a beach to his right. Kashvi stood along the shore, her hands raised and fingers wiggling. The movement matched the motion of the four water jets behind her. Great. Here was the Corrupted, in a perfect place for her ability. So much for their trap.

Ji-young Kim sat in a rowboat on the sand, a few feet from the pier's edge. She huddled low, whimpering and looking around frantically. Demarcus ran past her, then doubled back and flew onto the beach. He dug his feet in, sending a spray of sand flying toward Kashvi.

She must not have anticipated that, because the grains flew over her, enveloping her in a brown cloud. The water spouts fell back to sea level, and Demarcus could make out shouts of "Run!" from the crowd behind him.

Demarcus reached his hand toward Ji-young. "Are you okay? I'm here to rescue you. Um, hopefully doing a better job this time."

Her eyes widened with fear and she cowered down. "Did you get the other guy?"

Oh snap.

Chapter 46

Lily stood in an intersection near school, huddled against the cool night air. She wrapped her arms around her bare shoulders and wondered where Harry was. A couple of people came out of the auditorium, asked around, and when people pointed her way, they started toward her. Great.

She had to wait for Harry, because this was where she'd asked him to pick her up. But that made her a sitting duck, and the adults storming up the hill didn't seem pleased.

Mr. Akhtar, an administrator with a serious comb-over, motioned at her. "Miss Beausoliel! We need to talk, young lady. What on earth did you do to Missy Austin?"

"In my defense, she hit me first. I have witnesses."

Mr. Akhtar huffed on his approach, and a woman in jacket and slacks followed right behind him. They looked really ticked.

"I don't care. Did you see what happened to her face? What did you hit her with? Chemicals?"

Oh, this was so not going to go well. Lily tried to keep her voice calm. "I can promise I didn't do that, sir. It was an accident.

Well, I meant to hit her, because she insulted my dead mother after hitting me. But the blisters were not intended. I mean it."

The man didn't know the meaning of personal space. Hopefully he could make out the lines of mascara down her face, showing her sincerity.

"So now you're lying? There's no way she could have that kind of injury without some kind of agent involved."

"I am very sorry for what happened. I did not mean to hurt Missy like that. But she has been bullying me and Clara since last year. Maybe that can be taken in consideration."

Mr. Akhtar's complexion turned beet red. "The only consideration right now is to have you come back to the school and wait for your parents to pick you up, so I can inform them of your indefinite suspension, pending the board's deliberation about possible expulsion."

This was lovely. And she did not have time for this.

A familiar warping of the air occurred behind her. The two officials both jumped back in shock. "What is that?" he said, pointing.

Harry took her elbow. "Are you ready?"

"More than ready." She fixed her gaze on Mr. Akhtar. "Sorry, sir. I've got my ride."

And they were gone. Lily would've given her allowance for a year to see the man's face when they disappeared.

They reappeared—on a boat. The vessel rocked with their sudden weight change and Lily stumbled back against the railing. "Harry! What did you do?"

He pointed to a lighted sign that said Hyde Street at the

beginning of the dock from where their landing point was docked. "Sorry. Sometimes when I'm in a hurry I'm close, but not exact."

Lily glanced to her side and found SJ. "You look amazing, Lily!"

"Thanks. You look great too. But let's talk about our dates after we survive this, okay?" They scrambled to the dock and piled out of the boat, Harry having to assist her up in her stupid dress and heels. Thank goodness she had worn dance shorts, so she wouldn't expose herself.

They'd made it to the pier. Had they made it in time? And with no plan, as usual. Her mind scrambled to think of what their next move should be.

"Harry, go find John," Lily said. "We're going to need his wisdom. Demarcus is on his way here. SJ and I will go show ourselves. You'll be right back anyway, right?"

His eyes darted from the shore and back to them. "Are you sure?"

"Yes. We'll be fine. Now go!"

He disappeared, leaving the two girls standing on the wooden planks. "Are you up for this, SJ?"

She shook her head. "When will we ever be ready for this? But we need to go and see what's going on."

Lily and SJ started walking as fast as possible. The slats of the dock made it impossible for Lily to run in her heels. She shot a cone of light from her palm to illuminate their path better. She reached into the other pocket hidden in the folds of her skirt and pulled out her special gloves.

"SJ, do you have your bracelets from Ratchet? They might come in handy tonight."

SJ's eyes grew wide. "You're probably right. I have them in here somewhere." She fished in her little purse. It was cute with her flower print skirt and light-yellow blouse, but not ideal for battle. Lily glanced down at SJ's flats. At least she had more reasonable footwear.

They reached a cement walkway, so they started running their best toward the screams they heard at the water's edge, near the streams shooting above the building and blocking their view.

"I told Clara I shouldn't have worn the heels tonight," Lily grumbled.

SJ flashed her a look. "Really? Like she could have predicted this?"

The walkway opened up into a parking lot. They kept going past the few cars there. It was a ways to the street, but SJ tugged at her arm. "Here to the right. I think we can squeeze through there."

Sure enough, there was barely enough room for them between two buildings. They came out on the Hyde Street Pier as a spray of sand covered someone standing on the beach. The water spouts fell back to the earth, which could only mean that Kashvi had been taken out.

Lily's eyes searched frantically for Demarcus. There he was, next to a rowboat on the beach. The girl in the boat had to be Ji-young. *Good. Let's rescue the girl and get out of here.*

Before Demarcus could take her away, a piercing sound ripped through the air. Lily's hands went reflexively to her ears as Demarcus flew through the air, skidding to a stop along the water's edge.

Aasif! Where was the sound guy?

They rushed to the edge of sand next to the pier. "SJ, can you get her? I can't walk in the sand, but I can cover you."

Her friend nodded, her pupils dilated wide. Demarcus rolled over to push himself up, shaking off sand as he did. Kashvi rubbed at her eyes. Nice. She was distracted for a minute. Now to find . . .

There, ducked behind the edge of the pier, ready to ambush someone. Aasif crouched down. He turned his head and caught sight of Lily. Not this time. She thrust her palms out and caught him in the chest with a blast of plasma. He tumbled back and managed to knock Kashvi over like a bowling pin. Yes! What a shot! Those days of playing video games with her brother hadn't been wasted after all.

The two teens flopped into the water, rendering them harmless for the time being. SJ came running back with Ji-young. The journalist's face was splotchy with tears. A tangle of black hair fell to her shoulders.

"Come on, we need to get away from the water if we can." Lily threw out an orb of brilliant light to float between them and the Corrupted. Hopefully that gave them some extra cover. Gasps sounded from the people standing around, watching the show like it was some special effects extravaganza. Did they not realize that they were in danger?

Demarcus zipped up behind them. "Nice work with the shot. I saw that as I coughed sand up."

"Thanks. Now what do we do?" Her planning had only gotten them this far.

He looked around. "If we find a corner without people, we can have Harry get us out of here. Where is he, anyway?"

"I asked him to find John. If these two are wreaking havoc here, I don't know what to do."

Ji-young caught her breath enough to talk. "Thank you. Are you the teens that saved me in Japantown?" Her voice came ragged, the sound hushed. The determined look she had in her videos had washed away with the raw power of Kashvi and Aasif. Now her head was on a swivel, eyes darting every which way, looking for danger.

Lily shrugged at Demarcus. Their plan to hide their identities was toast anyway. "Yeah, we are."

The woman's eyes grew big. "It is you. I'm so sorry this happened. I'm not even sure how they knew. I was working on a story and these two and another man found me. One scream from the boy and the next thing I know I'm waking up in that rowboat on the beach."

Demarcus glanced back toward the water's edge. "Speaking of them, let's get you someplace safe and see if we can get you out here."

Lily and SJ worked together to support Ji-young as they moved up Hyde Street, away from the pier. What did she mean by another man? All they had ever seen was the two teens. Was there someone else involved?

A black metal object was in a display just ahead—it looked like an old steam engine. No one was checking it out, so Lily pointed there. "If we hide there, Harry can find us."

"Too late!" Demarcus yelled. He picked up Ji-young and disappeared ahead. Lily ducked and spun around. Water rushed at them. Not again. She imagined a solar shield acting as a barrier when she aimed and fired. Steam rose from where the sea and rays met. It created a mini fog bank, which helped hide them.

SJ said, "What do we . . ." and she was gone too. Then Lily felt Demarcus's strong arms scoop her up, and they dashed away in a blur. Before she knew it, they were standing on a street corner. A wooden pirate figure stood to their left, next to a shop. There was a park kitty-corner to where they stood. Across the street a blue neon sign read "The Blue Mermaid."

Someone shouted her name. Under the mermaid sign Harry and John motioned for them. "Where are SJ and Ji-young?"

"I took them over to the park," Demarcus said. "I figured we'd get away from the water and figure things out from there. Now that we have Harry, we can regroup and retreat."

Panicked cries came from behind them. More water poured up the alley. Some kind of projectile whistled past Lily and smashed into a window near Harry and John.

There were a lot of people around. How would they use their powers and stay undercover?

Before Lily could ask Demarcus about it, he grabbed her arm and led her across the street, out of range of the rising water. They reached the corner of the park, and Lily did the thing she should have the second she arrived at the waterfront—she slipped out of her heels. How the movies showed a girl running around in such stupid shoes was crazy. The cool grass soothed her sore feet. Running around on asphalt wouldn't be great, but she'd be in better condition to maneuver.

A group of trees grew in this corner of the park. Under their cover, SJ was soothing Ji-young when Harry and John joined them. Lily and Demarcus completed the group and drew everyone into a huddle.

"What is going on, my children?" John asked.

Demarcus leaned forward. "It's my bad, sir. I encouraged the group to find a way to confront these Corrupted kids on our own terms. A trap. But they turned the tables on us somehow and drew us here."

A scream reverberated through the air. Windows shattered a block away, glass shards raining down over a group of terrified Japanese tourists. People started running in different directions, trying to flee the confusion.

John spoke up, his voice clear with authority over the din of the crowd. "Corrupted? You mean the youth with powers coming against you? They are deceived and tormented, yes. But don't be fooled. All of us have the potential for corruption if we use our gifts for evil instead of the Lord's kingdom."

Lily blushed from the thought of the prank she pulled on Missy. In that situation, she wasn't any better than her enemy.

"My children, you may need to sacrifice dearly. Now that these two have been unleashed in public, you will need to confront them to protect the innocent here. But keep each other in mind. You are a team. More than that—family. Know the Lord is with you. Even in the chaos, listen to his voice.

"Now go, help the innocent out there, and come back to me, my dear ones."

Chapter 47

Water shot randomly from behind the boat club across the street, hitting different people and causing increased panic in the crowds. Demarcus saw a couple trying to run, only to be caught by a wave of water and knocked into a parked car. The man slumped to the ground while the woman held her arm close to her body, obviously wracked by pain.

John spoke up over the noise. "I'll stay with our friend here. Go aid those in need." He put a hand on Ji-young's shoulder, intoning quiet words of comfort to her.

Demarcus had daydreamed of using his powers to help people. The images from superhero movies didn't paint the true picture of the chaos going on, the fear in the air, or the hesitation from uncertainty. There was no training ground that prepared for this. But they had to start somewhere.

"Sarah Jane, let's help them," he shouted, pointing toward the couple he'd just observed. She nodded, so he picked her up and dashed over. Water foamed and sloshed around when they got to the car. "Can we help?"

The woman cried out. "J.J. won't wake up, and I can't move my arm. What is this, an earthquake?"

Not quite, lady. "I'm not sure. But I'll get J.J."

Sarah Jane put an arm around the woman. "I'll help you out of here. What's your name?"

"Wendy," she choked out.

Sarah Jane led her toward the park. Demarcus could tell her lips were already moving in prayer. He grunted with the effort of getting J.J. over his shoulder. The man was solidly built, so Demarcus didn't dare use his speed to risk a worse accident. He took halting steps to get the man past the puddles on the street and out of harm's way.

They reached the grass and Demarcus went to his knees to deposit J.J. Sarah Jane knelt by him and kept her prayer going. Demarcus looked back to see Wendy moving her arm as if nothing had happened.

"The pain, it's gone. How did that happen?"

He swung his own shoulder, trying to figure out an excuse. "Uh, maybe it had popped out and now is back in?" Good a guess as any. "Look, weird things are happening at the waterfront. You should find high ground."

"What about my J.J.?"

Just then J.J. sat up and rubbed his head. "What happened?"

Demarcus pointed away from the waterfront. "There's your answer, miss. You two make your escape. We'll see if we can help others."

Sarah Jane stood and surveyed the commotion. "We can keep trying to help people, or we can stop the source. I'll stay around here to help people and keep an eye on you guys. Go find Lily and Harry and see what you can do to shut them down."

Demarcus stared into her eyes. "Are you sure?"

Her pupils were wide, but she nodded with certainty.

Time to bring the speed to the battle.

Chapter 48

Lily pulled Harry over to the corner of the park after Demarcus and SJ rescued a couple.

Harry yelled, "How do we get the public out of here?"

What had they gotten themselves into? Lily's stomach rolled at the craziness. Here they pretended to be superheroes when they were just a group of teens. Sure, with special abilities, but sorely underprepared for a conflict like this. John had been right—they weren't ready.

There was nothing to do now but try their hardest.

Two figures slowly approached up Hyde Street. Water flowed around Kashvi as the girl waved her arms back and forth, creating sweeping waves of destruction. Aasif blew a couple of police offers over with a sonic blast.

"Harry, see if you can help people over there." She pointed up Jefferson Street. "I'll cover this side." He gave a thumbs-up sign. In a flash he started popping in and out of the screaming people, making a couple of them disappear each time. Poor folks probably thought that was worse than what was coming for them.

Lily scanned the scene, looking for the best place to jump in and help. Without shoes, she had to watch for broken glass. A thought came to her. She made a light design that said, "RUN" in pink neon and raised it into the sky. People that had been gawking at the confusion saw her message and began moving away.

Except for one man in front of a shop, standing still. Slightly hunched, he stared at Lily. Something about him made her skin crawl. His light brown hair had a close cut, but looked unkempt. The shirt was partially tucked in. He craned his neck to the side, and the change in position allowed Lily to see the black halo around his head.

Her discernment! She could pick up when people were being influenced directly by darkness. Ji-young had mentioned three people involved in her kidnapping. Was this guy the other person? Was he with the Corrupted?

He flicked a hand in her direction. Immediately Kashvi appeared around the corner and a jet of water followed, coming right at her. Before she could react, a rush of air carried her out of the way.

Demarcus. Zooming in to save the day. "Watch out for bad guys," he called as he disappeared again.

Lily turned to aim at the guy and shoot a blast at him. He had vanished. What was this new threat? She ducked behind a car, trying to keep Kashvi at bay and figure out how they were going to end this situation without losing someone.

Chapter 49

Demarcus zipped another woman fleeing from the damage up a couple of blocks. "Here. You should be able to get away now." Before the confused lady could say anything, he ran back into the fray. He could see Harry porting people around. But there, a kid had fallen behind his family, with a whip of liquid coming for him.

Demarcus shot forward, ready to skim over the water covering the road at this point. But the water suddenly froze solid, creating a super slick surface. He tried to skid to a stop, but fell on his hip and slid past the child, right toward a bench on the sidewalk. It was going to take his head off!

He threw his hands up to try and absorb the blow. Instead, he felt a frantic grab for his shirt and he ended up skidding along the grass with Harry in tow. Harry groaned and brushed blades of grass from his face.

"Nice save! That was too close," Demarcus said with a sigh of relief.

Spittle laced with green hit the ground. "Blech! No problem," Harry said.

They turned their attention back to Jefferson Street where tourists were trying to flee. That's what Demarcus had to keep doing—running.

Harry caught his arm and pulled him close. "Dude, we've got to get the Corrupted out of here. We have to worry about innocents, so we can't really fight them. What if we got them to a neutral location? Maybe where we can lock them up until we can figure out what to do with them?"

Demarcus stared at his friend. "What do you have in mind?"

His finger pointed to a few points of light suspended over the harbor. "Alcatraz."

"Seriously?"

"Dude, I've done the tour twice. If Lily can weld a lock, we can put them away for the time being! We've got to do something."

"What's the plan?"

"You ran on water—so you take Lily across. I'll port them over and we'll make sure to get them into a cell."

There was one major question for Harry. "Do you know where to put them?"

His eyes widened. "Not exactly. I can get them to the island, but I'll have to do a quick scouting run to find where we can stick them."

More screams sounded, following an explosion of glass from another building. "Okay, but you'll have to move fast. I'll provide a little distraction."

"Good. I'll give you a few seconds. I'll tell Lily to be ready for you."

"What about Sarah Jane?"

He heaved a deep breath. "I don't want her in harm's way."

Demarcus didn't want her there either, but Harry was willing to put Lily in the danger zone? They couldn't keep debating things, though. "Let's go."

He ran over to a demolished wooden bench. He picked up a couple of boards from the destruction and flung them as fast as he could at the Corrupted. He didn't wait to see what happened—he just kept hurling a barrage of projectiles at the two of them. They took turns picking off the objects, with either a water blast or sonic scream knocking the debris off course. Good, he had them on the defensive for a minute.

The next piece shattered against a sheet of ice. Oh snap. She can freeze stuff, and she had made an effective barrier against his attack. He could just make out their silhouettes behind the ice barricade.

A blast of light hit the wall and it started to droop. Lily kept pouring on the heat and the makeshift cover quickly vaporized. Kashvi prepared a water whip to strike out, but Harry used the opportunity to make his move. He appeared behind the two and disappeared again.

Demarcus didn't wait to ask Lily if she knew the plan. He flashed over to her, scooped her up, and took off down the pier again.

"Whoa. I guess that's a way to be swept off my feet," she teased. He felt his cheeks warm.

The salt water fanned out under his feet again, covering poor Lily and her beautiful dress. *Will she kill me over wrecking it?* That was probably a dumb thought, considering the stakes.

"I can't believe this! You're running on water. So cool!"

He couldn't suppress a grin. It was pretty sweet.

The island loomed large as he approached. Where did Harry go with them? Hopefully he went for high ground. The lighthouse flashed its occasional signal, a throwback to when ship captains needed it as a sentinel warning sailors of potential danger. There, the dock for the ferries. It looked like it would work, but it was hard to see.

Oh. He had someone who could help with that. "Can you light the side of the island so I can see how to get on land?"

She jutted a hand out and the darkness gave way to a bright sweeping light. Yep, that would work. He slowed just enough to account for the change from water to the dock. They hit land and he continued up on the dock by a long building. Skidding to a stop, he frantically searched for Harry.

"Do you see him?"

Lily scanned as well. "Look!" She pointed toward the other side of the island. Two streams of water flowed up and over them to higher ground. "Follow that! It should take us to Kashvi."

She used her hand to project a beam like a headlight. It revealed a switchback path that led up the island. Demarcus sped up it as fast as he could while keeping Lily from suffering whiplash.

A flat area extended by the lighthouse. In the center, Aasif stood over Harry, who writhed under a sonic blast of some kind. Kashvi had her water poised to strike.

Demarcus raced forward. No one was going to take out his friend.

Chapter 50

L ily tried to warn Demarcus as he made his dash forward to help Harry. Too late. All Aasif had to do was aim his vertigo scream at Demarcus and he pitched forward onto the ground. The sudden disorientation and nausea that resulted from Aasif's power would be worse with Demarcus tumbling around. Great.

Now instead of getting them into a safer situation, they were on the infamous Alcatraz without anyone else to help them, and two of the Anointed were hurt. But Lily noticed Aasif had to keep switching from Harry to Demarcus to keep them incapacitated. He couldn't do anything about her.

The ocean breeze whipped her hair and dress, the cool air chilling her damp skin. She'd never been to Alcatraz before. Not the tourist visit she expected. Lily ran toward the lighthouse and fired a blast to knock Aasif over. The boy took it in the belly. He wrapped his arms around his gut and dropped to the ground.

Kashvi growled at her. "I'm tired of you messing things up."

Maybe a different tactic would work. "Why are you doing this?

Can we talk about things? What have we done to make you attack us?"

"Our master wants you dead." A curt response.

Lily backed up to the edge of the lighthouse. This gave her coverage for her back at least.

"Who is your master?"

Two blasts of water aimed for her head. She made her solar shield again, which worked, keeping the pillars of liquid from pummeling her. That line of questioning wasn't going anywhere.

Demarcus shoved Kashvi down and grabbed Harry, who had only made it to his hands and knees. He dragged Harry away from them and down the stairs from the large platform and toward Lily's position. Lily tried another photon blast, but Kashvi threw up a clear piece of ice that reflected her beam back into the edge of the lighthouse, knocking some debris down to the ground. Lily felt some fine bits of concrete trickle over her shoulders.

She hadn't anticipated a counter for that move. Time to be more creative and think further ahead. At least it gave time for Demarcus to pull Harry over to the lighthouse steps.

Aasif tried to get up, but Lily aimed for him again. He was pushed back into the railing, a loud grunt sounding on impact.

"Any luck with Harry?" Lily asked.

The redhead could barely stand. "Dang, that scream of his scrambles your brain." He caught the side of the lighthouse to steady himself. "I need to clear this spinning in my head or I won't be able to port at all."

Lily and Demarcus looked at each other. This wasn't in the plan.

A loud rumble came from the south side of the island. What now?

Kashvi stood at the railing with her back to them. That was stupid, leaving herself exposed. Now was their chance to stop them.

The sound was getting louder, and Lily looked around the corner of the lighthouse.

A large wave went from twenty to at least fifty feet in seconds. Kashvi pushed her arms toward Fisherman's Wharf, and the wave started rushing in toward the shore. If that wasn't bad enough, Aasif's sonic blast sounded, and it seemed to propel it faster.

Lily put her hand on Harry's shoulder. "Harry, we've got to get back and clear the area!"

He tried to stand straight, but he slumped against the wall. "Sorry. I'm still out of it."

What could they do?

Demarcus crouched. "I could try to run past it and warn people."

The answer loomed over them. She grabbed his arm. "No. I need you to get me to the top of the lighthouse right now."

He tried to turn the doorknob, but it rattled. Locked. Demarcus's hand started vibrating so fast it turned into a blur. In a moment the rattling stopped and the door opened. They pulled Harry just inside. Then Demarcus took her in his arms again and dashed up the stairs.

A girl could get used to this.

They reached the top, and the large lens shone bright in the twilight. To Lily's eyes it was nothing, but Demarcus had to slip on his special shades from Ratchet. Okay, where was her target?

The wave had become a tsunami. Numerous city blocks would be instantly crushed by the deluge if this didn't work. *Oh Lord, give me strength.*

She put her hands on either side of the lens and powered the light up beyond anything the electricity on the island could produce. "You might want to get back," she called to Demarcus. The luminosity swelled to a blinding level. She had to make this work, because one shot would probably be all she had. Her temples throbbed with her heartbeat, a thunderous pulse pounding with her nerves.

The wave had a fairly narrow base, being caused by a person instead of a whole section of the earth shaking. That may be her saving grace. The water was three-quarters of the way to land. What would John and SJ be thinking, seeing the monster wave coming in?

Lily could feel the lens vibrating wildly. Any more and she'd shatter it instead of using it to her advantage. *Get the aim straight. Three, two, one.*

The lens turned into a focuser for a huge solar beam that melted the glass of the lighthouse top. The light blazed to the base of the wave and a huge cloud of steam instantly formed. The tingling in Lily's hands turned to a stabbing pain, but she had to keep it going. With a primal yell, she sent one more intense pulse out onto the bay to destroy the momentum of the wave.

A huge splash came from the top part of the wave dropping without anything to propel it now. The threat had been stopped.

She pulled her hands back and tried to shake them out. That wasn't fun. The throbbing made her wince as it thrummed up her arms. If only she could collapse in her bed. Her body was drained of energy and her legs wobbled.

They had stopped the Corrupted for a moment. Lily took a deep breath. The amount of light she had poured out reminded her of being strapped in the Source back at Simon's headquarters during the Launch Conference. A weary grin came over her when she realized she could do that on her own, without something like his machine sucking it out of her.

Her celebration was cut short as she grabbed for something. The whole lighthouse had begun a violent tremor.

Chapter 51

Demarcus wanted to whoop for joy when he saw how Lily had stopped the tsunami. But a jolt through the whole structure bounced him back and forth on the stairwell. A horrible sound reverberated through the concrete and the metal, and it was going to shake the whole thing down. He tried to get his feet under him to get Lily out of there, but he couldn't get level without being thrown down again.

Lily clung to the railing next to the lens, her eyes wide in fear. "Demarcus!"

How was he going to help her?

The air warped and Harry stood between them. The trembling promptly knocked him down as well. He took Demarcus's hand and reached for Lily. She couldn't let go of the railing enough to get the reach needed.

Cement started pelting them as the structure came apart.

"Just get her, whatever you do!" Demarcus screamed. Harry let go and lunged for her hand. They connected and disappeared.

A moment later Demarcus felt something wrap around his leg

before he appeared back on the grass of the park near Hyde Street. He coughed away the dust from the lighthouse. Sarah Jane ran over to them, with John trailing behind.

"Are you guys okay? What happened?"

Lily rolled on to her back with a groan, the cement dust from the lighthouse forming a thin layer of mud on her dress. "Apparently a combination of Kashvi's and Aasif's powers can cause a tidal wave. We couldn't get them in a cell."

Demarcus sucked in fresh air. His body felt battered from the beating he'd taken with the water. His ears rang. Sarah Jane was already on it, scanning each of them and offering prayers. "You have labyrinthitis. I have no idea what that is, but I'll pray for you anyway." She laid hands on him and in a moment his aches and fuzzy head cleared. But he had never exerted his gift like he had tonight. His legs started to feel wobbly, and his back and chest burned.

John waited for Sarah Jane to use her gift on each of the others. "You kids did admirably in stopping that wave. Many people would have been lost if you hadn't. We've cleared most of the pedestrians and workers. Police are starting to arrive. We should probably leave for tonight."

Was it time to admit this was another draw? Demarcus didn't like the idea of backing down, but maybe it was the wiser choice.

Lily scanned the water. "John, they're coming. I can see in the infrared range, so I can tell two heat signatures are approaching from the island. If they come back, what if they keep causing problems? I don't know if the police can handle them."

She was right. They had a responsibility to stay and make sure no trouble happened.

"I feel that we should leave. The Lord will take care of things. And we need to discuss what happened here tonight, if you were truly leading them into a trap." His voice quivered with sadness. "I am very surprised that you would not tell me."

Demarcus stared at his toes as he kicked at the grass. He didn't like disappointing John. They'd done enough of that today.

"Sir, you're right. We need to talk about what happened. It wasn't the best idea. But I really feel uncomfortable about leaving. We don't have to immediately engage them. We can hide and make sure they're not causing more havoc. If things stay calm, we leave. If not, then we're here to help with things."

John held his ground. "That sounds reasonable, but I have a strong sense that we should leave. Come with me. There's an alley close by where we can have Harry teleport us away."

A fog was rolling in from the ocean. The visibility was starting to drop. It probably made sense to slip away now. Demarcus was ready to agree, until he saw a face that chilled him to the bone.

Why would his father be standing a block away, watching him?

Chapter 52

L ily was ready to concede to John about retreating, until she
saw the color drain from Demarcus's face.

She put a hand on his arm. "What is it?" She'd never
seen him like this before.

He shook his head and focused on some man standing a few
hundred feet away. "See that man with the shaved head? That's my
dad. What the heck is he doing here?"

Demarcus turned to everyone. "I've got to check this out. Go
on without me. I can get myself back to the church." Before anyone
could argue, he zipped over to the man. Oh boy, as if he needed
anything else to deal with.

Lily took another look at the Corrupted. Instead of faint red
dots standing out over the cool blue of the sea, now they were
outlines rapidly approaching. If they were going to leave, they'd
better do it now. But she didn't like the idea of leaving Demarcus.

A desperate yell sounded from behind them. She whipped
around, switching to her normal vision.

One of the San Francisco trolleys was plummeting through the air toward them.

"Harry!"

He glanced up to see they were about to be crushed. Harry dove and caught them all in time to port farther toward the pier. A huge crack sounded when the trolley landed and skidded in the grass, dirt flying out from under it. A couple seconds later and they all would have been crushed.

A shorter figure stood where the trolley had its turnaround. Otherwise the area was vacant. Lily raised the light over there so she could make out who it was.

No, it couldn't be! Her heart dropped and sweat broke out even though the night air and water had chilled her in her soaked dress.

Rosa Gonzales, a dark halo encircling her head, started walking down the hill toward them. Wasn't she supposed to be dead? The last time Lily had seen her, the girl had plunged off the roof at Alturas from Lily's blast. All this time, the guilt she'd wrestled with—for nothing?

If Rosa was nearby, that could mean only one thing: so was Simon Mazor.

Lily's heart raced with the thought of him being around. What he did to her. And the information from the CD in her dad's office—that somehow Alturas was involved in her mother's death?

Lily had to have some answers. And Rosa would tell her where to find Simon.

Chapter 53

The dust billowed with his rapid stop in front of Tony Carter. His dad didn't flinch. He just stood there, his eyes zeroed in on Demarcus.

"What are you doing here? Of all nights, you're right here tonight?" Demarcus demanded.

Tony held his ground, but his eyes shifted around. "Someone told me I should be here tonight. I didn't know why. Until now."

"Yeah, well you shouldn't be listening to that person. I've only been trying to save lives and stop some maniacs from tearing up the piers here. And I can't believe it's an accident to see you now."

He was aware of a rushing sound on the water. Kashvi would touch down in just a minute. What was Demarcus going to do about his dad? He couldn't care less about the man, but he couldn't bear to see him hurt tonight. Not like this, at least.

"Obviously, you've found some kind of steroid like I've never heard of before, but I need to warn you, son."

That was so messed up, coming from him. "Dude, I am not taking steroids, or any drug. My ability is a gift from God.

Probably nothing you'd understand. So, don't go warning me about this, because you have no stinking idea what's going on." A red hue cloaked Demarcus's vision, and he could feel the pulse pounding in his neck.

Tony raised a hand. "You're right, I don't. But neither do you. There's a man that let me know about you—he made arrangements for me to get to the Bay Area and to see you. But I can tell when guys are playing an angle. And this sucker's all about that. So that's why I need to warn you."

Demarcus stepped forward and grabbed his father's shirt with both hands and gave a strong shake. "I don't care what you have to say. You stay away from me, and if I ever catch you messing with Mom, then you will really regret it." He gave a shove as he let go and turned around.

The sound of metal and wood crunching alerted him to something new going on from the park. He saw the trolley tumble along the ground. Now what?

Before he could investigate anything, Tony cried out, "Demarcus, run!"

Demarcus whirled back. A man with his neck cocked to the side swung at Tony and knocked him sprawling into the road. Despite his anger at his father, Demarcus didn't want to see him taken out.

The man strode right up to Demarcus, who was ready and willing to take his own swing. But Demarcus's attempt was dodged easily, even though he had put a lot of heat into the punch. Before Demarcus could try again, the man closed the gap and placed his hand on Demarcus's chest, wearing a sneering smile.

And Demarcus felt something rip from inside of him.

Chapter 54

Roberto fought against the monster controlling him.

Yet it was pointless. He had no strength against the Hoshek. He felt like a flea riding along with a dog, less than consequential. At least a dog would scratch at a flea. The Hoshek paid him no mind whatsoever.

He'd thought there could be no new horrors, until the Hoshek attacked the boy with dreads. Somehow the Hoshek siphoned off some of the boy's power. Roberto had been amazed, watching the supernatural actions of these teens in person. But now a new force rippled through the Hoshek.

What did it mean?

Lily heard John speak, but her mind had one focus: stop Rosa and get some answers. The girl still had that strong black halo radiating around her head. So where was Simon hiding?

SJ called her name. "Lily, what are you doing?"

"Get back!"

SJ would probably freak at seeing the girl who had almost killed her at the conference. Well, according to John and the boys, had killed her.

Rosa stopped at the edge of the street. "You wanna go again? I know what you can do this time, and I'm not on top of a building. I've been looking forward to this."

Lily shook her head. "You have no idea. If you answer my question, then I won't have to hurt you. Where. Is. Simon?"

Her opponent ran over to a street lamp, ripped it from the ground, and launched it at Lily. Lily aimed her gloved finger and cleaved the post in two with a laser, the halves clanging harmlessly behind her. Was it her imagination, or did Rosa flinch a little?

A voice sounded behind her. John called her name, but she didn't want to listen. Lily had been in shock the days immediately after the conference, grieving the idea that she had killed Rosa and Simon. Certain thoughts triggered panic inside her. But now that Rosa stood before her, it seemed that Lily's feelings had been misdirected. Rosa had a darkness in her, and maybe Lily needed to take care of it once and for all.

Lily shot with her laser again, but missed. If she could take out a knee or something, that wouldn't be too bad. But Rosa moved pretty quick, dodging into the street. Not as fast as Demarcus, but she was definitely faster than Lily.

A man's scream sounded from behind her.

She turned to see Demarcus stagger back from a man, clutch his chest, and topple. No! What was this new craziness?

She heard Rosa charging forward. Lily spun around to find Rosa jumping and coming down to slam the road with her fist.

The shockwave buckled the road, and a cracked piece of asphalt kicked Lily into the air. She stretched her arms out to catch herself.

One hand landed on a loose piece of rock and instead of rolling through the impact, she bent her wrist at a funny angle. Pain shot up her right arm, and she flopped on the ground, skidding a leg against the road.

Rosa laughed and headed toward her. Lily tried to push herself up, but her right hand wouldn't support any weight. She had to roll to get her good arm under her to push up. Lily followed with bright pulses of light, which stopped Rosa for a moment. The girl halted to claw at her eyes.

Lily stumbled back down toward the pier, her feet continually jabbed by scattered debris littered on the road. Where was SJ? Her wrist felt like it was broken, and her leg seared from the road rash.

A large wave crashed onto the beach area. Out of the spray stepped Kashvi and Aasif. This was going bad in a hurry. Crazy powered teens on both sides.

Another sound alerted her to someone on her left. She turned to see the man that had just taken Demarcus down.

His hand reached for her.

Chapter 55

The man's hand opened a crevice inside of Demarcus, a wound that leaked poison into his body. His breath caught and his muscles jerked in unison. One light touch, and it felt like he'd been ripped in half.

Demarcus's legs faltered, and he staggered back before falling. Now his blood felt like liquid fire running through his veins. He couldn't help but loose a scream at the utter devastation wracking his body. Instinctively he curled up in a fetal position, trying to hold in the pain somehow.

Then, as quickly as it had come, the pain stopped. Demarcus shuddered and stretched out. Oh man, that was no fun. But at least it was gone. Wait, no. The severe pain had fled, but a gaping hole remained inside him. It felt as if he needed something to soothe a deep, gnawing hunger. But he had a sense that no food would help him.

The man walked purposefully toward Lily, who appeared to be having a face-off with Rosa. Demarcus wanted to rush and help her, but he felt drained of his speed. His voice croaked toward Harry. "Stop him! He's going for the girls."

Harry disappeared and reappeared next to the man. He was going to take him on? Demarcus tried to shout a warning, but the man's hand caught Harry, who reacted in the same way. Harry writhed on the ground, his guttural cry a fresh reminder of what Demarcus had just gone through.

The man turned his attention toward Sarah Jane, who was watching Lily stand her ground against Rosa. Sarah Jane would have no idea what the strange dude had done. Demarcus tried to dash over and get her, but it was like his extremities were encased in cement.

Demarcus pumped as hard as he could. He only moved forward at average human speed at first, but the effort seemed to push something hindering his muscles out of his system. Before the stranger could get to Sarah Jane, Demarcus felt his speed break free and he rushed forward, scooping Sarah Jane up and moving her over to the end of the park.

"Whoa, what was that for?" Sarah Jane asked as he set her down.

"That dude just caused some serious pain to both Harry and me. He was coming for you."

"Who is he? How many people do we have against us?"

Demarcus shrugged. "I don't know, but—"

The sound of pavement being ripped up tore his attention away. A blur of blue flew in the air and crashed against the ground. Lily! Demarcus started for her, but another loud bang sounded behind him. He twirled. Kashvi and Aasif strode from the water's edge with fury in their eyes. A screech came from Aasif and knocked both Sarah Jane and Demarcus into the air. They tumbled in a heap at the gutter.

Demarcus sat up to see the stranger grab Lily by the neck.

A brilliant flash of light, then the ambient light vanished, plunging the area into a bubble of blackness. Demarcus couldn't see anything, but Lily's cries made it plain that she was suffering the same pain he and Harry had just experienced.

Demarcus followed the sound until he bumped against the man. He unleashed his fists at full speed, pummeling the man, who reeled back.

Lily fell to the ground, her soft voice whimpering. Light slowly seeped back into the bubble that she had created. Demarcus blinked and dropped to her.

"Are you okay? Oh my gosh, I'm sorry I couldn't get to you."

"What was that?" She wiped tears off her cheek with her left hand. "It felt like he ripped my guts out for a moment."

"He did it to me too." The dull ache inside him wouldn't subside.

"Where is he now?"

Good question. Demarcus stood and scanned for the man. Where was he? Rosa had retreated at the sight of him, and now stood a ways off, watching everything.

Kashvi and Aasif continued to march toward Sarah Jane. She pulled herself up and ran for Harry, who was barely sitting up where the stranger had dropped him.

They had two super-powered freaks behind them. One in front of them. And this stranger who was doing weird things to them, but then leaving them alone.

Demarcus took a moment to catch his breath. Something in him inspired him to pray. *Lord, we've really messed up. We need your help to get out of this situation tonight. Give us strength!*

Chapter 56

Simon sat in a car parked next to the maritime museum, eating another gummy bear. His glasses pulled a signal through a special dashboard cam, giving him a panoramic view of the carnage going on before him. When he gave the Council the information about the plan to trap their powered teens, they curtly thanked him and said they'd be in touch.

But the computer worm he'd inserted into the data he sent allowed him to track further communication. That's how he found out about this Roberto Pearce acting as the agent controlling the teens they were using. He didn't know where Pearce had come from, but it became a simple matter to track the plan to kidnap Ji-young Kim and lead the Anointed to the Fisherman's Wharf area for a confrontation.

This was the time he'd waited for. He had planned to be patient until he could sneak in amidst the confusion and have Sarah Jane taken. Unfortunately, he and Rosa had arrived later than he would have liked, and a major battle had already begun. Rosa didn't function best under his control in a dynamic situation. Instead of waiting to stealthily pluck their target away, she'd broken his influence enough to go after Lily.

Not that he could blame her.

At this point the best bet would be to let her burn off some of her aggression by targeting Lily.

Simon marveled at the way Demarcus, Lily, and Harry were using their abilities. At least his system had worked—they were potent individuals and they truly could change the world. But where had these other teens come from? He wished that he had picked up on them as well.

Pearce dropped Demarcus and Harry in quick succession. Now he was after Sarah Jane. Simon tapped some controls into his tablet and focused the camera on the man. This was the guy the Council had used to replace him? The man was barely put together, with his shirt half tucked in, his hair wild, and an odd gait. What was wrong with him?

If Pearce damaged his prize, Simon would be very upset. But before Pearce could get there, a blur whisked Sarah Jane away. Good, Demarcus still had his speed. Whatever Pearce was doing, it didn't seem to harm the teens for long.

The anticipation of finally getting his eyes back ate at him. He'd been working toward this for months. He needed it to happen.

A sudden blackout enveloped the area. Simon checked the rear-view mirror. His vision was blurry, but up Hyde Street there were lights. Was this a trick of Lily's? Her abilities had really grown in the few months since she had been strapped to the Source to power the spread of his influence around the world.

Energy slowly seeped back into the lights. Lily lay on the ground with the speedster next to her. He couldn't tell where Sarah Jane was. She couldn't have gotten away in the few moments without light. He concentrated, asking Rosa to investigate where she was. He switched to a lapel camera she wore to give him an up-close view of what she encountered.

A bunch of foliage was all he could see. Strange. He inputted a new command: find Sarah Jane. The girl was resisting him this time. His head started to pulse with pain, but he managed to release her inhibition and get her to move down toward the ocean.

Rosa turned suddenly, and the lapel cam took a second to focus. Pearce reached out and placed a hand just below the camera. The viewpoint started shaking violently. He heard Rosa's howl of pain as her body pitched backwards. Now all he had was a tremoring view of the night sky. Why would Pearce be attacking both the Anointed and Rosa? Could he not see they were against each other?

Simon clutched his head for the mental feedback from Rosa kicking into his head. Her pain and terror squeezed his brain. And then, gone. As quickly as it had started.

Okay, he officially had sympathy for his charge, wherever she was. He tapped on the tablet to go back to the dashboard cam. There. She lay on the grass, barely moving.

The car shuddered and a sound of snapping metal shocked him. The passenger door was ripped off—by Pearce!

"Hey, we're both working for the same team. I'm trying to help the Archai too." Simon held his hands up to show he meant no harm.

The definition from his glasses was poor, but he could tell something wasn't right in the man's face. And whoever this Roberto was, Simon sensed he wasn't in control.

A hand grabbed his shirt, and he was ripped out of his seat into the night air. Simon tried to call for help, but Pearce's other hand touched his face, and a horrible shock tore through his body, ripping through his whole being with terrible agony.

Chapter 57

Lily forced herself up with Demarcus's help. The insane pain from the man's touch had dissipated, but something else stayed in its wake. Something inside that made her feel incomplete, a nagging ache or something, deep inside. She tried pressing on her sternum hard, but that didn't do anything to make it subside.

"You too?" Demarcus asked.

She searched his eyes. Yes, they had both experienced something terrible. And Lily had a horrible sense that this was only the beginning.

A new shriek sounded. They both whirled to see Rosa fall victim to the stranger. Seeing Rosa drop to the ground in agony almost made Lily feel sorry for her. Almost. But why was this guy targeting them? How did he play into things?

A stream of water ran under their feet. Before Lily could react, the water turned into tentacles around their legs and whipped them upside down. She panicked focused on keeping her skirt from flying down. Demarcus pulled himself up to try and grab at the watery arms, but that didn't seem to do anything.

Lily flashed as brightly as she could, letting her whole body turn into a giant spotlight. The water lowered them closer to the ground, but didn't fully let go.

Harry ported between Kashvi and Aasif and slammed the pair's heads together. That did the trick, dumping both Lily and Demarcus unceremoniously to the ground. Her wrist barked with new pain, her hand tingling more than when she used her power. She held her arm close to her body as she swiveled to see where the strange man was.

There, tearing a door off a car. Was this guy stealing powers somehow? He'd just tagged Rosa, and now displayed her strength. He pulled a man out of the car.

Lily gasped. He looked different with his shaggy hair and glasses, but she wouldn't mistake Simon Mazor anywhere. Especially when she used to idolize him and perhaps harbored a girlish crush on the psychopath.

A noticeable spike in her pulse hit on seeing him. Sweat broke out all over her body. She had to force her breathing to calm down. As much as she wanted to question him, even hurt him, she knew he wasn't the priority right now.

"Demarcus, that guy is targeting everyone with powers. And I think he's stealing them. He just ripped the door from Simon's car."

He looked at her incredulously. "Simon? You mean he's here? Oh, great."

"Who do you think's controlling Rosa? We need to retreat for sure."

Lily shuddered as she heard Simon moan from the man's attack. She really didn't want to feel empathy for him, but the ache inside her swelled anew at the thought of someone else being struck with it.

Harry ported next to them. "Guys, this is getting a little crazy. I don't know about you, but I think getting out of here is the best plan."

Demarcus nodded. "We were just saying the same thing. Where are Sarah Jane and John?"

A sixth sense tickled Lily's brain with a message: turn around. Kashvi knelt down by pools of water she had drawn near her. She started pumping her arms at them, as if she were throwing things. Darts of water streamed through the air, morphing into ice projectiles as they flew.

Lily took aim and blasted each one with her laser. Most of the ice darts vaporized when she hit them, but an occasional one got past her. Demarcus dodged them easily. "You guys get SJ and John. I'll hold her off," Lily called.

"I'm not leaving you alone. Harry can get them," Demarcus called in between ducking back and forth.

"No, I'm okay. Really, we need to get out of here. The faster the better."

He was silent for a minute. Then he answered, "Fine. But you holler if you need anything at all. I can't stand the idea of something happening to you."

Despite the ache in her chest, a flutter of warmth ran through Lily as he sped off.

Chapter 58

Demarcus came to John's side. "John, we want to get out of here. There's too much going on, and it seems like it's all focused on us anyway."

The old man put a hand on his shoulder. "There's something else at work here. A conflict beyond everything you four are dealing with. Remember that."

What did that mean? "So . . . are you ready?"

His eyes radiated sadness. "There's another play to be made. And son, know that you are loved, that your friends are loved. And scars can be healed. Look to your Father."

A cry sounded, the very thing Demarcus didn't want to hear. He swiveled to see Lily get pinned down by some kind of ice net. Snap!

"I've got to help Lily!"

John caught his arm. "Son, let her fight her battles. She is capable. Look to where you are needed."

Demarcus pulled away. "I can't let anything happen to her, sir. I . . . I just can't."

He left John and arrived at Lily's side. A lattice of ice had pinned her to the ground. Blood trickled from a cut above her eyebrow, and her legs had multiple scrapes and bruises. He bent down to lift it up, but the heavy ice didn't want to budge. Water had seeped into the ground and frozen, anchoring it and Lily solid.

"Just a second. I'll get you out of there."

"No! Get SJ. That guy hasn't gotten her yet."

He sighed. Sorry, Sarah Jane, but this came first. He zigzagged toward the Corrupted, dodging every water and sonic blast they threw at him. He neared them, ready to knock Kashvi out. That always affected her control over water.

Before he could reach her, the stranger appeared right in front of him, just like Harry would.

Demarcus tried to stop, but he ran into a sweep of the man's arm. He arced through the air and bounced off a nearby wall. His whole body throbbed from the impact. He looked up to see Aasif recoil in fear before the man caught both him and Kashvi in his grip. The two simultaneously wailed in pain as the man did to them the same he had to his friends.

What was going on?

Demarcus stumbled as he got to his feet. Man, he'd never felt so pummeled from football or anything. Demarcus willed his body to get him over to Lily. The ice had turned to water when he arrived, and it washed off of her into the ground. She sat up, favoring her right wrist.

Lily groaned. "I could have sworn that guy was with the Corrupted. But he just turned on them too."

The man let the two kids go and they collapsed. Kashvi pushed herself up on her elbows, and Demarcus could make out her voice, "Why did you do that? Did we not do what you wanted?"

Lily said, "Look at their eyes. There's something different there."

Sure enough. For the first time their eyes seemed clear.

Chapter 59

Lily felt for the source of the sharp pain over her eye. Yep, blood. Why not? This dress was ruined anyway. What was a little more blood on it?

Their biggest problem now was the stranger, who apparently stole powers from gifted people, even his own two helpers. Only one person was left untouched: Sarah Jane.

"Demarcus, he's after SJ."

"Where is she?"

Lily pointed near the park. "There, helping a man." The black man she prayed for sat up and shook his head.

"She did what?" Demarcus exclaimed.

"What do you mean? That's what she does, help people."

"I know, but I didn't expect her to help my dad."

Lily forced herself up and started moving toward her friend, limping as she ran. "SJ, let's get out of here!"

SJ turned and was surprised by the stranger materializing in front of her. She took a step back, her fists raised in defense.

Lily shot a blast of light at the man. The bolt thudded into his back, which drew his attention away from SJ. The man acted more annoyed than hurt—that blast would have sent a normal person flying—but he only sneered in contempt. He flicked his hand toward Lily and a sphere of darkness smashed into her, knocking her backwards into Demarcus's arms.

What in the world was that? It was like a . . . corruption of her power?

Thankfully her distraction worked. Harry ported behind SJ and disappeared with her, reappearing next to John in the middle of the park.

All she and Demarcus had to do was get to the park and they could escape. "We're coming!" She waved in their direction.

Only the stranger appeared behind Harry. He grabbed him, punched him in the face, and tossed him aside like a rag doll. SJ screamed, but John placed himself in front of the man.

"In the name of the Lord Jesus, you must leave. Be gone!"

She'd never heard John speak so forcefully.

The man reeled. He growled and arched his back, like he was in pain. "What are you trying to do, old man?"

"Greater is He that is in us, than he who is in the world. The light shines in the darkness, and the darkness cannot overcome it."

Another roar came from the stranger as he swayed on his feet. His voice didn't sound normal. It was more like an unearthly rumble, vibrating through the air. Fear lanced through her at the sound. Lily picked up a scent of something like rotten eggs.

John was fighting this man with words? Lily recalled the story of Jesus quoting the Old Testament to the devil. Was that what John was doing?

"Salvation belongs to our God who is seated on the throne, and to the Lamb who is worthy. He is the Alpha and Omega."

The man jerked back with each statement, as if they were physical blows. Their adversary was being beaten back. They had almost won!

The ground shook and the sky thundered. The stranger planted his feet and let out a hellish curse, then slipped into a strange tongue, rattling off harsh-sounding words. Even John stumbled back from the shaking.

Thick black smoke started fuming around the man. What, could he do fire? No, the smoke was coming out of the man's mouth. Like in a horror movie, the dark substance billowed from his face until it formed something new. Something terrifying.

A hulking body formed, the smoke snaking around to fill the frame with substance. The stranger flopped backward when his creature had taken shape.

With each breath, the new being's size grew and diminished. Fear and loathing emanated from it in pulses. The hair on Lily's neck stood on end, and she chilled at the sight of it.

The monster had broad shoulders but no neck, a head that protruded forward, jackhammer arms, and legs like tree trunks. Little bursts of electricity or lightning darted around it in random patterns.

John stood his ground. "You will not harm these youth today. They have been bought by the blood of the Lamb, and they are under my protection."

The beast wheezed. Was it laughing? "They may be out of my master's hands, but they still house darkness. Don't you see? They helped make me. And now my master wants you out of the way. Finally."

The next moments proceeded in slow motion. Demarcus rushed forward with a warrior's cry, but a mere flick of the creature's finger sent a wall of brackish water washing him back. Harry hadn't recovered from his beating. Lily tried aiming her laser at the thing's head, but it dodged as fast as Demarcus, and the beam zipped right past it. The beast turned, his eyes blood red, and fixed his gaze on her.

It felt like Simon's voice was in her head, telling her to relax, but with an eerie quality to it, like it had been modified with a filter. Her knees gave out and her arms slumped to her sides. There was nothing she could do as she dropped to the ground. She tried to move, but her limbs wouldn't respond.

John started to speak again, but the monster lashed out with a fearsome backhand. John's greying head jerked back and he sprawled out on the grass. Before he could recover, the beast bent down and picked him up.

Lily felt strength returning to her arms and legs. If only she could get a hand out.

The beast held John aloft, his huge frame dwarfing their mentor. John held on to the creature's arms, struggling to speak. Lily heard a few faint words spoken.

"Unless a grain of wheat falls to the ground and dies, it is alone. But if it dies, it bears much fruit."

The monster chuckled, a horrid, wet hack. "Then let it be as you said, old man." A blackened arm struck John in the chest, flinging him through the air until he bounced off a tree. He crumpled into an unmoving heap.

A barbaric cry came from the beast. "It was said he could not die. Yet I have vanquished him! Now let me deal with the rest of your servants!"

Shock flooded her body. John was down? How powerful was this crazy beast, and how would they stop such a thing?

One idea came to Lily's mind. Pushing through the temporary weakness, she thrust out her palms and focused as hard as she could on what she needed to do.

Chapter 60

Demarcus shook the foul water off by vibrating as fast as he could. The very touch of the water felt like it was choking his skin. He tried to get his body to move, to help somehow, but when he looked up, the beast had already struck John.

Demarcus watched helplessly as John struck a tree and collapsed to the ground. A cry stuck in his throat at seeing their mentor fall. The beast roared, and his words sent chills through Demarcus's heart.

Now the thing was coming after them. If it could do that to John, what hope did they have?

An intense figure of light swooped from the sky. Feathery wings left a trail of illumination in its wake. Its strong face looked determined, and it held a flaming sword in its hand.

The smoke monster yelled a curse in surprise, and ducked to the side as the angel dove at his position and swung its sword. The weapon sliced through the air, missing by inches. The heavenly being then flew over the shoreline above the piers of Fisherman's Wharf.

The monster picked up its human host around the waist and leapt into the air, landing on the tops of buildings and pursuing the point of light as it vanished in the distance. Relief washed over Demarcus, even as he wanted to collapse right there on the grass.

Wait, he had to check on Lily.

He raced over to where she lay, her arms outstretched in front of her with palms up. "Lily, are you okay?"

Her eyes wouldn't focus on him. He pulled her into his lap. "I flap moist uncle," she replied weakly.

Oh no. She didn't.

"Did you use your holograms?"

Lily nodded.

How would she be reset with Ratchet down? And what about John? He picked Lily up with a grunt due to the battering he'd taken during the night. It took a few seconds to limp over to where John lay, face down on the ground. He set Lily down gently as she babbled gibberish. At least her eyes weren't closing.

"Nooo! No, no, no. This can't be happening. John!" Demarcus cried. "Harry, get over here! Sarah Jane, where are you?"

He checked John carefully. His body moved with his breathing. Barely. "John, can you hear me?" A soft groan sounded. Demarcus wasn't sure if he should move him, but it seemed hard for him to breathe on his belly. He carefully kept John's head steady as he rolled him over.

"We're getting Sarah Jane. It will be all right."

John wheezed, and red spittle sprayed from his lips. "No, my son. She is gone." His voice was barely a whisper.

"Harry! Where is Sarah Jane?" he hollered.

His friend appeared beside him, his face a mask of panic. "Demarcus, I can't find her anywhere."

John's hand rested on Demarcus's. His breaths grew ragged. "I saw her . . . taken away. She was alive, but she is in great danger."

Demarcus wanted to vomit. Lily was out of it, Sarah Jane was missing, and John . . . it didn't look good. "Harry, port in the air and see if you can get a better vantage point. Are you okay to do that?"

Harry looked frantic, biting his lip and trembling, but he nodded and then disappeared.

Oh Lord, please come and touch John. We need him, more than ever. The world needs him, with that foul creature loose who knows where. Tears welled up in Demarcus's eyes.

Lily asked, "Did frapping mucho gasbat?"

John wagged his finger to have Demarcus lean in closer. "I am in God's hands. You are too. Remember that. You all need to stand in that, for dark days are here. I'm sorry to leave you." More coughing and blood erupted.

Demarcus wiped the liquid from his face, a metallic taste on his lips. "Let me get you to a hospital. Or Harry. Please, we can't lose you."

The air warped and Harry appeared again. "No sign of her. Demarcus, what happened to her?"

"Dude," Demarcus pointed at John.

"Oh no. No!"

John's face crinkled up, his eyes squeezed shut tight for a moment. Then, he relaxed a little. "Boys, be strong. Be humble. You must . . . seek the light . . ."

His head lolled to the side, his eyes unfocused.

Demarcus and Harry looked at each other, both in shock. What had happened? His chest caught, each breath a battle. Everything tonight was too much to process. Lily incapacitated. Sarah Jane missing. John . . . gone.

Where were the Corrupted? Demarcus scanned the area where he'd last seen them. No sign of them. Could they have taken Sarah Jane?

Demarcus reached down and pulled Lily up close to him. Was she aware of what had happened? "Lily, how are you?"

Her eyes crossed. "Ahh, shazafrazz."

Each new thought was a blow. What would they do now? Realization dawned on Demarcus how much of a horrible mistake they had all made, coming down here, thinking they could face the Corrupted. Their arrogance and foolishness had cost them so much. And as he considered the night, he realized how much of it was *his* arrogance. *Oh Lord, how did this happen?*

Tears started to drip down his face while he cradled Lily and searched John for signs of life. Harry knelt on the ground, pounding his fist against the grass. The crowds around had fled, leaving them a huddled, wounded crew. The moment seared into his memory.

Demarcus felt a hand on his shoulder. He looked up at whomever it was that was comforting him.

Tony Carter stood above him. "I don't know what happened tonight, but you and your friends were very brave. That other girl, she did something to me. I haven't felt this way in a long time. I know she healed my body, but there's something else. She touched my mind and I can think clearly.

"I need to know; how do you do this?"

Demarcus tried to slow his breathing, and used a ragged sleeve to wipe tears away. Where to begin? After all the trouble of the night, his father was standing before him, claiming to be healed?

Before he could answer, flashing lights and sound of sirens arriving punctuated the air. Police, firemen, and paramedics started pouring out into the streets. How would they even begin to explain what happened? It didn't seem like a good idea to stick around and try.

His voice croaked. "Dad, it's a long story from a long time ago. It's about a carpenter—a real blue-collar guy. Maybe you'd like it. But we should probably do it somewhere else. I need to get Lily help." He looked at Harry, who nodded. "Take my hand, and you'll see something amazing."

Demarcus wrapped an arm around Lily's waist and took his father's hand. Harry took Tony's hand and stood. "Have you eaten lately? Because this may not feel good."

Before his father could answer, the awful scene in front of them shuddered and they disappeared.

Chapter 61

Simon clutched his chest, the rawness inside him hard to fathom. It literally felt like he had a hole inside of him. Whatever Pearce had done, it had left a lasting mark.

The air rushed by through the open space where the door had been. People glanced at their vehicle as they drove by. Simon just hoped the seat belt was strong enough. The chaos at the pier should keep the police from stopping their vehicle for being out of code.

He caught Rosa rubbing her chest as well. She drove without speaking, which surprised him. If he relaxed, she could really give it to him. Tonight must have affected her as well. But he didn't feel like discussing feelings with her.

He glanced in the back seat. Their passenger was out cold. At least Pearce hadn't gotten to her.

A smile formed. At last. Simon would have peace. His eyes would be whole.

And he could truly face the Archai again, and reclaim his proper place: leading their foray into controlling the world.

Discussion Questions

1. *Launch* is a work of fiction but set in a present day world. Did this book seem realistic to you? Why or why not?

2. What did you like best about this book? What did you like least about this book?

3. In the first chapter Demarcus is checking out his gift of speed, and wonders what to do with it. What are your gifts-music, sports, writing, baking, etc.? Do you wonder what to do with gifts you're given? Make a list of ways you can use your gifts to show kindness or as a ministry to others.

4. Demarcus helps the homeless alcoholic by getting him to the hospital, but while there, he's questioned by a police officer and he fudges his answers and takes off to avoid questioning. He even asks for forgiveness as he does it. Do you agree with how he handled things? Why or why not?

5. Lily is dealing with sadness and depression when we first meet her. How have you handled things when you are down? How do you think you could help someone like Lily in your life?

6. Simon Mazor has a quirk of ascribing luck to whatever color of gummy bear he pulls out. Do you have any beliefs that influence you? What's a fun quirk or habit that you have?

7. Demarcus is asked what traits he thinks are most important in a man and woman during his interview at the conference. What do you think is the most important character trait for a man to have? For a woman?

8. Out of all of the "powers" revealed in Launch, which one would you like to have? Or is there some other power not mentioned?

9. Simon has a gift to influence people, even to the point of mind-control when he tries his hardest. Who are the people that influence you in life? Do they point you toward good things, or have you allowed negative influencers to have sway over you?

10. Flare is the social media the kids used in the book. Social media has become a huge part of our world in just the last decade. What do you think are the benefits of social media? What are the drawbacks?

11. There are a lot of geeky references in the book. Part of the fun of writing it was slipping in icons, quotes and

other references in the story. What are your favorite pop culture references you found?

12. Both Lily and Demarcus have experiences where they see something miraculous. Have you ever seen something miraculous happen?

13. What do you think of the book's title? How does it relate to the book's contents? What other title might you choose?

14. What was your favorite quote or passage from the book? Who said it?

15. If you were making a movie of this book, who would you cast? Why?

Author Acknowledgments

Abook is a huge challenge. A series? That is another mountain to climb. I'm so thankful to have others helping me ascend to higher elevations.

Thank you to Rachel and Lindsay at Little Lamb Books. The work put in, the heart behind the sweat, and the vision to see it through —it is so appreciated. The whole flock of authors at LLB are so encouraging.

My Mastermind group is invaluable to me. Thanks to Becky, J.J., Josh S., Josh H., Steve, Liberty, and Tina for laughs, GIF battles, and keeping me on the straight and narrow.

Writers are a precious community. I wouldn't be here without my tribe at Realm Makers. Thanks to Scott and Becky for all your hard work. Thank you to the Guardians of the RM Galaxy for all you do.

Shout-outs specifically to Lindsay Franklin, Peter Leavell, Matt Mikalatos, Jake Tyson, Ann Fryer, and Randy Streu for friendship and support.

A special thank you to Becky Dean for being an awesome critique partner. Your insights are so helpful.

Thanks to Jenna Head for beta reads and being a fan.

My church family at Blackfoot Christian Fellowship is so support-ive. Thanks Pastor Kevin and everyone for letting me be weird.

Sorry to say, but I have four of the greatest kids out there. Nathan, Matthew, Caleb, and Micaiah give me story fodder for days. Keep running the race with faith!

To Beccy, my love and anchor. Thank you so much for believing in me, even when I get that far-off look in my eyes when story ideas run by.

Finally, it's all for Jesus. Without him, I would be dust. Thank you, Lord, for life.

About the Author

J ason C. Joyner is a physician assistant, a writer, a Jesus-lover, and a Star Wars geek. He's traveled from the jungles of Thailand to the cities of Australia and the Bavarian Alps of Germany. He lives in Idaho with his lovely wife, three boys, and daughter managing the chaos of sports and super-heroes in his home. His first book, *Launch*, is an award-winning YA superhero novel and the first book in the Rise of the Anointed series. Get updates at www.jasoncjoyner.com, or follow him on Facebook, Twitter, or Instagram.

Fractures is available as an eBook in 2021

BOOK 3
RISE OF THE ANOINTED

ANOINTED

COMING
SPRING
2021

JASON C. JOYNER

For all the latest information regarding
Anointed, Book 3 in the *Rise of the Anointed* series, visit
www.JasonCJoyner.com or www.LittleLambBooks.com

CPSIA information can be obtained
at www.ICGtesting.com
Printed in the USA
LVHW111602021220
673228LV00040B/1154